SUMMER KISSES AT MERMAIDS POINT

SARAH BENNETT

Boldwood

First published in Great Britain in 2021 by Boldwood Books Ltd.

Copyright © Sarah Bennett, 2021

Cover Design by The Brewster Project

Cover Photography: Shutterstock

A CIP catalogue record for this book is available from the British Library.

Paperback ISBN 978-1-83889-918-9

Large Print ISBN 978-1-83889-914-1

Hardback ISBN 978-1-80162-614-9

Ebook ISBN 978-1-83889-912-7

Kindle ISBN 978-1-83889-913-4

Audio CD ISBN 978-1-83889-919-6

MP3 CD ISBN 978-1-83889-916-5

Digital audio download ISBN 978-1-83889-911-0

Boldwood Books Ltd
23 Bowerdean Street
London SW6 3TN
www.boldwoodbooks.com

For M – my happiest of happy endings

1

Laurie Morgan surveyed the mostly empty tables on the opposite side of the counter. Barbara Mitchell and her best friend, Kitty Duke, were at their usual spot in the corner, knitting tiny hats for a charity which donated them to premature baby units around the country, but other than them she'd had nobody in since the breakfast rush. Turning her gaze to the raindrops streaking the plate-glass window of her café, Laurie squinted through the rivulets of water. She could just about make out the view beyond the window. With the clouds so thick and low, it was all but impossible to distinguish where the sky met the sea, turning everything into a wall of miserable grey. *What a difference a day makes.*

This time yesterday she'd barely been able to hear herself think over the hubbub of conversation, teacups rattling on saucers and forks scraping on plates, thanks to a visiting WI coach trip. They'd all but eaten her out of that day's baking, and she'd had to hastily defrost a couple of emergency Victoria sponges to make sure her lunchtime regulars had something to go with their sandwiches. It wasn't only her cake stock which had taken a beating; one look at the queue snaking halfway around the café from the visitors' bathroom had her scrambling for her phone to send an SOS text to her brother, Nick, begging him to do an emergency run to the corner shop to replenish her dwindling supply of toilet paper. Of course, he'd found the whole thing hilarious and insisted on making a big entrance through the front door like some white knight come to save the day, rather than sneaking in through the back entrance and leaving them in the stock room, which also served the gift shop their parents ran next door.

A ripple of laughter from the corner table drew Laurie's attention from the gloomy weather. She watched Barbara and Kitty for a few minutes, full of admiration for the way their needles flashed back and forth without hesitation. Neither woman spared much more than the odd glance to their knitting as they chatted. Her nan had tried to teach Laurie to knit as a child but, as with all the other crafty type activities she'd tried over the years, she'd found it impossible to get to grips with. Being the only left-hander in the family hadn't helped as everything they tried to show her felt awkward and clumsy. Even now, at just shy of twenty-three, she had to concentrate when using her knife and fork or she would find herself pulling things apart with the fork in her naturally dominant left hand. Thankfully, when it came to cooking and baking it didn't matter which hand she held a knife with and she'd spent many happy hours at her nan's knee learning the basics and discovering a true passion. It had been a gamble on her parents' part when she'd come to them with the idea of converting one end of their sprawling seafront shop into a café, but they'd decided it was one worth taking. If they hadn't, it would've left Laurie facing the prospect of leaving

Mermaids Point to seek employment in one of the bigger towns and cities. Having grown up a stone's throw away from the ever-changing tides of the Atlantic Ocean, the prospect of moving inland had filled her with dread.

She'd always been drawn to the sea. Whatever the season, there was beauty to be found. From the balmy summer days when the shiny white triangles of pleasure boat sails dotted the gentle waves, to the roiling majesty of a winter storm in full tumult when even the hardiest of the local fishermen kept their boats secured in the sheltered bay. Even on a filthy day like today, she'd rather be out than in. Her eyes roamed the café once more. If business didn't pick up after lunch, maybe she'd flick the closed sign over, tug on a hat, turn up her collar and snatch a few moments of peace on the wet sands of the beach.

If things were this quiet in the café, they were likely just as dull in the adjacent shop. Laurie checked the clock above the counter. It would be at least an hour before the first visitors looking for lunch showed up. Pulling down one of the reusable mugs she kept for locals who didn't have time to stop on their way to and from their own places of work, she brewed a cappuccino with an extra shot on the fancy machine she'd invested in. With a stencil she decorated the top with a chocolate powder smiley face, before screwing on the lid. Designer coffee had become the norm – even in a little village like theirs. When the tourists came, they expected the same kind of choice they got in the big retail coffee chains of their hometowns. Her dad had wrinkled his nose at the cost when she'd told him, but one sip of the first cappuccino she'd made for him had him hooked. Though he'd worked his way through the entire menu, the creamy delight of the frothy Italian staple was his first love. Pausing only to wrap a small square of flapjack in a napkin, Laurie called out a request to Barbara to keep an eye on things for her – not that there was anything to keep an eye on – and made her way through the low archway that linked the café to her parents' shop.

The scent of baking and fresh-brewed coffee gave way to the earthier fragrance of the essential oils and baskets of dried herbs and flowers from a large table to her left. Hessian sacks in three different sizes and small gauzy sachets hung above the table, ready for visitors to create their own potpourri or scented drawer bags. Crystals of every shape, size and colour filled the next display she passed, each with a hand-written card beside them describing the purported beneficial properties of each type of stone. The soft strains of traditional Celtic music came from speakers hidden in the uneven stone walls and ceiling of the shop.

When they'd agreed to partition the original building to create the café, her parents had decided to rebrand and refurbish the shop at the same time, moving away from the more traditional branded tea towels, fridge magnets and other touristy nick-nacks and instead focusing on the 'new-age hippy stuff', as her dad called it. This kind of fare had become increasingly popular with visitors drawn to the area by the stories of mythical sea creatures which had given their village the more fanciful part of its name. Thus Morgan's Gifts and Souvenirs had been transformed into The Mermaid's Cave.

The dark stone walls might be nothing more than the clever application of a fake veneer, but together with uplights in shades of green, blue and purple and the installation of a gold-lined water feature the size of a small pond surrounded by more fake boulders, the interior of the shop had been transformed into a magical underground cavern. Crystals and figurines of mythical gods and monsters winked up from the base of the pond – a mermaid's hidden treasures and the perfect showcase for items of stock her father wanted to draw attention to.

As long as men had been going to sea, they'd been making up tales of mermaids, and the ancestors of families like hers who could trace their roots back to the origins of the village, were no exception. Though he scoffed at it, Laurie thought there was a tiny corner of her father's heart, which wanted to believe in those legends. Why else had he persuaded Mum to christen her Lorelai? Not that anyone other than her nan had called her that, not unless she was in big trouble. The use of her full name – Lorelai Christina Morgan – by either of her parents still had the power to make Laurie quake in her shoes. Smiling at the thought of her gentle giant of a dad actually bringing himself to punish either of his children, Laurie wove between a rack of CDs and mythology books, skimmed past the gorgeous glittering confections of silver and glass beads created by a gifted local woman who'd begun making jewellery after being made redundant several years previously, and finally reached the large sales desk.

Perched on his usual stool, eyes fixed on the phone in his left hand as he stroked the greying strands of his neat beard with the other, Andrew Morgan didn't notice her arrival until Laurie plonked his metal coffee mug down on the counter with a clunk. Eyes, as dark as her own, creased in delight as her dad looked first at Laurie and then at the silver mug. 'Is that for me?'

'Who else would it be for, hey?' Laurie asked as she circled around the desk to peck a kiss on his cheek. Leaning into the solid weight of his side as he circled an arm about her waist, she peered over to see what had been keeping his attention fixated on his phone. 'Checking your followers again?' After the refurbishment, her parents had branched out into cyberspace, creating a simple website through which people could order anything being sold in the shop. Dad had also become something of an Instagram addict and loved nothing more than posting photos of different items of stock, as well as gorgeous black and white landscape shots of the village and the surrounding area. He'd built up quite a decent following and had persuaded Laurie to get on board with her own page for the café where she could share pictures and recipes.

'Not sure what's going on, love. I posted a picture of those new polished agate bookends and my likes have gone crazy. It doesn't make sense.' He tilted the screen so she could see it better.

Laurie studied the image. The striated waves of red, orange and gold were certainly striking, but no more eye-catching than many of the other pictures he'd posted. Dad had a knack with a camera she couldn't dream of matching. She glanced at the number of likes registered beneath the photo and did a double take. Over a thousand when they were lucky to hit a tenth of that usually. The number of comments was even more surprising. They had a few regular followers who tended to respond to posts, but she could count those on the fingers of one hand. 'There's nearly three hundred comments, Dad.' It was impossible to keep the disbelief from her voice. 'Have you read any of them?'

He shook his head. 'I haven't had a chance. I'd only just opened my phone when you came in.' He pulled the phone back and tapped the screen. Unable to see it from where she was standing, Laurie watched his expression instead. Every time his thumb flicked to scroll further through the comments, the frown line between his brows deepened. 'Have I seen who?' he muttered. 'Is someone on a wind up?' Looking thoroughly puzzled, he offered her the phone. 'Everyone is using the Mermaids Point hashtag for some reason and they're all asking if I've seen a mermaid.'

Taking the phone, Laurie flicked up and down the list of comments. He was right. Along with the usual hashtag for the village, which they used for all their posts, the replies were full of stuff like #mermaids #mermaidsarereal #mermaidsquad #thetruthisoutthere. Bemused, she clicked on #MermaidsPoint and almost dropped the phone. 'What the hell is that?' Beneath her dad's post showing the agate stones was a murky image completely at odds with the usual sharp focused, carefully curated and staged images she was used to seeing on the website.

Selecting the post, she found it was a series of pictures, most of them blurred, as though the person holding the camera had been clicking too fast to focus properly or had expanded their phone to the maximum zoom capacity. The number of likes was over 150,000 and climbing rapidly, unheard of for anything other than a celebrity's account. The original poster didn't have a handle she recognised, and when Laurie clicked to their page it held only a handful of posts, all dated that morning. The first picture showed a cluster of islands, the furthest little more than a twisting spire. She recognised it instantly as the grouping known locally as the Seven Sisters. The Sisters marked the far end of the scattering of unoccupied islands stretching several miles off the end of Mermaids Point that were a haven for seals, seabirds and other wildlife. Beyond them lay nothing except several thousand miles of ocean.

The second photo was a zoomed shot showing the blurred outline of what looked to be a person sitting on the edge of one of the rocks. *Rather them than me.* There were no landing points out on the Sisters as far as Laurie knew so there was no way to access them other than swimming. Even if a small boat had steered close to the rocks the water temperature would be frigid at this time of year. It only really became bearable at the very height of summer, if there'd been weeks of hot sunshine to warm the waters by a few degrees – something that had been in painfully short supply the past couple of summers. Plenty of hardy souls went for a dip throughout the year, but never that far from shore, and rarely without a wetsuit.

The next couple of photos showed the figure – a woman from the masses of long blonde hair on display – slipping down from the rocks and into the water, nothing remarkable beyond the location and, from the amount of skin on display, the fact she appeared to be topless. It wasn't until Laurie scrolled to the last of the photos that she suddenly understood what the fuss was all about. The woman had dived beneath the water leaving what looked to be a long fish-like tail covered in silvery-green scales sticking out of the water. *A mermaid's tail.*

'It's just someone's idea of a joke.' Laurie handed the phone back to her dad. 'A hoaxer with too much time on their hands. Looks like it's gone viral, which is why you've got more people than usual looking at related posts.'

Her dad flicked back and forth through the group of photos, shaking his head. 'They're not even very good quality, are they? Almost as blurry as those old photos of the Loch Ness Monster that did the rounds back in the day.' He closed the app and tucked his phone in the top pocket of his shirt.

'Oh well, it keeps whoever it is off the streets, I suppose, and with any luck, it'll send a bit of extra business our way.'

Laughing, Laurie rounded the counter. 'You can dream, Dad! It'll be like everything else on the internet, here and gone in a flash. I'd better get back next door. I left Barbara holding the fort.' She pushed the silver mug and wrapped slice of flapjack towards him. 'Don't let your coffee go cold.'

Her dad raised an eyebrow at the piece of flapjack. 'What happened to your mother's ban on mid-morning snacks?'

'I can take it back...' Laurie's hand had barely extended before her dad slapped his palm down over the sweet treat. 'Or not,' she said with a laugh, heading back towards the café. 'I won't tell if you don't,' she added over her shoulder.

'You know I tell her everything.' It was true, she'd never known either of them to keep a secret from the other, and she and Nick had been raised with the same levels of openness and honesty. The fact he'd confess to it wouldn't stop him eating the flapjack, though.

Pausing next to the display of homemade jewellery, Laurie spun on her heel to face her father. 'Tell her after you tell her about our newest resident. She'll be too busy thinking about mermaids to be cross with you.'

'Good idea, love!' Her dad popped the corner he'd broken off the sticky square into his mouth and gave her a thumbs-up.

2

Laurie's prediction that the story of the mermaid would be just a fly-by-night sensation proved wide of the mark. As word went around the village, the café filled up with people dropping in for a bite to eat and to add to the gossip and speculation. Most were of the same opinion as her – that it was someone messing around – and the talk soon turned to likely culprits. It was little surprise to her when Nick's name cropped up more than once in the conversation. Like generations of men from the village, he earned his living from the sea, though he'd moved in recent years from the harsh world of deep-sea fishing to running a sightseeing and day-tripping service for tourists. The islands off the end of the Point teemed with wildlife and were popular with general visitors who came to enjoy the beaches, as well as the more discerning enthusiasts.

It'd been a sad day when their uncle sold the trawler Nick had crewed on since turning sixteen, but the ever-increasing pressure from government quotas as well as greater competitiveness from boats coming over from France, Spain and the

Nordic countries had proven to be too much. It wasn't only Laurie who'd heaved a secret sigh of relief when they'd stopped, either. Though Mum had never said anything, she had always been restless and lacking in her usual bubbly warmth on those weeks Uncle Tony, Nick and the rest of the crew had been out at sea. Things had only grown more tense following a terrible accident on one of the other trawlers, resulting in the loss of one crew member and debilitating injuries to another. There'd been tears of relief when Tony and Nick had announced their new venture, and for the first couple of years, they'd raked it in as the sun beamed down and visitor numbers grew and grew.

Then, on top of a general economic downturn, they'd had two of the worst summers in living memory, weather-wise. Bed and breakfast rooms stayed empty and the local camping sites were barren of their usual motley collection of bright tents and shiny white caravans. The few hardy souls who ventured to the coast were greeted with warning flags on the beaches and views as disappointing and grey as the one outside the café's windows today. Everyone had felt the bite, and only a few businesses like her parents' shop had the option to diversify online. Like many others in the village, Laurie had watched her profits dwindle to nothing. If she hadn't still lived at home, there was no way her business would've survived. Offering special deals to groups like the WI had helped a bit, but if they didn't get a good spell of decent weather soon, the future looked grim.

As the lunchtime gossipers drifted home again, the only sound in the café was the incessant rattle of the rain against the windows and the quiet swish of her mop over the tiled floor as she washed away the mess of shoe and boot prints no door mat could cope with on a day like today. By the time closing time arrived, Laurie had cleaned every available surface, rearranged her display cabinets and rewritten the chalkboard menu. Adding a few bright flowers to decorate the board had done nothing to lift her mood and she was feeling thoroughly sorry for herself when her dad called out to ask if she was ready to join him for their short walk home.

Forcing a smile, she tucked her long black hair under a more practical than stylish wide-brimmed hat and snuggled into her dad's side. As he'd always done, he walked on the seaward side, using his body to shield her from the worst of the rain and freezing-cold spray the wind was whipping in.

'Urgh! Right in my bloody ear.' Shuddering, her dad ducked his head deeper into the raised collar of his oilskin jacket and they increased their pace until they were all but running up the cobbled hill of whitewashed cottages to their house. A more modern brick addition to the village, the house the Morgans called home might not be as aesthetically pleasing as the traditional fishermen's cottages, but with both Dad and Nick topping out at six foot, at least the higher ceilings saved them both from knocking their heads on the oak beams so beloved of visitors to the village. Most of the cottages were rental properties these days, their quirkiness attractive enough for a week or two, but not very practical for modern family life.

* * *

Laurie's dad pushed open the front door and ushered her into a bright, familiar warmth. As they toed off their boots and hung up their dripping jackets in the inner porch, the strains of the radio – and Mum's enthusiastic accompaniment to an old eighties pop classic reached their ears. Beaming, her dad padded down the hall in his socks and reached the open kitchen door just in time to join in with the chorus. As she followed in his wake, Laurie could hear her mum laughing as she scolded her husband for making her jump. When she entered the kitchen, it was to find her dad with his arms around her mum's waist, pressing kisses to her cheek as she tried to fend him off with ineffectual flicks of the tea towel she'd been using to dry her hands. 'Come on, Sylvia, my love, give your poor husband a proper kiss.'

Rolling her eyes, Laurie turned away, though her heart sang at the pure love they still held for each other after nearly thirty years together. They'd always been the same, full of easy, open affection, and though she adored the way they were together, Laurie suspected one of the reasons both she and Nick were serially single was because of the high relationship bar their parents had set. That, and... *no.* Laurie shook the memory away before it could settle and spoil her mood.

'How was your day, darling?' Having extracted herself from Dad's clutches, her mum came over to give her a hug and a kiss.

'A bit quiet, apart from a flurry at lunchtime when everyone came in to talk about the mermaid.' Taking the tea towel from her mum's hands, Laurie crossed to the draining board to dry the couple of pans and dishes still dripping, which her mum had obviously been using to make dinner. During termtime, when the shop was quieter, Sylvia Morgan volunteered at the local combined primary and junior school on Mondays, Wednesdays and Fridays. She helped the children with their reading and writing just as she'd been doing for the past twenty years. She'd started when Laurie had been old enough to join Nick at the village school and had stayed on after they'd both transitioned to secondary education. Like all the children from the villages scattered along their part of the coast, they'd been bused to a comprehensive school some twenty miles away. Laurie's stomach gave an uneasy twinge at memories of those queasy journeys, the winding roads and the smell of diesel from the old bus an unhappy combination she'd never grown accustomed to.

On school days, Mum was usually the first home, so she cooked. The other two weekdays, Laurie and Nick split the task between them, with their dad in charge at weekends when he had time to experiment with his ever-expanding collection of cookery books. Like Laurie, Nan had taught him to cook as soon as he was old enough and he'd helped develop their palates with everything from elaborate Thai curries to homemade sushi. He was on a bit of a vegan kick at the moment, part of a drive for the whole family to try to eat more healthily, which was why Laurie didn't feel too guilty about sneaking him the odd bit of flapjack or thin sliver of cake.

'What mermaid?' Mum asked, coming over to take the pot Laurie had just dried from her hands.

'Look here, I'll show you.' Her dad took out his phone and opened it. 'Bloody hell, it's got nearly quarter of a million likes now. Mermaids Point is well and truly viral.'

Abandoning her chore to retrieve her own phone, Laurie started clicking through her various social media apps. 'It's everywhere. Look, Dad, it's even trending on Twitter.' She showed her parents the list of the current most talked about topics in the UK. 'It's crazy.'

The front door opened, sending a draft of cold air into the kitchen. 'Did you guys hear the news? A mermaid's supposedly been spotted out by the Sisters.' Nick appeared in the doorway, still wearing his bright yellow raincoat, though he'd had the sense to kick off his boots rather than traipsing wet footprints across the carpet.

'Hear it?' Dad raised an eyebrow at the same time as their mum told Nick off for dripping on the floor and started tugging his coat off.

Grinning down at their diminutive mother, Nick obediently held out his arms to let her pull the soggy jacket off. 'It was on the local news just now, and it's all over the internet. Whoever dreamed it up must be having a right laugh.'

'Whoever?' Laurie gave her older brother a suspicious glance. Since she'd first seen it that morning, it had seemed like the kind of prank her brother and his friends might try and pull off. Who knew the islands better than the people who sailed out to them most days? And who else would be daft enough to do it? Unless it was some random stranger who'd picked their village purely based on its name, there were few likely suspects, and Nick's name was close to the top of the list.

'Don't give me that look, Lorelai!' Nick shifted his hands to his hips. 'It's nothing to do with me.'

'Just like painting the front of The Sailor's Rest bright pink last year wasn't anything to do with you?'

He gave her a grin. 'That was a matter of honour.' Nick's best friend, Stu, had got into a fight with a tourist and the whole of their little gang had been kicked out by the landlord. The tourist had been at fault for groping Stu's girlfriend as he'd squeezed past on the way to the bar. Like everyone else, Pete Bray relied on the holiday makers who frequented the pub in the summer months and so he'd barred Stu, Nick and the rest without giving them chance to explain. They'd all gone back to Stu's and after a few more beers, this time from his fridge, they'd raided the supply of paint in the back of Stu's van and given the pub a makeover. Pete had been furious at first, but the neon pink had drawn so many curious new faces across the pub's threshold that he'd kept it that way for the rest of the summer. Their ban hadn't been lifted until Nick and the rest had repainted the pub – and not just the front, but all the window frames and the door, too.

'It was an act of sheer foolishness,' Mum countered, giving his arm a flick with her fingers as she returned from hanging up his coat. 'Don't stand there making the place look untidy, set the table. And I hope for your sake that you didn't have anything to do with this mermaid nonsense. Things like this have a habit of backfiring, and you know what the internet is like, they'll already be hunting out whoever is behind the account.'

'Well, I hope they don't find out too soon,' Dad said, placing a stack of dinner plates in the centre of the scarred wooden table they ate at during the week, the dining room being reserved for Sunday night dinners and special celebrations such as birthdays and Christmas. 'I posted a few pictures of the mermaid-themed items we stock on our page this afternoon, and I've had over a dozen orders on the website.'

'Look at you go, Dad,' Nick said, giving his shoulder a friendly shove as he worked his way around the table laying out the cutlery and place mats. 'You'll be an internet billionaire in no time.'

'I'll be happy if it keeps us ticking over. About time we had a bit of good luck around here. Maybe those old stories about the mermaids protecting the village have a ring of truth to them after all.'

'That's a nice thought, love.' Mum placed a rectangular

ceramic dish of lasagne in the centre of the table, the sauce on the top still bubbling. 'It's been such a miserable day, I thought we could all do with something to warm us up. It's butternut squash and spinach before you ask.' She took her usual chair at the head of the table. 'Who knows, maybe it'll bring a few visitors down at the weekend. I checked the forecast earlier and this rain is supposed to blow through tomorrow and then it's clear skies.'

'Let's all cross our fingers and hope so,' Nick said, accepting the spoon from their mum and dishing himself up a huge slab of pasta and sauce. 'We haven't had a booking since that ornithology group we took out last week. Uncle Tony was even talking about looking to see if any of the trawlers need temporary crew.'

'Oh, it hasn't come to that, has it?' Mum's fork clattered against her plate, her face pale with worry.

Nick raised one shoulder in an unhappy shrug. 'We can't pay the bills with fresh air. I told him if anyone's going out, it'll be me. He shouldn't be hauling nets at his age, not when he captained his own boat. It'd be too much of a comedown. Besides, he could've done anything he wanted with the proceeds of the sale, he didn't have to establish a business and try and make sure we all still had work. I owe him.'

'You're a good lad.' Dad placed a broad palm over the back of Nick's hand and gave it a pat. 'A couple of weeks out on the boats wouldn't be too bad this time of year.'

'I've been out in worse, that's for sure.' Never one for dwelling on his worries, Nick gave them his trademark broad grin. 'Who knows, maybe I'll haul in a mermaid in the nets and she'll fall madly in love with me – about the only chance I've got of getting a girlfriend these days!'

'See if you can catch a merman for me, while you're at it,'

Laurie chipped in. Having grown up with the few eligible prospects around the village, it was hard to see them as anything more than her brother's friends. She'd been asked out now and again by visitors to the village, but one failed summer fling was more than enough to put her off for life. The way things were going, she'd end up alone like Aunt Nerissa, Dad's younger sister.

Laughter rippled around the table, the way it had on so many evenings past.

* * *

Laurie wasn't laughing the next morning when she opened the front door just after 7.30 to see a queue of cars snaking down the hill in front of the house. *What in the world?*

The driver's window of the nearest one slid open. "Scuse me, love, but are you local?'

Bending at the waist, she met the excited gazes of a family of four. 'Umm, yes, I am.'

The man in the driver's seat beamed at her. 'Any idea where we can park? All the roads seem to be double-yellows.' In order to save the residents' sanity and to prevent parked cars from blocking the narrow streets, the local council had confined parking to authorised car parks, apart from a couple of loading bays that the local businesses used for deliveries.

'There's a council car park not far from the front.' Laurie pointed down the hill. 'Although it looks like you might be in the queue for it already. If you don't get any luck there, there's another one back the way you came. It's a bit of a longer walk, but not too far.'

The blonde woman poked the driver in the arm. 'I told you I saw a sign just as we were coming into the village.' She leaned across him to smile at Laurie. 'Looks like we're not the only ones who have come mermaid spotting. We thought we'd be ahead of the game by setting off early but seems like everyone else had the same idea.'

'Have you seen it?' A little girl, the spitting image of her mother, poked her head between the front seats. 'The mermaid? Is she pretty?'

The driver rolled his eyes, but the indulgent grin on his face didn't waver. 'Mermaid-mad, that one. Aren't you, Rosie?'

Nodding, the little girl waved what looked like a Barbie doll with an iridescent fish tail at Laurie. 'They're sooo beautiful. I wish I was a mermaid.'

Mermaid spotting? Laurie glanced up and down the row of cars stretching as far as she could see. 'I... umm... I haven't seen the mermaid, no. Would you excuse me a moment?' Without waiting for an answer, she dashed back inside. 'Dad? Nick?'

'In the kitchen, love.'

Rushing in, she found the rest of the family finishing off their breakfast. 'You'd better shake yourselves and get down the shop,' she said to her parents. 'And you need to call Uncle Tony,' she added to Nick.

'What's going on?' Her brother asked, rising from his seat to place his crumb-covered plate in the dishwasher.

'I think Dad was right. I think that mermaid might be bringing good luck to the Point.'

3

Jake Smith stared at the candid shots littering the table before him, feeling sicker by the minute. He felt grubby and dirty as though he'd been one of the pathetic men who'd used and abused the sad-eyed women being ushered into the back of a van by a border force official. Whatever sense of satisfaction he'd had over playing a part in their discovery and rescue was buried under an avalanche of guilt. *Yeah, you're some bloody hero, all right.* He'd ignored their plight for weeks. At the time he'd justified it, knowing there was a bigger story to uncover. The authorities had had their chance and blown it. The story only landed on Jake's desk thanks to a call to the *Eastern Comet*'s tip line. If the police hadn't ignored Mrs Rodgers' complaints about suspicious activity across the street, the women would've been in safe hands long ago. Knowing that didn't make Jake feel any better.

Like the cops, he'd thought it a dead-end at first, just some bored old lady twitching her net curtains, and been furious at Mac, his editor, for assigning him a non-story any of the juniors should've been able to deal with. But Mac had a nose for a story, and the moment Mrs Rodgers had opened her front door, Jake had felt that familiar buzz of adrenaline he only got when he knew he was onto something good. Over a pot of tea, Mrs Rodgers had told him about the comings and goings at all hours. The strange cars parked in the street, the odd glimpse of women at the windows when she'd been told a couple of brothers had bought the place. He might still have thought it nothing more than a figment of a bored imagination if he hadn't witnessed the arrival and departure of three cars in the hour he'd spent with her.

Delighted to have someone take her seriously, Mrs Rodgers had been only too happy to turn over her spare front bedroom for Jake to use as an observation point. After a couple of nights camped out in there, he'd come to the same conclusion as her – someone was operating a brothel in this quiet little street. He'd happened to spot a man leaving on foot, just as he was departing one morning after wolfing down the full English Mrs Rodgers had laid on, and followed him to a mini cab firm operating out of a rundown shop on the high street. Jake had dug around and found the taxi company was registered to two brothers, along with several other small businesses, including a couple of takeaways, a barber shop and a dry cleaners. All the kind of places it would be easy enough for someone with the right knowledge to launder illegal money through. And as the investigation continued, his focus became less and less about the women behind that anonymous front door and more about the shadowy activities of the brothers. Jake watched the same 'customers' using the barber's week in and week out, though they seemed to spend more time chatting than anything else and their appearances were unaltered when they left. He'd even posed as a customer to take a closer look, leaving twenty minutes later with a disastrous buzz cut, and the conviction the bloke wielding the clippers knew no more about cutting hair than Jake himself did.

The taxi company proved trickier to dig into. There were plenty of legitimate drivers on the books – Jake's expenses at the end of the month could attest to that. Using a cover story about his own car being written off in an accident and having to wait for the insurance to sort it out, he'd gone everywhere in taxis for three weeks solid. A couple of the drivers were bored and eager to chat, especially after he'd been picked up by the same ones a few times. Before too long they were airing complaints about a couple of the other drivers who weren't pulling their weight, always on the road but never available to pick up any of the jobs called in. He started feeding information back about his suspicions to a reliable contact on the local police force who shared intelligence off the record about cabs being a possible source of drug dealing in the area. More pieces of the puzzle fell into place, and Jake's entire focus narrowed to building a story of the two brothers running a major crime ring in the town.

He studied the abject misery and desperation etched on the women's faces before him. Finally convinced he had enough proof, he'd gone back to his contact on the force and persuaded him to let Jake and a photographer he trusted tag along when they raided any of the properties. Weeks had passed while the police carried out their own investigations and Jake focused on drafting and polishing what would now be a series of exposés, not just on the crime and corruption surrounding this case, but also on the rise in these types of crimes in other small towns. It wasn't until he'd seen the first woman being led from the house by an immigration officer that the true human cost behind the story hit home. A couple of the younger women – no more than girls from the look of them – had been in tears. Another had started kicking and screaming the moment she saw the black immigration van with its caged interior, as though she knew this wasn't a rescue mission, simply a transfer from one type of confinement to another. But what had struck Jake the most was the blankness on the faces of the rest of the dozen or so women. There was no hope in their eyes, no relief. As he stared at them now, trying to narrow down the selection of photos before he sent them to Mac for final approval, he felt only disgust. Not for them, but with himself for extending the horrors they'd been put through in pursuit of a *better* story.

Snatching off his glasses, he chucked them down on the table and rubbed at the pinch of pain on the bridge of his nose. There was always a point in the day when he couldn't stand wearing them a moment longer, but he'd never got on with contact lenses and he couldn't focus on his computer screen without them. Or maybe he was just looking for any excuse to avoid the accusation he swore he could see in those women's faces. Knowing Mac would be expecting his latest draft and the narrowed down selection of photos within the hour, Jake gave himself a mental kick in the backside and stretched out a hand to retrieve his glasses.

A knock on the open door of the conference room gave him the excuse he'd been looking for. Glancing up, he found Mac propped against the frame, arms crossed, his checked open-necked shirt almost as creased as Jake's own. 'You look terrible,' his editor said by way of greeting.

'Cheers, I feel it.' Jake waved a hand over the scattered images. 'I thought I had until 4 p.m. to get these to you.'

Unfolding his arms, Mac took a couple of strides into the room and began shuffling through the photos. 'This one,' he said, sliding a picture of the two crying girls towards Jake. 'And... this one.' He added a haunting portrait of a woman looking back over her shoulder as she was being helped into the van by two burly uniformed immigration officers.

The contrast between the thin fragility of her arms held in their large fists, the lace white of her top – little more than a scrap of underwear – against the jet black of their uniforms was striking. Though both Jake and Colin, the photographer, had been standing on the outside of the cordon of official vehicles, it had felt like she was staring straight at them, when in reality, he doubted she'd even noticed them at all. *The joys of a guilty conscience*, Jake supposed.

'Right,' Mac said, with a decisive nod. 'Now that's done, perhaps you can tell me why you've been faffing around in here for the past hour looking like a cow with a smacked arse instead of pounding that keyboard to meet your deadline.'

'The story's done.'

Mac propped his hip against the edge of the table. 'Then why isn't it on my desk, and why aren't you down the pub celebrating?'

Jake shrugged. 'Doesn't feel like there's much to celebrate.'

'Other than the biggest story of your career,' Mac scoffed. 'Bloody hell, man, I've got interest from news syndicates across the country. This is going to break everywhere, and once it does, the nationals will be knocking on your door and you won't give us a backward glance.' There was no malice in his tone, only resignation and maybe even a hint of gruff pride. 'Mind you, you'll have to do something about that thin skin of yours. There's no room for hearts and flowers in Fleet Street.'

Working for one of the national papers had been a dream

of Jake's since he'd first decided to study journalism after leaving college. Working at the *Eastern Comet* had always been a stepping-stone along the path, and Mac had known that. A veteran of the business, he'd seen several protégés make the leap to the capital, and for all his grumbling about it, the walls of his office were plastered with copies of their major successes. Jake had always imagined himself earning a place on Mac's wall of glory, but now, when it was within touching distance, he just felt tired.

Perhaps something of his ambivalence showed on his face, or perhaps Mac was a canny operator who'd been around the block more times than most. Whatever it was, he watched Jake in silence for a few moments before clapping his hands together. 'Right. Get your jacket, I'm taking you for a drink.'

Ten minutes later, Mac pushed open the front door of The Horse and Jockey and ushered Jake inside with a wave of his hand. The bite of fresh air on the walk to the pub had lifted some of the gloom from Jake's spirit and he managed a proper smile and a wave to Jilly behind the bar when she called a greeting and said she'd be over with 'the usual' in a minute. Slipping off his jacket, Jake hooked it over the back of one of the chairs at a table in the corner and took a seat on a bench beneath a large opaque glass window etched with an outline of a sleek racehorse, its rider hunched over its neck, urging it on.

Mac hung his own jacket on the other free chair and bookended the other end of the bench, slinging one arm across the low cushioned top of the seat. 'Thanks, Jilly, you're an angel,' he said, reaching for the pint of bitter she placed before him. 'Ah, that's better.' He smacked his lips together, the upper one bearing a trace of foam from the head of the freshly poured beer.

Tilting his bottle of lager, ice-cold from the fridge and the neck already beading with condensation, Jake took a decent swig of his own then set it back on the cardboard beer mat. 'Cheers.'

Mac settled his back more comfortably against the seat then turned a gimlet eye to Jake. 'Come on then, lad, spit it out.'

Rubbing a hand over his aching eyes, Jake sighed. 'I forgot about them. I got so caught up in the bigger picture, I forgot all about those poor bloody women.' He sighed again. 'No, that's a lie. I chose to ignore them, to not think about the consequences because it didn't suit me at the time.'

'And now you're feeling guilty.'

There was no question there, but he answered it anyway. 'Yeah.'

Mac shrugged. 'You didn't put them there. And if you hadn't followed the story, they'd still be there now.'

'But I could've got them out earlier,' Jake protested.

'Oh, take off your bloody cape, Superman, and get over yourself.' Mac snorted as he reached for his pint once more. 'It's not up to us to make the news, it's our job to report it. And I'm not sure those women are going to be any better off than if I'd ignored that call from Mrs Rodgers, rather than sending you to talk to her.'

Jake could only stare for a moment, unable to believe what he was hearing. 'You can't mean that.'

Mac took a long swallow of beer, then shook his head. 'Probably not, but I don't like their future prospects. Immigration are overwhelmed. They've likely registered them all and turfed them back onto the streets with instructions to report. Most will end up on the game again because what else are they going to be able to do to support themselves? It's a bloody nasty business, but it's not something the likes of you and me can do anything about other than highlight it.'

'Christ. Now I'm really depressed.' Jake took a morose swig from his bottle. 'So, what's the point?'

'The point, my lad, is to tell the truth. And to keep on telling the truth until the public get outraged enough to put pressure on someone who *can* do something about it.'

'And what if that never happens?'

'Then we move onto the next terrible thing, and we report on that. And we keep on reporting because that's our job. We're here to bear witness, to hold up a mirror to society and reflect it back in all its ugliness.'

Jake sat silent, contemplating the stark truth behind his mentor's words. Seemingly unconcerned, Mac settled back to enjoy the rest of his pint, his gaze never still as he studied the other patrons in the pub. He might be getting a bit long in the tooth, but there was a sharpness in those blue eyes that said he didn't miss a thing. Jake bet himself that if he quizzed his boss on their way back to the office, Mac would be able to describe everyone in detail. That's what people like them did; they observed, and catalogued, and reported. Nothing more.

'But what if I can't do it?' he asked, at last. 'What if I can't leave it to somebody else to fix the problems?'

'Then you're in the wrong job,' Mac fired straight back at him. 'Though for what my opinion's worth, I don't believe that. You've got a gift, Jake. Sometimes words speak louder than actions. Your words have power, I've thought that since you first started working at the *Comet*.' Setting down his empty glass, Mac turned his body more fully towards Jake, his elbow resting on the table. 'Look, lad, you've been working flat out on this for months, it's bound to take a toll. We'll put you on something lighter for a bit, something less stressful to give you time to think things over.'

'Fluff pieces, you mean? Local dog shows and bonny-bloody-baby comps? No, thanks!' Jake took a mouthful of his beer, grimacing because it'd gone warm and flat.

Mac grinned. 'Nothing that bad. What else would I torture the cub reporters with?' A wicked glint shone in his eye. 'What if I told you there was a way to combine a story with a holiday? A bit of sunshine will do you the world of good.'

A break in the sun sounded just like what he needed. But from the way Mac was showing him more teeth than a Great White lurking beneath a group of teenage swimmers, he knew there was a catch. 'Why do I have a bad feeling about this?'

'Fetch me another pint, lad, and then you can tell me everything you think you know about mermaids.'

'So I can have it until the end of August?' Jake picked up the ugliest vase he'd ever seen from the clutter lining the mantelpiece and turned it over. Expecting it to say 'Made in Taiwan' he saw instead some kind of gold maker's mark and the sort of symbols he'd seen on expensive bits of pottery on *Antiques Roadshow*. Placing it back with rather more care than he'd used picking it up, he made a mental note to find a cupboard to store it and all the other nick-nacks scattered across every available surface. The minimalist movement had clearly bypassed Mrs Walker.

'Well, I've got a couple of enquiries pencilled in the diary for July, but nobody's paid a deposit, so if you're sure you really want it for the whole summer?' The way her tone rose at the end of the question made it obvious his potential landlady was dying to know why a single man wanted to blockbook a holiday rental cottage.

'I'm definitely interested, I've got a couple of other places to look at, but I prefer this location. Privacy is important to me. I'm a writer and I need somewhere I can shut myself away and get on with things.' The cover story he'd concocted with Mac was close enough to the truth to be plausible.

'Oh, how wonderful! My very own artist in residence.' Mrs Walker perched on the arm of the large chocolate-brown sofa and stared up at him with interest. 'Do you mind me asking what you're working on, or is it top secret?'

'It's a guide to myths and legends around Britain.' Another strand to the tale he and his editor had concocted that would make his choice of Mermaids Point seem credible. Propping his hands on the back of an armchair, he laid a bit more groundwork. 'I'll be writing more about how and why the same stories crop up in different parts of the country when they often date back to a time when people didn't travel much. Like, I didn't realise how many versions there are of big cat legends stretching all the way from Scotland to Exmoor.' *Thank you, Wikipedia.* 'Around the coast, it's all sea monsters and mermaids.'

'And when our very own mermaid hit the headlines, you couldn't resist coming to look for yourself, I take it?' When he nodded, Mrs Walker laughed. 'You and half the country, or so it's felt like the last couple of weekends. We're never normally this busy at the start of the season, but it's been a bit like being under siege.'

The journey from east to west had been pretty straight-forward and Jake hadn't noticed much traffic on the roads, but then again it was a Monday and still in termtime, so most visitors would come and go at the weekends. 'I hadn't really thought about that. One of the other places I am supposed to look at is right in the heart of the village.'

When he'd been building his shortlist from Airbnb, and a couple of other holiday rental sites, a central location had been top of the list. He'd only added this cottage located within the grounds of Walkers' Farm because the photos of the rear garden demanded a closer look. Not a large space, it was mostly patio and would need almost no effort from him to keep up. What had really caught his eye, though, was the spectacular view over the end of the Point and out across the ocean. As well as a table and chairs, the large patio held a swing seat and a small gas barbecue. Huge pots filled with ferns and other greenery, he had no names for, gave it a tropical feel, and even he could manage to sprinkle them with a watering can a couple of times a week.

'If you're talking about the Coopers' place, you won't find much peace and quiet there.' Mrs Walker rose and glanced up the full length of him. Jake doubted she was much taller than five feet two from the way she craned her neck to meet his eye. 'And you'll concuss yourself on all those low beams. You'll have the best of both worlds here,' she said, warming to her sales pitch. 'Peace and quiet when you want it, with easy access to the beach at the same time. There's a decent pathway that'll take you down into the village, and although we prefer to use the local shops you might not have the time or the inclination. The big Tesco delivers out here for when you want to stock up.' Raising a finger, she tapped it against her lip, considering for a moment. 'It wouldn't be much extra effort to add a portion to whatever I'm fixing Alan and me for dinner. I could freeze them for you and you could pop by once a week and pick them up. Or one of us could drop them in, but then you'd probably not want us disturbing your work.'

Home-cooked meals on tap, instead of microwave meals and takeaways? Okay, she was really selling this place to him. 'That's very generous of you. We'd have to come to a suitable arrangement to cover the cost as well as for your time.' He did a quick mental calculation of his weekly takeaway costs. 'Would fifty pounds a week do it?'

She flushed. 'Oh, that's far too much money, I couldn't possibly. Like I said, I'd only be adding a bit extra to what I was already going to make. I just thought it might help you out, give you one less thing to worry about so you can get on with your work.'

If Mrs Walker's friendly warmth was an example of what the people of Mermaids Point were like, Jake was glad he'd let Mac talk him into what he still thought was a wild goose chase. 'Well, if you could throw in a couple of hours cleaning with the deal then I'd call an extra fifty quid a week on the rental price, a bargain.'

Mrs Walker looked troubled. 'I'd have to service the place anyway if I was doing the usual weekly rentals and that's factored into the rent... an extra thirty pounds would more than cover it.'

It was all he could do not to laugh. He didn't think he'd ever dealt with someone who tried to bargain him down to a *lower* offer before. He shook his head. 'Fifty. I'm a messy bachelor.'

She pursed her lips before finally nodding. 'Fifty then. I'll change the bedding and towels twice a week on Wednesdays and Saturdays and if you've anything else you want putting through the wash, leave it the laundry basket in the bathroom.'

Jake was sure he'd spotted a washing machine and dryer in the small utility room off the kitchen, but he wasn't going to argue the toss with her. He hadn't had someone fuss about after him since, well, ever really. His mum's entire focus had been on making sure his dad had everything just the way he liked it. Jake had only ever been an afterthought. Not having to fend for himself would make a nice change, even if he was paying for the privilege.

Besides, this *was* supposed to be a holiday as well as a chance to dig around and try and get to the bottom of who was behind the mermaid hoax. Though he liked to keep an open mind going into any story, he was starting from the point of the video being staged, because really what was the alternative? It would be interesting to uncover *why* they'd done it as much as finding out who it was. Hence his cover story. If he started barging around the place, asking loads of questions he risked not only spooking the hoaxers, but getting the backs up of the local people. No one liked the idea of a reporter snooping around, even when the story was a bit of nonsense. The myths and legends angle gave him a legitimate reason to interview people about what they might know without arousing suspicion.

Holding out his hand, he grinned down at Mrs Walker. 'You've got yourself a deal.'

She took his hand, but instead of shaking it she gave it a pat. 'Oh, Jake, I *am* pleased. Why don't you come over with me to the farmhouse and we can sort the paperwork out? Alan will be in anytime for his afternoon tea so you can meet him, too. I've got scones baked fresh this morning.'

Oh, he was really going to like living here. 'Lead the way, Mrs Walker. Lead the way.'

* * *

It wasn't until the next morning that Jake got his first proper look around the village itself. Afternoon tea with Alan and Carolyn – Mrs Walker having insisted on first names – had been followed by a trip around the farm in Alan's battered but serviceable four-wheel drive. He hadn't appreciated the extent of their holding, but it stretched out for acres beyond the funny dogleg of land that held the main farmhouse and what was now Jake's cottage for the next few months. Alan's father had sold some of the land to help the village expand in the sixties, leaving the farmhouse and its outbuildings almost isolated from the rest of it. Alan had sold a bit more off when the old schoolhouse had outlived its usefulness to allow for a newer one to be built in the mid-eighties, and said he and Carolyn liked the division of their living space from the working part of the farm.

They'd been out for a couple of hours, Alan stopping every now and then to point out some feature of the landscape, or to check one bit or another of the miles and miles of dry-stone walls crisscrossing his land. Most of the farm was given over to grazing, sheep for the main part, but to Jake's delight Alan also raised a small herd of alpacas. The sheep had mostly ignored them, but the alpacas had headed over the moment Alan stopped his truck, and they'd soon been encircled by the herd. Not really used to being around animals, especially ones of that size, Jake had been a bit wary, but with a bit of encouragement from Alan he'd soon been scratching their ears and stroking their backs. Wending his way down the rocky path into the village, Jake found himself smiling at the memory. He might not find any mermaids during his stay, but he'd had a different kind of unexpected encounter, that was for sure.

Reaching a fork in the path, he opted for the left-hand route as the other looked as though it led down to the beach. He would explore that later, but for now he wanted to get his bearings and hopefully meet a few other residents. There was no promenade to speak of; the shops facing towards the sea were situated along a cobbled street edged with a narrow footpath. The only thing separating the street from quite a steep drop down to the beach was a black metal fence.

The shops were a mixture of practical services for the residents – a butcher, a fishmonger, an independent chemist's – and those focused entirely on tourists. The sight of an old-fashioned penny slot arcade filled Jake with nostalgia for his own childhood trips to Great Yarmouth and Blackpool. His parents had always favoured package holidays somewhere hot with a pristine azure-blue swimming pool surrounded by banks of sun loungers and a kids' club they could dump Jake in to keep him out of his father's way. He'd much preferred the rest of his summer holidays when he'd been packed off to his maternal grandparents. Like a plant starved of sunlight, he'd soaked up the attention they lavished on him. They hadn't had a lot of money to spare, but they'd always worked hard to make those summers a special time with day trips and short breaks to holiday resorts closer to home. They'd stopped not long after Jake went to secondary school. His grandfather had got sick – too sick to cope with a boisterous teenager. The last two visits he'd made had been to the nondescript brick chapel next to the crematorium.

Raising one hand to shield his eyes, Jake peered through the plate-glass window of the arcade and wondered how much of his pocket money he'd wasted shoving coins in the machines. His belly tightened, a muscle memory stirred by the remembered thrill as the stacks of five- and ten-pence pieces hovered on the end of the slot, luring him, telling him with every miniscule quiver as the mechanical slider edged back and forth that one more coin, *just one more*, would cause a fortune to tumble down into the collection tray. A large glass cabinet full of stuffed toys caught his eye, and he couldn't help but grin. It was one of those games with a large grabbing claw used to fish the hapless bears, rabbits and other garishly coloured toys out of the pile and carry them to a collection chute. Only the claw never quite had the strength to get the toys all the way to the end.

Deciding a nostalgia visit to the arcade was on the cards at some point, Jake tucked his hands in the pocket of his lightweight jacket and continued to stroll past the shops. The butcher had a small queue, and a couple of guys were loading small wooden crates full of fresh vegetables into the back of a white van outside the grocer. If they did home delivery, it might be worth checking out as a way to supplement the meals his landlady was going to supply. It would make a nice change to get something local rather than using a supermarket all the time.

Beyond the grocer's was a newsagent, the pavement in front of it filled with racks of postcards. Nets hung from its bright, striped awning, filled with balls of all sizes, buckets and spades and other beach essentials. Jake found himself walking through the front door, the temptation of newsprint a siren's call. Though he subscribed to just about every online news service going, there was still something about holding an actual newspaper that he loved. They were a staple of his life, and not simply because of what he did for a living. His parents still had their paper of choice delivered, his mum saving the weekend supplements all week as she worked her way through the articles she wanted to read. Breakfast at his grandparents' had always been accompanied by a running commentary from his grandfather on whatever article he was reading, his gran hmming along in what sounded like agreement, though as he'd grown older he'd realised she had her own opinions on things and just let those morning rants wash right over her.

Ignoring the national titles, Jake picked up a couple of the local papers and carried them over to the large glass-fronted counter. Behind the glass, he was delighted to see a couple of Airfix model kits, along with some board games he remembered playing on rainy afternoons with his grandparents. The shelves behind were packed with jars of traditional sweets and, never one to resist temptation, Jake requested a quarter of mint imperials. After tucking the paper bag of sweets in one pocket and securing the papers under his arm, he shared a cheery farewell with the newsagent and carried on exploring.

A few feet further on there was a pedestrian crossing leading across the street to a gap in the railings and a wide set of steps going down to the beach. As there was only one car coming, Jake didn't bother to press the button on the crossing, but the approaching car slowed nonetheless and flashed its headlights to indicate he should cross. Round where he lived, the drivers barely gave you chance to cross even when the light was green. Raising a hand in thanks, which turned into an exchange of friendly waves with the lady driving the vehicle, Jake strode across the road and jogged down the steps.

The beach was a mixture of larger rocks and shingle, which crunched beneath his shoes as he made his way down to the thin strip of dark sand edging the waterline. Close to shore, the lapping waves looked benign enough, but away from the shelter of the buildings there was a breeze stiff enough to make Jake tuck his newspapers against his chest and zip up his jacket. Further out to sea, white horses were racing in on some impressive waves, and the bases of the dark islands he could just about make out were ringed with white surf. Jake crouched to dip his hand in the water, drawing it back instantly as the icy chill registered. *Not a day for paddling.* Shaking the droplets off his fingers, Jake dried them on the front of his jeans as he stood up. The beach was deserted for the most part, a couple of dog walkers and a man dressed in green overalls who looked to be litter-picking the only people in sight. From his vantage point he could see another set of steps further along and decided to brave the biting edge of the wind for the reward of the freshness of the salty air.

He was maybe halfway to his destination when a golden retriever who'd been splashing in and out of the surf bounded up and dropped a well-chewed stick at his feet. Laughing at the expectant look on the dog's face, Jake retrieved the stick and tossed it behind him, making sure it didn't land too deep in the water in the same manner he'd watched the dog's owner do. The retriever raced off after it, barking madly. Continuing, Jake smiled as the owner approached and he readied himself for a brief exchange of greetings. 'Beautiful morning, isn't it?'

'Yes, it is, glorious.' To his surprise, the woman stopped rather than carrying on her way. She tucked in a stray curl of dark hair which had escaped from the knitted beret covering her ears.

'It might be sunny, but it's a bit chillier than I'd anticipated,' he admitted. Jake was sure the tips of his ears must be glowing bright red and was quietly jealous of the way women wore hats with such ease. He hated baseball caps, or rather hated the way he felt stupid in them, and flat caps might be trendy but he couldn't get over feeling he looked like his grandfather whenever he'd tried them on in the shops. He settled for turning up the collar on his jacket instead.

The woman smiled, the edges of her mouth and eyes crinkling in a way that hinted she was a bit older than he'd first estimated. 'The sun can be deceiving when you're not used to the climate around here.' It wasn't quite a question, but there was a curiosity in her gaze that said she knew everyone around these parts and had him pegged for a stranger.

Remembering he was supposed to be working and not just sightseeing, Jake took the cue to extend the conversation. 'I only arrived yesterday. I've taken the cottage at Walkers' Farm for the season. I'm a writer, you see.' Realising he'd told her everything but the most important part, he gave a sheepish grin. 'I'm Jake.'

'Nice to meet you, Jake, and welcome to the Point. I'm Nerissa Morgan.' The retriever came running up at that moment and she crouched down to wrestle it for the stick before throwing it once more. 'You'll find me here most mornings around this time,' she continued, wiping her wet fingers on the leg of her jeans. 'I bring Toby down for a run while Doc has his coffee break. It does us both good to escape for a bit.' She blushed as though she hadn't meant to add the last bit. 'Anyway, if you're going to be with us for a while, you might want to consider a temporary registration with the surgery.'

It hadn't even crossed his mind, and now he thought about it, he couldn't even remember the last time he'd visited his own GP. 'I didn't realise that was something you could do,' he said, not wishing to be rude.

She nodded. 'We get a few longish term visitors, though many of them are retired so probably more in need of a regular doctor than a young man like you.' She laughed. 'Although the way you're shivering, you'll catch your death if I keep you standing around much longer.' Pointing back the way she'd come, she indicated a large white building at the far end of the street. 'That's the surgery. If you do decide to register, just pop in and see me anytime, I do all the admin.'

'Cheers. I might just do that. Right now, though, I'm going to hunt out a cup of coffee to warm up.' Jake tugged again at the collar of his jacket, a fruitless gesture as the wind was cutting straight through the thin cotton. 'And then I'm going to buy myself a fleece!'

'Sounds like a plan! I can help you out with the first one at least, there's a café almost opposite the next set of steps. It's run by my niece, Laurie. Tell her I sent you.'

If the forthcoming weekend was going to be anything like the previous couple, Laurie was going to have to seriously consider taking on another member of staff to help. She always hired a handful of local teenagers for the summer holiday peak but managed on her own most of the rest of the time. Her mum did her best, splitting her time between the shop and the café for the very busiest hours and Aunt Nerissa had popped in and helped for a bit on Sunday, but it wasn't fair on either of them when they had their own jobs to do. Wednesdays were half-day closing so she'd do a bit of brainstorming and see if she could come up with a shortlist of people to approach. Failing that, she'd have to place an ad in the local paper. For now, though, she was taking advantage of a lull in customers to make a few batches of cookies and brownies. The timer on the counter dinged just as she was spooning the last bit of mix on the greased tray in front of her. *Perfect*.

She removed the two trays of piping-hot brownies from the oven and replaced them with the cookie batches. As she transferred the brownies onto a pair of cooling racks, she closed her eyes for a second to enjoy their rich chocolatey aroma. Though she tried to be good, these choc-cherry treats were her favourite and the reason she would never squeeze her bottom into a pair of size twelve jeans. It was a compromise she was willing to accept, she decided, popping one of the brownies onto a plate to enjoy with a cup of tea later. The front bell rang, and she wandered through from the kitchen, still wearing her dirty apron as she had a least two more batches she wanted to mix up.

Instead of one of her regulars, Laurie found herself staring into the eyes of possibly the most handsome man she'd ever seen. Well, not exactly into his eyes, more into the salt-spattered lenses of the wire-framed glasses perched on the bridge of an impressive Roman nose. Tall and broad through the shoulders, with his brown hair cut close to his scalp, he had a presence about him as though he somehow occupied more space than his physical frame. Wishing like hell she'd taken off her dirty apron, and that she was wearing something more flattering than the well-worn cotton t-shirt with a faded image of the Eiffel Tower she'd slung on with her favourite jeans, Laurie gave him her best smile.

'Take a seat and I'll be right with you.' She waved him towards one of the tables by the window then shot back into the kitchen to tug off the apron and hang it up. Pausing to check her reflection in the small mirror hanging on the wall next to the hook, she sighed over the big smear of cake mix on her chin and how flushed her cheeks were from the heat of the oven. Wiping off the mess, she washed her hands at the sink, considered retying her ponytail but that would mean washing her hands again and leaving the poor chap waiting even longer. He'd just have to take her as she was.

Chance'd be a fine thing.

Grinning at the naughty thought, Laurie hurried back into the café, grabbing a menu on her way past the counter. When she stopped beside the table he'd chosen, it was to find he'd removed his jacket and was wiping the lenses of his glasses on the front of his red and blue checked shirt. Glancing up with a smile, he gave Laurie the full force of eyes as blue as the sky at midsummer and she had to rest a hand on the table – casually, she hoped – to stop her knees wobbling.

Instead of putting them back on and giving her some protection from those devastating eyes, the man set his glasses to one side on top of a couple of newspapers and smiled. 'You must be Laurie, your Aunt Nerissa sent me. Even if she hadn't said you two were related, I'd know it from the shape of your face.'

'Thanks.' *Maybe.* Not able to help herself, Laurie raised a hand to shield her chin. Both she and her aunt were blessed – or cursed – with a heart-shaped face which tapered into a jaw more than one person had referred to as stubborn. She'd been conscious of it since one of the boys at school had teased her about its prominence, although she'd grown more assured and accepting of her looks since escaping the trials of the playground.

'Is that for me?' He nodded to the menu her other hand was pinning to the table, a grin teasing the corner of his mouth. Gorgeous and amusing? Oh boy, she was in real trouble.

'What? Oh, yes.' She pushed it across to him, resisting the urge to use it to fan the heat she could feel rising on her cheeks. 'There's specials on the chalkboard, but you can have anything you fancy.'

'Well, there's an offer I wasn't expecting today.' Honestly, the creases in his cheeks had no right to be so attractive, especially when he was making fun of her, even in such a sweet way.

Hoping attack was better than retreat, Laurie decided to up the ante. 'I was referring to the contents of my fridge, but I'm free most Friday nights after seven.' She gave herself a moment to enjoy the surprise widening his eyes before continuing. 'I'll give you a few moments to choose and then I'll be back to take your order.' Turning on her heel, Laurie beat a hasty retreat for the safety of the kitchen before he had chance to respond. Meeting her flustered gaze in the little mirror, she shook her head at herself. 'Lorelai Morgan, what on earth are you thinking, flirting with a customer like that?' she whispered at her reflection.

It was an unwritten rule of hers not to respond to any attempts by visitors to try to pick her up, and inevitably a few would try to do that every year. Some of them didn't even hide their wedding rings as they leaned on the top of her counter, thinking she would be charmed by their run-of-the-mill comments when all she wanted to do was yell at them for getting bits of sand and greasy sun cream residue all over her nice clean surfaces. Even the few she found attractive she never pursued because what was the point? They'd be gone in a few days, and casual hook-ups were not her thing. She'd been there, done that and been left with too many regrets. She wasn't on holiday, after all, and while it might be fine for the local lads to have a bit of fun, the community of Mermaids Point was a long way from the anonymity and liberal attitudes of big city life. Tongues wagged.

Determined to be more professional, Laurie gathered up

a notepad and pen, took a deep breath and headed back to the man's table. 'Are you ready to order?'

The smile lighting his face dimmed a little when she kept her own expression flat, pen poised over a blank page of the notepad. 'Umm, a large cappuccino, with an extra shot, will be fine, please.'

'I'll be right back with that.' She'd barely made it behind the counter before she heard the scrape of chair legs as he rose and followed her. Though it went against her nature to be rude, Laurie didn't turn around to acknowledge his presence, making a beeline instead for the large industrial coffee machine.

'I met her on the beach, just now, your aunt, I mean.' Even his voice was nice. Not too deep, its rich tone softened by a hint of an accent she couldn't quite place. A slight drawl on some of the vowels, but nothing as pronounced as the deep west country burrs many of the local people carried.

Adding the extra shot to the machine, Laurie set it brewing before setting a polite smile and turning to face him. He was a customer, and it wasn't his fault she'd steered their conversation in the wrong direction. At least he wasn't leaning on the counter, his hands tucked neatly in the front pockets of his jeans. Another point in his favour, they really were starting to rack up. 'Taking Toby out for a run?' she guessed.

He nodded. 'Lovely natured dog.'

Laurie snorted. 'Only because she takes care of him. I don't know why Doc got him, because Toby spends more time with Nerissa than anywhere near his so-called owner. I knew it would happen as soon as she mentioned he was getting a dog.' Laurie folded her arms, the old impatience at the way Doc treated her aunt flaring up. 'She's supposed to be his housekeeper, not his nursemaid, but she does everything for that blasted man.'

'Not a fan, I take it.'

Realising she'd forgotten her sense of propriety yet again, Laurie pulled a face. 'Sorry, but he needs to retire. He should've gone at least five years ago, probably more, but everyone indulges him because of his age – including Nerissa.'

'I suppose it can be hard to let go sometimes.' It was a reasonable observation, but it didn't soothe the feathers thoughts of Doc had ruffled up.

'Maybe so, but the community is entitled to someone who doesn't think the answer to everything is "women's problems",' she said, turning back to the coffee machine with a huff.

'A bit of a dinosaur, then?' He didn't seem fazed by the topic.

'I think his best friend is Fred Flintstone,' she joked, flashing him a quick grin over her shoulder. She took her time, making sure the milk was really hot and frothy before gently adding it to the double espresso shot in the mug. 'Chocolate?'

'Yes, please. And is there any chance of a slice of whatever it is that smells so divine?' He asked as she slid the coffee onto the counter in front of him.

'Chocolate-cherry brownies. I was making them ready for the weekend, but I can spare you one. I'll bring it over.'

Returning from the kitchen with the brownie she'd set aside for herself, Laurie placed it on the table together with a fork and a fresh cotton napkin. She'd switched over to them the previous year, deciding to try to cut down on her paper usage, and had been pleasantly surprised with the results. Customers often commented on what a nice touch it was, and where they might have taken handfuls of paper ones from the dispenser without thinking, they very rarely used more than one of the fabric ones. 'I hope you enjoy it.' She hesitated over revisiting the topic, but decided she owed him something of an apology for blowing hot and cold. 'I did promise you anything you fancied, after all.'

He fixed her with that laser stare. 'I hadn't forgotten.' *Oh, boy.*

'Yes, well, I'm sorry for overstepping the mark.' Noticing the way she was wringing her hands together, she tucked them behind her back.

'I don't think I've ever been asked out by a woman before, at least not before she even knew my name.'

'I didn't ask you out!' she retorted too fast to notice the teasing grin on his face. 'I don't date my customers. It's not appropriate.'

'Such a shame, because this brownie looks amazing.' With a mournful sigh, he pushed away his cup and plate.

'What are you doing?'

Standing, he reached for the jacket he'd hung on the back of his chair. 'Well, if you're not going to date me if I'm one of your customers, I'd better not eat this.'

Laurie couldn't help but laugh at the word trap he'd well and truly caught her in. 'Oh, sit down and eat your brownie. I'm not going to date you anyway so you might as well enjoy it.' The timer in the kitchen dinged. 'And that's my cue.' She headed back towards the kitchen, trying to ignore the butterflies fluttering in her belly.

The legs of the chair scraped once more as he sat down. 'It's Jake, by the way.'

She paused by the counter to turn and give him a grin over her shoulder. 'I didn't ask.'

He started to laugh as he forked a piece of the brownie into his mouth, the sound breaking off into a moan. 'Bloody hell, Laurie, this is the best thing I've ever tasted. Looks like we're never going out together, because I'm going to be eating in here every day for the rest of the summer.'

The rest of the summer? Escaping into the kitchen, Laurie grabbed a tea towel and fanned her red-hot face. How on earth was she going to deal with him – *Jake* – on a daily basis? The timer dinged again, and she rushed over to the oven to rescue the cookies before the edges caught.

Maybe some rules were made to be broken...

6

The taste of the chocolate brownie lingered on his tongue as Jake reluctantly continued his exploration of the village. It would've been nice to stay and flirt with pretty Laurie Morgan, but he hadn't wanted to push his luck. He'd earmarked the café as a prime location to gather local gossip about the mermaid sighting and there would be plenty of time in the coming days to hopefully get to know her a little better. Sheltered from the wind in the leeward shade of the buildings, he could enjoy the sun's warmth and so he left his jacket hanging open. He strolled the full length of the street, making note of shops he wanted to explore further – he would make his way around them all eventually, but a few in particular caught his eye. The most touristy ones he would save for the weekend when he could blend in with other visitors and listen in to any chatter about the mermaid while browsing the shelves.

He made a pit stop in the grocer's, where he introduced himself and, once he explained his situation, they were only too happy to add a small veg box to their delivery schedule.

'I'll add you to Monday's round, if that works for you,' Jim, the owner said. 'We do a delivery to the farm that day so it won't be any trouble at all.' He fished around in one of the pockets of his brown overall for a moment then produced a card, which he handed to Jake. 'We try to do it all online these days. You'll find a registration link on the website, just fill it in and if you've any specific likes or dislikes there's a box where you can make a note. It's local, seasonal produce and not always pretty to look at, but it all tastes delicious. We also do a fruit bowl option and have a contract with a dairy if you want milk, butter, yoghurts and the like.'

Jake hadn't even thought about stuff like that, and now it looked like he wouldn't have to. 'Sounds great, I'll take a look when I get back and put my order in before the end of the day. Will that be soon enough to start next week?'

'Plenty of time.' Jim beamed at him. 'I hope you enjoy your stay here.'

'I'm sure I will. Everyone I've met has been so friendly. I only arrived yesterday, and I already feel at home.'

'That's what I like to hear. What are your plans for the rest of the day, then?'

Jake was a little taken aback at the directness of the question, but then realised it wasn't a demand for information, more the kind of everyday enquiry Jim likely made to all his customers. It would also be another great way to get the word spreading about him so when he started asking questions, the locals would already be aware of the 'writer' in their midst.

'I'm spending today and the rest of this week getting my bearings. I'm supposed to be working on a book, so I'll be knuckling down next week but wanted to take a few days to familiarise myself with the area.' Jake cast a brief glance over his shoulder at the sea. 'I'm doing a study of myths and legends, and you certainly seem to have a myth of your own around here.'

The grocer chuckled. 'Aye, our mermaid is causing a stir, all right. Not everyone around here is thrilled about it, but if you ask me she's brought some much-needed good luck with her. Past two summers were a washout with all those terrible storms so we're sorely in need of the extra visitors she's attracting. A lot of the bed and breakfast places are booked up solid right through until September.'

Jake nodded. 'Mrs Walker was saying the same thing. I'm glad I got in quick with the cottage or I might have been out of luck.' He smiled when he realised what he'd just said. 'Perhaps the mermaid will be a good luck charm for me, too.'

'A muse for your book, perhaps. Isn't that what they call it?'

'If I'm going to get this book written, I'll certainly need one!' Although, if he was going to have a muse, she was more likely to have a bouncy jet-black ponytail, a devil-may-care grin and the baking skills of an angel, but Jake would keep that information to himself. He tucked the business card into his back pocket then took a step towards the door. 'Thanks again for this, Jim, I'll get that order in and look forward to my first delivery.'

'Glad to be doing business with you, Jake. You take care now, and good luck with the writing.'

Feeling a slight pang of guilt, Jake left with a smile and a wave. What was the matter with him? Getting people to talk to him was part of the job, and if it took a white lie here and there, well it had never been a problem before. Besides, he wasn't doing any harm. Something Jim had mentioned stuck in his brain, about the previous two summers being ruined by the weather. If that was the case, perhaps there was more to the hoax than someone messing around. Perhaps it was a deliberate attempt to draw attention to the village. Jake's pace quickened to match the racing thoughts in his head. Exploring the rest of the village could wait. It felt like he might have found the first thread to begin unravelling the mystery, and he knew right where he needed to start. Clutching the newspapers he'd bought tighter under his arm, he jogged up the winding path that would take him back to the cottage. Everyone had websites these days, even tiny little greengrocer shops like Jim's, and most definitely local newspapers who relied as much on their online advertisers as print ones to keep afloat.

* * *

It was mid-afternoon by the time Jake cast his hated glasses onto the table and raised his arms overhead to stretch out the ache in his lower back. As he rubbed the pinch marks at the bridge of his nose, he considered the progress he'd made. He had a folder on his desktop full of links to a whole host of articles, both local and national, as well as useful sites. The Met Office website was a treasure trove of forecasts and data he would be able to mine for supporting facts and figures if this weather angle to the story proved fruitful. He shifted uncomfortably. The kitchen table and chairs were a long way from the ergonomic desk and seat in his little corner of the busy office at the *Eastern Comet*. He also hadn't anticipated how quiet it would be. The office was always full of chatter and music, and when he worked at home he had music or the TV on.

He hadn't got around to setting everything up the

previous evening, so as an excuse to get away from his screen – and the bum-numbing hardness of the wooden kitchen chair – he spent the next half an hour linking his smart speaker to the cottage's internet. The décor might be traditional, but the Walkers had installed plenty of up-to-date technology, including a smart TV in both the cosy lounge and the main bedroom and he soon had both connected to his Netflix account. They'd also invested in a decent mattress, if the fantastic sleep he'd had the previous night, was anything to go by. Eyeing the bed, he was tempted for a moment to settle back against the mountain of soft pillows and while away the next couple of hours bingeing *Mindhunter*. His stomach chose that moment to remind him he hadn't eaten anything since the chocolate brownie at Laurie's café by rumbling loud enough that he was glad there was no one else around to hear it.

He hadn't got anything in for dinner, having planned to pick something up during his wander around the village. Would it be too obvious to nip back down to the café and get something? Probably. He also needed a few other staples to see him through until his first delivery from the grocer's, and the meals he'd arranged from Mrs Walker weren't going to start until after the weekend. She'd mentioned a big Tesco doing deliveries to the village, so it couldn't be that far. With any luck he'd be able to pick up a fleece or something similar at the same time. When trawling through the Met Office website, he'd noticed on their long range forecast some changeable weather for the coming couple of weeks so he would need something other than the summer-weight jacket he'd brought.

* * *

A few minutes later he was reversing his car carefully out of the farmyard, the postcode for the supermarket plugged into his satnav. Heading back out of the village, it took him a few minutes to realise he was on the same route he'd taken on the way in yesterday. It was another thirty minutes before the slightly robotic voice directed him off the dual carriageway at the next junction, around a large roundabout and he spotted one of those edge-of-town shopping centres. As well as the supermarket, there was a large furniture warehouse, an electronics store, a DIY chain store and an office supplies outlet. *Perfect*.

A quick browse around the office outlet and a chat with one of the staff who assured him the self-assembly was easy enough and Jake was the proud owner of a reasonably priced office chair, which promised full lumbar support. He wasn't sure how effective it could be at less than a hundred quid, but the arms could be folded back out of the way and the padded seat felt like heaven compared to what he'd been sitting on all afternoon. The lad who'd advised him even helped him wrestle the box into the back of his car with only minimal swearing (on Jake's part).

As he'd hoped, the supermarket included a large clothing range where he found a black waterproof jacket with a cosy fleece lining. Heading down the aisle towards the food section, he paused by a display of hats. Most of the rack was dedicated to baseball caps and the kind of wide-brimmed sunhats favoured by cricketers, but next to a selection of tweedy flat caps hanging on the bottom row he spotted a dark fedora. Unhooking it on a whim, he popped it on his head and glanced around for a mirror. To his surprise, it didn't look as bad as he'd feared and he had almost convinced himself he could get away with wearing it when he turned his head to the side and spotted a ridiculous yellow feather sticking up from the band encircling the crown.

'Suits you!' Startled, he glanced around to find a middle-aged woman smiling at him. 'It suits you,' she repeated. 'I could tell you weren't sure about it from your expression, but I like it on you.'

'Oh, thanks.' Jake turned back for another look at his reflection. 'Not a fan of the feather, though.'

'Then pull it off once you've paid for it,' she said, like it was the most obvious thing in the world. Which he supposed it was, though he'd never have thought to do it himself.

'Good point, thanks.'

'My pleasure.' And off she went with a cheery wave.

Though he'd only planned on picking up a few essentials, Jake's small trolley was soon full to overflowing. Balancing a slab of beer on the handle, he steered unsteadily towards the tills. His preference was the self-checkout but the queue was longer there than for the normal tills, and he realised with a mental smack to the forehead that he'd left his reusable shopping bags at home in his flat. Grabbing a few from underneath the conveyer belt, he started to unpack the trolley. As the jars of herbs and spices, boxes of rice, packets of pasta and other cupboard staples mounted up it occurred to him just how underprepared he'd been for this trip. He'd treated it as more of a holiday and not given due consideration to the reality of relocating for three months. Duplicates of what he was busily stuffing into shopping bags were sitting in his kitchen at home and he wanted to kick himself for not planning things better. He'd not thought beyond packing clothes, a wash kit and his electrical essentials, and even then he'd been in holiday mode as his new jacket and hat could testify. Trying not to wince at the cost, he slid his debit card into the reader, punched in his pin and thanked the man behind the till. Though he'd agreed essential expenses with Mac, he'd blown his daily food allowance for the entire trip in one shop. Oh, well, it wasn't as though he had much else to spend his money on. Unless he could get the lovely Laurie to change her mind about that no dating rule...

7

The next morning, Laurie loaded the last of the cups and plates from breakfast into the dishwasher, switched it on and then checked her watch. Her regular delivery from the supermarket was due anytime within the next hour, and after her marathon baking session the day before she was in urgent need of it. When she'd first opened, she'd signed up for the cash and carry, but it was a forty-minute drive there and back and with the cost of the fuel and losing the best part of half a day traipsing around the aisles, she'd found it more convenient and economical to order online and have everything delivered straight to the door. Popping out the back, she unlocked the rear door and poked her head out to double-check the loading bay was empty. It was a fine, warm morning so she left the door ajar. It was nearly always the same couple of drivers, and they would give her a shout when they arrived and start transferring the delivery to the storeroom if she was busy with a customer.

Not that she was likely to get many this time of day. It wasn't a knitting circle day and there was always a bit of lull between breakfast and the early lunch crowd. There was Jake, of course, but she doubted he'd been serious when he'd said she could expect to see him every day during his stay. And after her madcap behaviour towards him, she wouldn't blame him if he gave the place a wide berth. She gave her watch another quick glance. Besides, it'd been nearly eleven when he'd called in yesterday so even if he was going to come back, it was probably too early yet.

Without enough flour to even prep anything, there wasn't much she could do other than wait, something she was never very good at. The front bell dinged, and she jumped like a scalded cat. Rushing into the café, she was only slightly disappointed to see Barbara, Kitty and the other knitting circle ladies making a beeline for their usual corner tables. 'Morning, ladies! What a treat, I wasn't expecting you today.'

'After the washout the other day, we decided to reschedule. It's too nice a day not to get out and about,' Barbara said, hanging her pretty flower-covered mac on the coat stand near their tables.

'Well, you're in luck as I've made a load of extras ready for the weekend, so there's plenty of choice. How about a lovely carrot cake?' She placed a friendly hand on Kitty's shoulder. 'And before you say anything, I used low-fat crème fraiche for the icing so it's sin-free.'

'You are a good girl.' Smiling up at her, Kitty raised a hand to pat hers. 'Always so thoughtful.'

'I need you all fit and healthy, Kitty. I can't go killing off my best customers, now, can I?'

Laughter rippled around the tables. 'I knew you only wanted us for our money,' Barbara said.

'Pshh. You know your visits are the highlight of my day. Now, who wants tea?'

Having delivered two large pots of tea, a jug of milk and the carrot cake to their tables, together with cutlery, plates and proper cups with matching saucers, Laurie left the ladies to serve themselves, as was their preference. Looking at the pair of small vases with artificial posies in them she'd removed from their tables to make more room, she decided they could do with a good wash. After popping them on the counter, she did a sweep round other tables to gather the rest up, pausing by the front door for a quick glance outside.

'Looking for someone in particular?' Barbara called, making Laurie jump.

Juggling the vases in her hands, she hurried quickly away from the door. 'No. Just looking. The Tesco man will be along any minute with a delivery.'

'I thought he came to the back door.' The older woman's tone was arch with interest.

'Well, yes, of course he does. I was just saying in case I had to disappear. I wasn't looking for him... or for anyone else, for that matter.' Laurie had spent a long time waiting for sleep to come the previous night. Lying there in the dark, she'd admitted the instant attraction to Jake. It had been a long time since a man had sparked her interest, but though she'd joked with him about not dating visitors, beneath the smile she'd been deadly serious. *Once bitten...* And she'd been bitten hard enough to suffer a nasty scar. Thinking about it was enough to drag her away from the window. If Jake came in again, she would keep things professional. For one thing it wasn't fair to lead him on, and for another, the last thing she wanted was Barbara and the rest of the knitting circle to start speculating.

Keeping one ear out in case the knitting ladies needed anything, Laurie took the vases out to the kitchen and set them next to the sink. Separating the little stems of artificial sweet peas and lily of the valley from the vases, she lay them out on a tea towel ready to sponge them off with a damp cloth. It was silly to let Barbara get under her skin. Like several of the other older ladies in the village, she took an interest in the personal lives of the younger generation and often teased Laurie about needing to find a boyfriend.

Still, it rankled to be on the wrong end of gossip, as she knew to her detriment. There was no reason to suspect Barbara, or anyone else for that matter would think she was attracted to Jake, why would they? No one else had been in the café yesterday during his visit, and as he'd only just arrived it was too early for word about the new arrival to have got around. She was just being silly, letting the lingering embarrassment over her uncharacteristic flirting with him colour her judgement. When he came in, *if* he came in, she would treat him just like any other customer.

Feeling a bit better for the internal pep talk, Laurie filled the sink with hot, soapy water and carefully set the little vases to soak. They'd probably go through the dishwasher, but she didn't want to take the risk. It wouldn't take long to wash and dry them by hand; they'd be back on the tables in no time.

'Gooood morning!' *Or maybe not.*

Drying her hands on a towel, Laurie hurried through to the back to greet Malcolm, the delivery driver, as he wheeled the first stack of trays into the storeroom. Semi-retired after years out on the boats, he kept himself busy with this part-time driving job. Exposure to the elements had weathered his skin to a leathery brown, making him appear older than his years. 'Hi, Malcolm. You're a life saver. I was down to my last bag of self-raising.'

Malcolm smiled. 'I noticed your order was bigger than usual. Been cooking up a storm, have we?'

She nodded. 'It's been really busy the past couple of weekends, and I'm hoping it'll be the same for the foreseeable future.'

'You and everyone else, girl, though the council will have to do something about enforcing the parking if it keeps up. The car park was full to overflowing and after the wet weather we've had, some of the verges are in a terrible state from people parking where they shouldn't be.' Shaking his head, he wheeled his little barrow back out to his van to collect the next load.

As she busied herself unpacking the crates, Laurie pondered what he'd said. It wasn't the first complaint she'd heard about damage caused by day-trippers. There'd been a few grumbles about the amount of rubbish being left on the beach. Though some of the holiday makers who came to stay could be thoughtless, the vast majority were respectful of the environment – probably because they were staying for a few days and didn't want to see rubbish strewn around any more than the locals did. The surge of interest about the mermaid was bringing in a different type of crowd, people who didn't much care about the village itself and were only interested in finding the perfect vantage point to take an 'I was there' selfie to share with their friends. A number of people had come into the café looking for a charging point and ordered the bare minimum to justify occupying a table.

Though she was grateful for the business, she silently hoped they'd find a nice middle ground once the initial excitement died down – people who found out about the existence of Mermaids Point via the publicity but who chose to visit for other reasons, and, fingers crossed, stayed for a few days to explore everything the village and its businesses had to offer.

Malcolm returned as she finished emptying the first batch of crates. 'This is the last of it. No substitutions this week, paperwork's on top here.'

Laurie swiped the invoice and receipt from the crate and folded it in half, ready to tuck in her bag before she had chance to mislay it. 'Thanks. If you wait two minutes, I'll make you a coffee to take with you.'

'Ah, you're a sweetheart. I'll unpack these for you, shall I? Schedule's full-on this morning.'

'If you don't mind? Stick it anywhere and I'll sort it out in a minute.' The front door opened as she re-entered the café and Laurie's silly heart skipped a beat at the sight of the tall male figure facing away from her. It was then she noticed the reason he was turned away was because he was helping a woman behind him lift a baby's buggy over the threshold, and that his hair was the wrong colour to be Jake. 'I'll be right with you!' Hurrying back behind the counter, she shoved the invoice inside her bag and brewed a tall Americano coffee into one of her reusable travel mugs, which she took back out to Malcolm. 'I've got one of those in the cab,' he said, giving her a sheepish grin. 'I'll fetch it in.'

'Drop it in the storeroom, will you? I've got customers.'

'No worries, love, and I'll lock up on my way out.'

* * *

Laurie had just finished serving the couple, including heating a jar of baby food for them in the microwave, when Barbara gave her a wave to indicate that the knitting ladies were ready for another pot of tea. Dumping the used tea leaves in the composting food bin, Laurie spotted the forgotten vases still soaking in now-cold water in the sink. *So much for having loads of time on my hands.* Tea brewed and delivered, Laurie rolled up her sleeves, refreshed the water in the sink and got stuck in. She'd got through about half the vases when she heard her mum's voice. 'I'm in here,' she called, glancing over her shoulder as her mum poked her head around the door.

'Hello, darling. It's quiet next door so I thought I'd pop over and make your dad and me a coffee. What've you got in there?' She raised an eyebrow at the soapy water in the sink.

'The vases off the table. I decided they needed a wash.' The front bell rang. 'Only I can't find five minutes to get them finished.'

'I'll see to them.' Her mum was already reaching for a pair of rubber gloves folded neatly beside the sink. She kept buying them in the hopes Laurie would wear them and stop 'ruining her nails', but Laurie hated the feel of them, as well as the funny smell they always left on her hands.

'You came for a coffee break, not to do my chores,' Laurie protested though she'd already yielded her space at the sink and was drying her hands. Trying to stop her mum from helping out was like trying to stop a steamroller, a sweet, loving steamroller. That tendency to take over irritated Laurie at times, but she took care never to show it. Not when it was clear how much pleasure it gave her mum.

'Helping you comes first,' Mum said, confirming exactly what Laurie had been thinking. 'Now go and see to your customer and I'll have these polished off in no time.'

After pecking a quick kiss on her mum's cheek, Laurie went out front to find Jake settling himself at one of the tables by the window. Unlike yesterday, he was carrying a backpack with him, from which he withdrew a slimline laptop as she reached his side. 'You're back, then?' *Smooth, Laurie. So much for treating him like any other customer.* 'Sorry, I mean, hello. It's nice to see you.' Heavens above, you'd think she'd never seen a good-looking man before, the way her tummy was fizzing.

'I couldn't stay away from the gorgeous... brownies.' He smiled, lighting up his whole face, and her good intentions melted to nothing. A little bit of light flirting wouldn't do either of them any harm, as long as she didn't get carried away.

Trying to ignore the little thrill zipping through her veins, Laurie shook her head sadly. 'No can do, I'm afraid. The rest went straight in the freezer as soon as they'd cooled. I thought I mentioned I was making them ready for the weekend. There's plenty of other things to choose from, though.' She nodded over her shoulder at the glass display cabinet beneath the counter.

Jake's face fell, like a cloud blocking the radiance of his smile. 'I've been thinking about those brownies all morning.' He sounded so mournful it was hard not to laugh.

Doing her best to sound as solemn as he had, Laurie nodded in mock-sympathy. 'They were very good brownies.'

Jake's brows rose, as though a marvellous idea had just occurred to him. 'Now I have an excuse to come back on Saturday morning.'

'Oh, I wasn't suggesting...' Laurie felt her cheeks heating.

'I know.' There was a gentleness to his tone as he sat back in his seat, creating extra space between them. 'I'm only teasing.'

'Oh, yes, me too!' She tried to laugh it off, but it came out a little too loudly. Really, she would have to give up flirting with him, because she was *hopeless* at it.

She withered a little inside as he shifted his chair in an obvious excuse to break eye contact with her. Having moved his seat all of two millimetres, he glanced back up, his smile dialled down to something best described as polite. 'Well, now we've cleared that up, I'll have a cappuccino and wait until I've worked up an appetite before I have anything else.' He indicated his laptop. 'If you don't mind me working here for a bit?'

'Not at all, make yourself at home.' *Leave the poor man alone, for goodness sake, Laurie.* 'Ha ha ha.' *And stop laughing like that!* 'I'll be back in a sec with your drink.' In her haste to get away, she caught the leg of a nearby chair with her toe, sending it flying and barely preventing herself from following it down onto the floor.

Wondering if it was possible to die from making an idiot of oneself, Laurie returned to the counter to find her mum standing there, drying one of the vases with a tea towel. She made no attempt to hide her grin as Laurie eased past her towards the coffee machine. The mirrored finish on the machine reflected her tomato-red cheeks, and she prayed silently for a moment's peace to settle her flustered nerves.

'Who's your friend?'

No peace, then. Stretching on tiptoe, she reached for a large cup and saucer stacked on the shelf above the machine and waited until she'd set them just so on the counter before casting what she hoped was a casual look towards her mum. 'What? Oh, that's Jake. He came in yesterday. He's rented the cottage up at Walkers' Farm while he's writing his book.' *Nothing to see; move along, please.*

Fat chance of that. Setting down the dried vase and cloth, her mum edged closer into Laurie's personal space. 'He'll be here for some time, then?' Open speculation on her face, she didn't even pretend not to stare at Jake.

'Stop it!' Laurie hissed as she turned on the hot steam to heat the milk for Jake's cappuccino. 'Don't ogle the poor man. And what difference does it make to you how long he's here for?' She banged the metal jug a bit harder on the counter than was strictly necessary to settle the froth before adding it to the cup in front of her.

When she glanced over it was to find her mum watching her with an amused smile. 'It makes no odds to me, darling, but given I can count on the fingers of one hand the times a man has made you behave this awkwardly, perhaps it ought to make a difference to you. I'll finish drying the last of those vases then be back out for my coffee.' She turned and walked back into the kitchen, leaving Laurie to stare open-mouthed after her.

8

While he waited for Laurie to return with his drink, Jake tried to make sense of her. Much as he liked watching her cheeks heat as they flirted, he didn't want to make things uncomfortable between them, and he'd come perilously close to that already. The café would make a good base of operations for him to work from when he was in the village, he didn't want to be outstaying his welcome on only his second visit. Even if he hadn't wanted to use the café as a way to meet people, he knew he'd find some other excuse to walk through the front door. Laurie was pretty as a picture, and funny, too, when she forgot to be nervous around him. If he wanted to get to know her better, he needed to be a bit more subtle about his attraction towards her.

Mind made up to keep things friendly, but not *too* friendly, he fiddled around with his laptop, plugging it in and connecting it to the mobile hotspot on his phone. He'd noticed the café had its own wireless hotspot, but he preferred to keep off an open network, especially when he was doing anything work-related. It was another sign of the times, he supposed, that a little local café was expected to lay-on free Wi-Fi for its customers. He hadn't thought twice about it when he used one of the big chains like Starbucks, but he found himself wondering how much it cost Laurie to provide it. It would be a bit rude to come out and ask her, but his journalistic radar had been tweaked and now he'd have to look it up and see if he could find out. He clicked on his favourite browser and was halfway through typing his enquiry when one of the women sitting in the corner called out to him.

'You that writer chap, then?'

Glancing up, he found all eyes in the café on him, including Laurie who cast him a little apologetic smile. Turning his attention to the ladies watching him over the stilled points of their knitting needles, he nodded. 'That's me.'

'Knew you were, soon as I saw the laptop. Staying up at Walkers' Farm, I hear.' *And so could everyone else in the place.* He'd been wondering how he was going to approach people and get them to talk to him, but it looked like he didn't need to worry about that thanks to Miss Marple in the corner. Turning in his seat to face her, Jake widened his smile a touch. 'It's a lovely little cottage, and perfect for when I want a bit of peace and quiet. It was too nice a morning to be cooped up, though.'

The woman nodded to the one next to her. 'Didn't we say exactly the same thing, Kitty?'

'We did.' Much softer spoken than her companion, the new speaker cast a couple of shy glances towards Jake before finally asking. 'Are we allowed to be nosy and ask what your book is about?'

Deciding to seize the moment, Jake rose and walked towards the group. He pointed at an empty chair. 'Jake Smith. May I?' There was a flurry of nods and introductions as the ladies shuffled their chairs to make more room for him. 'Thank you.' He leaned forward to rest his elbows on the table, conscious that the body language would make it seem like he was sharing something for their ears only. 'I'm writing about local myths and legends.'

'Another blooming mermaid hunter,' a woman whose name he hadn't caught snorted quietly.

He held up his hands. 'Guilty as charged. But I'm not only here because of those photos that are everywhere. Sure, they caught my attention, but a village with a name like yours must have stories about mermaids that date back generations, and that's the kind of thing I'm interested in, finding out where these things originated from and looking for common connections across communities with similar legends.' He looked from face to face, seeing he'd caught their interest. Even the disgruntled one was looking more friendly. 'Do any of you know how the village got its name?'

Barbara, the woman who'd first called out to him, shook her head. 'Can't say that I've ever given it much thought. There's always been stories about the mermaids, though, how they've come to the rescue of people from the village in times gone past.'

'Didn't do nothing to help the *Betsy Mae*, did they?' It was the grumpy lady again.

A few of the other women shot her shocked looks, but he was surprised when Kitty, the quieter one spoke out. 'Don't start, Bev. Peter Torpy should've never put out in that storm and you and everyone else around this table knows it.' She reached out and put her hand on Barbara's arm, a gesture of comfort if ever Jake saw one. His inner bloodhound caught the scent of a story and pricked up its ears.

'If that wife of his hadn't taken herself off in a huff, he wouldn't have been trying to support two households and been forced to take such risks,' Bev snapped back. 'She always thought too much of herself for my liking. Incomers don't settle in the Point, never have, never will.'

'If Peter hadn't been stepping out on her every time she turned her back then she wouldn't have had reason to leave him, so don't give me that incomer nonsense.' Kitty turned in her chair, deliberately giving Bev her back. 'Sorry, Jake, you didn't come over to listen to us dig up old gossip.' She shifted in her seat, radiating indignation like a ruffled hen.

He didn't like to tell her most of the best stories in his career had started off as gossip, nor that he would be Googling the words Betsy and Mae the moment he could escape back to his own table. Instead, he prompted her back to their original discussion. 'What about older stories? Is there anything that's been passed down in your family?'

Kitty shook her head. 'Only the same things everyone else knows, like Barbara said, the legend is that the mermaids will always come when the village needs them the most.' She glanced over his shoulder towards the counter. 'One person you could ask is Laurie, over there.'

Unable to resist the opportunity to look at the lovely woman who already occupied too many of his thoughts, Jake turned to see her chatting behind the counter with a woman who'd been watching him earlier. The two shared a smile before the older woman picked up two mugs from the counter, then leaned in to kiss Laurie with a familiar affection. Not wanting to be caught staring, he turned back to Kitty and the others. 'Why would I ask her?'

'Rumour has it there's some mermaid blood in her veins, through her father's side,' Kitty confided.

'Oh, stuff and nonsense,' her friend Barbara said with an exaggerated roll of her eyes.

Kitty got that ruffled hen look about her again. 'That's as maybe, but why else do the women on that side of the family all have those peculiar names? Lorelai, Nerissa, Merrow, God rest her, they're all named after mermaids.' She addressed the last to Jake.

Lorelai. It was such a beautiful name, he wondered why she shortened it, but then again the only time he used Jacob was on his byline. 'Fascinating.' He gave Kitty an encouraging smile. 'That's exactly the kind of titbit I'm after, thank you.' Extending the smile to the rest of the group, he rose. 'Well, I've taken up enough of your time, if you think of anything else that might help me with my research, please let me know.'

'I hope they weren't bothering you.' Laurie placed his cappuccino down on the table as he returned to his seat. 'I love them all to bits, but they have a tendency to make everyone else's business their own.'

'It's fine, in fact they were very helpful. I need local sources to help make my book as authentic as possible. Kitty mentioned you might have an interesting story to tell about the origin of some of the names in your family.'

Laurie frowned for a moment then shook her head. 'The mermaid thing? It's just a fairy tale someone made up that's been passed down.'

'I'd still like to hear it when you have some time to spare.'

She looked around the café which had filled up in the few minutes he'd been chatting to the ladies. 'Not at the moment.'

She held up a hand to acknowledge a greeting from another table. 'I have to go, sorry.'

'It'll keep.'

9

As tempted as he was to make it three days in a row, Jake forced himself to stay in the cottage on Friday and knuckle down to some work. He'd allowed himself to get completely side-tracked looking into the tragic story of the *Betsy Mae*, but after reading every article he could get his hands on, he concluded it was as Kitty had said, a nasty fishing accident leading to permanent and debilitating injuries to two crew on a fishing trawler that had set out in terrible conditions. Interesting, in as much as it would've had a devastating impact on a small community, but nothing of relevance to the mermaid pictures. He'd turned instead to his list of bookmarked articles and spent a tedious, but useful day going through them. By the time he'd finished, he didn't have the energy to do more than chuck a pizza in the oven and slouch in front of the TV with a cold beer or two.

* * *

When Saturday dawned bright and sunny, he was more than ready to escape from his laptop for what he hoped would be a fruitful day mingling with the tourists and finding out from a few what it was about mermaids they found so fascinating. Having been fooled by the brightness of the sun before, he checked a weather app on his phone to find it was claiming to already be 19C with a forecasted high in the mid-twenties after lunch. Not sure he believed it, Jake opened the front door of the cottage and stepped out into the yard. Moving from the shade of the overhang into full sunlight, he did a few laps and decided he wouldn't need his jacket.

He shrugged it off and was heading back inside when Carolyn called out his name. 'Jake! Oh, I'm glad I caught you. I just wanted to check what time would be okay for me to pop in and change the sheets.'

'Of course, come on in a minute.' Leaving the door open for her to follow him, Jake transferred his wallet and keys to his jeans, then hung his jacket on the back of one of the kitchen chairs. As Carolyn entered, he pointed to the washing basket he'd brought through from the bedroom earlier. 'I've stripped the bed and left everything in there ready for you. I'm off for a wander. I should be out for most of the morning, so whenever suits you.'

She smiled. 'Oh, you didn't need to do that, but thank you. I'll do it now, and then it'll be sorted for when you come back. Alan's up with the vet. One of those blooming alpacas of his has got an infected hoof so I'm at a loose end for a few hours. I'm going to get ahead of myself and prep some meals for next week. Give us a knock at the farmhouse when you're back and I should have some pots ready for your freezer.'

'You're very kind. I'll see you later.'

'Mind how you go. If it's anything like last weekend it'll be a bit of a madhouse down in the village.'

Hoping Carolyn was right and there'd be plenty of people to interview, Jake made his way to the coastal footpath and began his descent. To his surprise, the beach below looked pretty much deserted. This end was a bit rockier than the area closer to the shops, though, so perhaps visitors didn't come this far along. It was a similar story when he reached the steps. There were several people about, but nothing like the volume he'd been led to expect from the stories he'd heard the past few days. Rather than heading to the beach, he turned towards the centre of the village. There were more vehicles on the streets than he was used to seeing, but they were moving freely and he only had to wait about twenty seconds before there was a long enough gap for him to cross. He followed the direction of most of the traffic to the top of the street and the main car park. The front rows were full, but he estimated less than a quarter of the spaces were occupied.

A family of four decamped from a people carrier, loaded themselves up with rucksacks from the boot then headed not towards Jake and the direction of the beach, but across to the other side of the car park. Curious, he followed at a discreet distance. A large sandwich board standing next to the Pay and Display machine gave him the answer. In bold red letters it declared Mermaid Boat Tours as being the best and easiest way to get to the islands, with a huge black arrow at the bottom pointing the way. Beside a pedestrian exit, a smaller board bearing only the company name and another arrow sent him along a well-worn path and down to the edge of a large horseshoe shaped harbour.

Walking along the stone quay, Jake could see the area was split in two. The smaller area closest to him was reserved for yachts, motorboats and other pleasure craft and could've been mistaken for a harbour on the Côte d'Azur the way the sunlight reflected off the gleaming white hulls. Seagulls turned lazy arcs overhead, their raucous cries filling the air. Beyond a wooden jetty that served as a demarcation line, he could see what looked to be the working end of the harbour. Tangles of bright orange and blue netting decorated the quay next to where several industrial fishing boats were tied up, as if a giant had abandoned piles of knitting. The back of the harbour was lined with workshops and a couple of small warehouses, their metal sidings a mix of bright blue paint and rust spots. He recognised the scene from several stock photos he'd come across during his research into the *Betsy Mae* accident, but the angle they'd been taken at had fore-shortened the scene and it looked much larger in real life.

A few feet from him stood a basic white hut with Mermaid Tours painted in bright red across the front. The family he'd followed joined the back of a small group and Jake watched as they were all led along the quay to a smart-looking boat with a large open deck area at the back.

'You looking to tour the islands, mate?' A guy around his age wearing a branded t-shirt under a pair of blue dungarees ambled towards Jake, leaving his older co-worker to assist the last few people on board the boat.

'Maybe another day, I'm just having a look around for now and enjoying the sunshine.' He spotted a couple of matching boats moored up beside the one being loaded. 'Busy day?'

The man shook his head. 'Nah, this is only our second group of the morning. Last weekend you couldn't move on here for people, and now look at it.' He waved a hand to indicate the mostly deserted quay. 'So much for mermaid fever.'

'I thought it was quiet when I walked through the village just now.' Jake offered his hand and introduced himself. 'I'm staying up at Walkers' Farm at the other end of the Point.'

'Ah, the writer. My sister was telling me about you the other night. I'm Nick Morgan, my folks run the big gift shop on the front and my sister owns the café attached to it.'

The man smiled and Jake could see the resemblance; though his face was softer, a little rounder than Laurie's, his hair was that same raven's wing black. 'Nice to meet you.'

'You too.' Nick nodded towards the boat. 'You sure you don't want to join them?'

Jake shook his head. 'Not today, I haven't brought any gear with me. I wouldn't mind a tour another time, though. Do you go out during the week? I don't mind paying a bit extra for a private trip.'

'We go out any day the weather's half-decent and someone pays us.' A radio hooked onto the front pocket of his dungarees crackled, the message unintelligible to Jake's ears. Nick understood it, apparently, because he turned and waved towards the boat. 'Hold on a minute, I'll just see this lot off and then we can talk some more.'

Having consulted with the man on the boat, Nick did a few last-minute checks then untied the mooring lines. He watched the boat until it had made its way out towards the open water, one hand raised to shield his eyes from the glitter of the sun on the sea. Jake didn't know about steering anything bigger than a car, but he was impressed with the smooth passage the boat cut between the rows of moored vessels.

Hands tucked into the front bib of his dungarees, Nick strolled back to join him. 'We're not going to put more than two boats out today, so that's me done for a couple of hours.

I'll close things up here and then we can head to Laurie's if you like? I could murder a coffee.'

'Sounds like a plan.' With any luck, the café would be busier and with Nick as cover for going there, Laurie couldn't get the wrong – or right – impression about any ulterior motives he might have for making another visit.

Nick flipped the front shutter on the cabin closed, secured it with a padlock and turned the hands on a large clock with the words 'Time of next trip' under it to read one o'clock. 'Right, let's get that coffee and I'll see what kind of a deal I can do for you for an exclusive visit to the islands.'

10

Laurie added a couple of bright chalk squiggles to the mobile chalkboard, then sat back on her heels to read it over one last time. Glad she'd had the foresight to bring out a damp cloth with her, she erased and rewrote the word quiche, remembering to put the 'i' in it this time. Not that spelling errors mattered much when there wasn't anyone around to read them. Straightening up with a sigh, she cast a gloomy look over her shoulder along the quiet street. Where was everybody? Even if people were bored with looking for the non-existent mermaid, it was a glorious day and the sunshine normally saw people flocking to the village for a stroll along the beach. Perhaps their regular visitors had been put off by reports of the crowds over the past few weekends. Whatever it was, she couldn't remember a Saturday in June being this quiet, ever.

Hoping the chalkboard would catch one or two eyes and tempt them inside, Laurie propped open the café's front door to let some of the gorgeous fresh air in. She thanked the solitary couple who were gathering their things ready to leave and collected their dirty cups and plates on her way past.

'What am I going to do with all this cake?' It was hard to keep a note of despair out of her voice as Laurie surveyed the full-to-bursting display case stuffed with all the things she'd defrosted overnight in anticipation of another busy weekend. She stacked the dirty dishes in the dishwasher out back, then returned to help her aunt who was folding a stack of linen napkins into neat squares. Leaning over to grab a share of the pile, she gave Nerissa an apologetic smile. 'I feel even worse about asking you to come in and help me out today.' She'd had a number of responses already to the advert she'd placed in the local paper for part-time workers but needed time to go through them and arrange interviews.

Turning her head, Nerissa pressed a kiss to Laurie's cheek. 'It's no hardship to spend a few hours with my favourite niece.'

The familiar joke cheered Laurie somewhat, but she still felt guilty for encroaching into Nerissa's limited free time. 'I'm your *only* niece, and this is supposed to be your day off.'

Nerissa smiled. 'You're still my favourite.' Shadows crossed her face, wiping away the sweet warmth. 'Doc's got that obnoxious great-nephew of his visiting this weekend, so I'm glad of an excuse to be out of the house to be honest.'

Doc Gadd was several years past retirement, in Laurie's opinion, and he treated her aunt more like a servant than an employee. But as much as she wished he'd hand over the reins to someone younger, she knew Nerissa worried about her future. She'd lived in the little flat above the surgery for as long as Laurie could remember, and if Doc retired, she faced not only losing her job, but being without a roof over her head as well.

Michael, the great-nephew in question, was Doc's only living relative and had made it clear to Nerissa on several occasions he thought *she* was the one taking advantage of the situation. Which was a bloody cheek given everything her aunt did above and beyond her job description, like walking Doc's bloody dog for a start! Toby was as gorgeous and friendly as it was possible for a dog to be but looking after him was yet another imposition on Nerissa. And no doubt she'd be expected to cook dinner for them all tonight.

'Michael here for his quarterly visit to count the silver, is he? He'll be disappointed in how well Doc's doing.' Laurie didn't even try to hide her rancour. On a previous visit, Michael had had a meeting in the café with a local estate agent to discuss the viability of converting the surgery into holiday flats. Doc might be getting a bit doddery and forgetful, but there were plenty of years left in him yet. To overhear someone talking with such eagerness about a potential inheritance had left a sour taste in Laurie's mouth.

Nerissa rolled her eyes. 'The last time they were here I caught him nosing around my flat, horrible man. I've made sure I locked the door this time.' Her face fell once more. 'I know he's going to try to persuade Doc it's time to hang up his stethoscope.'

Putting her arms around her aunt's waist once more, Laurie rested her head against her shoulder. 'It must be awful for you, all this uncertainty.'

'It is and, oh, I know better than most that Doc needs to give up the practice, but the idea of that little weasel forcing him out in the hopes he can sell the place and get his sticky fingers on some of Doc's cash early makes me so cross!' Nerissa smoothed her hands over the napkin she'd accidentally crushed between her fingers.

'If he does decide to retire, you could always throw your lot in with me. I need to find a better balance to my days, and it would save me having to recruit anyone permanently.'

Nerissa placed the last napkin on the pile and turned to face her. 'Weren't you just bemoaning the waste of cake because visitor numbers are down again? Can you really afford two full-time salaries?'

'Well, yes, it's true things have been a bit tough lately, but if today's proven anything, it's that I need to diversify a bit. It would be a lot easier to try other things with someone I know and trust on board with me.' She'd been toying with a few ideas for a while, though the sudden influx of mermaid hunters had distracted her.

'What sort of thing do you have in mind?'

'Dad's been doing so well with his online sales I was thinking about trying something similar.'

Folding her arms, Nerissa leaned back against the counter. 'An online café? How would that work?'

'More like an online bakery as part of the café. I get lots of comments on the pictures I post about how delicious the cakes look, what if I could reply and say, "You can order them here," and then post a link?'

'Cake by post? Well, they do it with just about everything else these days, I suppose.' Nerissa smiled. 'You could be the next Interflora!'

'Nice thought, but a bit beyond my ambition. Even if I only get a few orders a week, it'd be something extra to offer, especially during the off season.' Laurie shrugged. 'Look, I'm not planning on doing anything about it immediately, and I definitely need to do some more research, but I just wanted you to know it's an option for the future should you need one.'

'You're a good girl.' Nerissa pulled Laurie into a hug. When she spoke next, her voice sounded husky with unshed tears. 'Thank you. I don't know what I'd do without you and the rest of the family.'

Laurie squeezed her back. 'Or us without you.' She swallowed down the lump forming in her throat and gave a little laugh. 'Although I'm sure we could all do without Nick, sometimes.'

'No fair! I'm the best big brother you've got.' A familiar voice called from behind them.

Turning, Laurie found her brother standing just inside the door, a broad grin on his tanned face. Her pulse fluttered when she realised who was standing next to him. It seemed a stupid thing to admit to herself after only a couple of days of knowing him, but she'd missed Jake when he hadn't come into the café the previous day. 'You're the only big brother I've got,' she deadpanned. 'Skiving off again?'

'Are you talking to me, or him?' Nick pointed a jokey finger at Jake. 'I found him wandering around on the quay.'

'I was doing research,' Jake protested. 'Well, I was planning on it until you distracted me with an invitation to have a coffee.' He cast a mischievous smile towards Laurie. 'I assume I'm allowed one of your brownies to go with it today?'

She knew he meant it as a joke, but the untimely reminder of her hubris at assuming she would be overrun with customers today stole all the happiness she'd felt at seeing him walk through her door. 'You can have as many as you can eat.' It came out sharper than she intended, and she was immediately sorry for taking out her worries on him.

Jake's features scrunched into an apologetic wince. 'It's quiet, huh? I was really surprised when I walked down a bit earlier. I was expecting the streets to be packed out.'

'Well, hopefully things will pick up a bit later.' Nerissa placed a comforting hand on Laurie's arm. 'Sit down, boys, and I'll sort out your drinks. Cappuccinos, is it?'

Nick tugged out a chair with his foot and plonked himself onto it with a laugh. 'I'm twenty-eight, Aunt Nerissa, hardly a boy.'

'You'll always be a boy to me, darling. I can remember the day your mum brought you home from the hospital like it was yesterday.' Nerissa scooped a measure of fresh coffee into the portafilter and began tamping it down.

'You were still at school then, weren't you?' Laurie asked her as she lifted a couple of brownie squares from the cabinet. 'I'm sure I've seen a photo of you in your school uniform holding Nick.'

'I was fifteen,' Nerissa confirmed. 'Your dad must've been about your age, Laurie.' She paused for a moment then huffed a little laugh. 'It never occurred to me before, but he would've been the age Nick is now when they had you. Where does the time go?'

Twenty-three and married with a baby? Laurie found it hard to imagine. Some days she wasn't sure she was old enough to run a business and take proper care of herself, never mind doing that and raising a family at the same time. Plus, there was the minor issue that in order to get married or have a baby you had to find someone you actually wanted to do either of those things with first, something both she and Nick had singularly failed to do.

'Rather them than us, eh?' Her brother tipped a wink at her as Laurie set the two plates of brownies down on the table between him and Jake.

'Not the marrying kind?' Laurie was grateful Jake

addressed the question towards Nick rather than her, in case her treacherous brain said something beyond embarrassing.

'Never found time for it. School wasn't for me, not that I didn't enjoy learning, just didn't see much point in going on to college or whatever. All I ever wanted to do was go out on Uncle Tony's boat. A lot of the girls around here don't like going out with a trawlerman. They've seen their mums, their aunties go through the stress and worry of it, grown up with their dads missing birthdays and whatever. The money's good when it's good but a couple of poor catches and the bills mount up.' Nick shrugged, then dug his fork into his brownie. 'By the time my uncle sold up and we switched to running the tour boats, all the women my age were spoken for.' He paused with the fork an inch from his mouth to offer Jake a wry grin. 'Not that there's a lot of choice in a small place like this.'

Laurie smirked at her brother's glossed-over version of the truth. 'You'd dated and dumped every girl in your class before your eighteenth birthday, so no wonder none of them wanted to sit around pining for you!' She shook her head. 'You had plenty of chances, and you blew them.'

'At least I went out, which is more than can be said for you.' He leaned across the table towards Jake. 'Justin Bieber's the only man who ever broke my sister's heart.'

Bieber? Oh my God, she was going to kill him. Not daring to look at Jake's face, for fear she'd see him laughing over her teenage crush, Laurie stalked back to the counter to fetch their drinks. Her ears pricked up, and she forgot her embarrassment when she heard Nick ask. 'What about you, Jake? No ring on your finger?'

'Been too focused on my career. Like you, I've worked lots

of unsociable hours,' Jake was saying as she returned with two frothy cups of cappuccino.

Nick frowned. 'I thought you were a writer? Doesn't that mean you get to choose your own working hours?'

'What? Oh, yeah, the book things more recent. Before that I was... ah... a freelancer.' He shifted in his seat. 'Lots of tight deadlines, so typing away into the evenings, you know.' Looking a little flustered, Jake reached for one of the coffees. 'Thanks, Laurie. These brownies are out of this world, any chance of another?'

'Absolutely, it's not like I haven't got plenty to spare.' She made sure to keep her tone light this time. She turned to Nick. 'What about you?'

'Make it two, and then I won't have to bother with any lunch.'

Anyone would think he was eight, rather than twenty-eight. 'Your eating habits are a nightmare.'

Nick flashed her an unrepentant grin. 'It's your fault. Hey, why don't you cut a couple up into bite-sized pieces and stick them in a Tupperware box. I'll take it back with me and when the boats come back in, I'll offer the passengers a taster and see if I can send a few of them your way.'

Laurie brightened. 'Sounds like a great idea. I've got some rocky road slices, I'll add some of those too.'

Nick groaned and made a fake grab of his stomach. 'Don't mention the rocky road.'

'There's millionaire's shortbread, as well.' Laughing, Laurie made her way back to the counter. Nick's sweet tooth was legendary, but at least she always had a willing taster on hand whenever she wanted to try out a new recipe.

Nerissa began lifting the plates of treats from the cabinet while Laurie rummaged in a cupboard for a box. 'While you're down there, see if you can find a cake stand. We could cut up a couple extra and put it on display beside the till next door.'

'Good idea. I know Mum and Dad always mention the café. I don't know why I didn't think about offering samples before.' She set the box on the counter above her, then shuffled sideways to the next cupboard to retrieve a decorative stand with a matching clear dome. They were nice in theory, but she'd found the chilled display cabinet more practical. 'I'll just give them a quick wash.'

As she stood at the kitchen sink, Laurie popped up on her tiptoes to see out of the window. There were a few people out and about on the beach now... she checked her watch. She had an hour before lunch, maybe she should take a taster box down and see if she could encourage a few more people to drop in. Nerissa could hold the fort here. Setting the Tupperware and stand on the rack to drain, she fetched another box from the cupboard and washed it out too.

11

'Just ring me if you need me to come back,' Laurie said to her aunt as she placed the laden cake stand on top of the box and tried to stretch her grip to carry them both at the same time. 'I won't go far. Along the street to the other steps, a quick lap of the beach and back.'

'I'll be fine, don't worry.'

'There's a couple of quiches prepped in the fridge. Can you pop them in the oven?'

Picking up a tea towel, Nerissa waved it at Laurie the way one might shoo off an annoying fly. 'Will you go already? It's not like this is the first time I've looked after the place, is it?'

'Sorry.' With a sheepish laugh, Laurie lifted her precious cargo, then put it straight back down when the cake stand started to wobble.

'Here, let me help you with that.' Jake reached around her to pluck the stand from the top of the box. This close, the warmth of his body sent a shiver of awareness tingling up her arm. She'd never noticed before how tall he was, how well she would tuck beneath his chin if he reached out and drew her close.

Heat scorched her cheeks at the errant thought, and she reached back to undo and refasten her ponytail, flustered and foolish at her inability to manage her feelings around him. He wasn't even that good looking up close, she lied to herself. His chin was too broad and darkened with stubble, his nose a little crooked, the bump at the bridge a bit too prominent. His eyebrows, scruffy at the corners, looked as though they'd never been acquainted with a pair of tweezers. As though she preferred the over-waxed, over-bronzed fakery of the men in those Top 100 sexiest males features in the magazines she occasionally treated herself to. Supressing a snort at the absolute nonsense swirling around her brain, she reached for the cake stand braced between his neat, capable hands. 'Oh, there's no need. I can pop that next door and come back for the rest of it.'

Lifting the stand away from her reach, Jake quirked one of those unkempt brows she'd been mentally critiquing. Raised like that, they didn't look so bad after all. 'I've got it now, so I might as well carry it.'

It would be silly to argue, and besides, there was no graceful way around what was after all a perfectly reasonable offer of help. 'Thank you.' The beam of a smile he graced her with sent her insides flip-flopping, and she turned away before she did something unconscionably stupid like lift her finger to touch the surprise dimple creasing his cheek. Needing something to do with her hands, she grabbed a handful of small paper napkins and stuffed them into the front pocket of her apron next to a box of cocktail sticks she'd found in the cupboard. *Breathe, Laurie*, she chided herself. *He's carrying a cake stand, not a bouquet of bloody flowers.*

Setting her shoulders back, she picked up the box on the counter and turned once more to face Jake. 'Straight through the arch at the back.' She nodded him in the right direction, then turned to Nerissa. 'You'll call me, right?'

Nerissa's laugh was warm. 'I'll call. *And* I'll put the quiches in the oven.' She shooed them away with another shake of the tea towel. 'Go on with you!'

* * *

'What's this?' Her dad's greeting boomed across the gift shop, turning all eyes towards them. Though nothing like as busy as it had been recently, Laurie was pleased to see a few people browsing.

'I thought your customers might enjoy a little sample of the treats we have on offer today in the café.' Laurie spoke with more force than usual, trying to ensure her naturally soft voice carried over the whale song echoing from the speakers, in the hopes she could draw the attention of the customers nearest her.

'Smashing idea, love. Let me move that out of your way and you can pop the stand down here.' Her dad slid a charity box for the RNLI to the opposite end of the counter and patted the empty space next to the till. He fixed an interested eye on Jake as he placed the cake stand on the counter with the same care he might have given to a priceless Ming vase. 'Hello, there. Don't believe we've met before. Andrew Morgan.' He thrust a beefy hand over the counter.

Laurie watched in amusement as Jake ignored the proffered hand until he'd positioned the stand to his exact liking in the centre of the cleared space. After turning the stand a fraction of an inch that made no difference to the aesthetic of the display but was clearly necessary by the way he tilted his head before giving a nod of satisfaction, Jake wiped his palm on the back of his crisp cotton chinos before reaching out to shake hands with her dad. 'Jake. Jake Smith, I'm—'

'Our writer in residence,' her dad cut in, his laughter filling the room. 'Heard all about you from my ladies.' He winked at Laurie, making her want to duck behind a display of mugs emblazoned with various boys' and girls' names. They were the kind of thing you could find in any gift shop and Laurie didn't understand the appeal, but they were a steady bestseller, so her parents kept restocking them.

'*Dad.*' Though she shook her head at him, Laurie couldn't help but laugh. There was nothing small or subtle about Andrew Morgan, and she'd long since given up trying to make him be anything other than himself. Even during the worst of her blushing, cringing teenage years, she'd known there was no mute function when it came to her dad, and now she wouldn't have him any other way. He drew people to him, with that big laugh and even bigger heart.

Giving her a wink he made no attempt to disguise, Andrew turned his attention back to Jake. 'What are you two up to, then?'

Before Laurie could point out the *two of them* weren't up to anything, Jake replied. 'It's a bit quiet next door so we're going to try to drum up a bit of extra business.' He turned the devastating smile with its oh-so-delicious dimple on her. 'Aren't we?'

Oh, hell, why was she even trying to fight the chance to spend a bit of time with him? So what if he was a relative stranger, a visitor and therefore off the Laurie Morgan list of suitable dating companions? There was no one else on the list, the eligible bachelors either boys from school who'd never transitioned in her mind from being rude and smelly and entirely avoidable, or well past their sell-by date proppers-up of the bar like Doc Gadd. Returning his smile, Laurie gave a conceding nod. 'We are.' When his eyes held hers for a moment longer than necessary, Laurie hid her tell-tale blush by rifling in her apron for a couple of napkins to set beside the cake stand. 'How's things with you?' she asked her dad, not quite ready to wonder about what that glance might or might not mean.

He twisted a big hand from side to side. 'So-so. Not a patch on last weekend, and I wish I'd held off on ordering more mermaid stock.' He cast a forlorn look towards a massive new display beside the door covered in mermaids of every possible size and colour. 'They cleared me out last week so, of course, I put a rush order in. Amateur move.'

'I think we all got a bit caught up with mermaid fever.' Laurie patted the back of his hand. 'Hopefully things will settle into a happy medium.'

'As long as the sun keeps shining, eh?' Her dad raised two pairs of crossed fingers to the sky.

'Don't jinx it.' Laurie clapped her hands over her ears. The one thing the occupants of Mermaids Point had learned the hard way was to never predict the weather.

Her dad laughed. 'I never said a word.' He drew his fingers across his lips as though zipping them tight.

'Come on, then, we'd better get going.' Laurie reached for the boxes of cake bites, but again Jake beat her to it, sweeping them off the counter before she had a chance to grasp them. 'All right, then, I'll see you later, Dad. Remember the cake is for the *customers*.' She nodded to the cake stand with a cheeky grin.

Her dad's laugh boomed around the shop. 'I make no

promises when it comes to your divine baking, lovely girl. No promises at all.' He gave them a wave. 'See you later, love. Bye, Jake.'

'Cheers, Mr Morgan.' Jake raised a friendly hand in return. 'Nice to meet you.'

'You, too.' They were halfway out the door when her dad called out. 'Get Laurie to bring you round for dinner one night, I'd love to hear more about this book of yours.'

'*Dad!*' Laurie cast an exasperated look over her shoulder. When all he did was waggle his bushy eyebrows in response, she mouthed, 'Behave,' at him and nudged Jake out the door.

On the pavement, she reached for the box. 'Look, you really don't need to carry that, I can manage.'

He once more moved his hands out of her reach. 'Okay, I'll confess, I had an ulterior motive when I offered to help.'

Her stupid pulse started hammering a mile a minute. Had he offered to help out in order to spend more time with her? Could there be something more to the look they'd shared just now other than a fancy of her imagination? Putting him on her list of eligible potential partners (could one name technically be called a list?) was one thing, contemplating she might be on Jake's equivalent list – which she would wager held a number of candidates at all times – was entirely something else. Choosing to ignore his comment for the moment, Laurie led the way, the narrowness of the pavement the perfect excuse to not walk side by side while she tried to sort out the muddle in her head.

What harm could there really be if she opened herself up to the possibility of a relationship with Jake? She wasn't a naïve seventeen-year-old, like last time. If she went into it with her eyes open and her expectations managed, it would be fine. Besides, it wasn't like he was only going to be around for a couple of weeks. He'd taken the cottage for the whole summer – plenty of time to find out if this attraction between them might mean something. As long as she took things slowly, kept her guard up and her heart safe, it didn't need to turn out badly.

With every justification she made, her quicksand resolve shifted a little more. The conversation earlier with Nick had struck a nerve. While her brother seemed content with his single status, Laurie knew she was missing something in her life. Jake Smith wasn't necessarily the answer, she wasn't naïve enough to believe that, but nor was turning her back on every opportunity for a little intimacy in her life. He didn't have to be her happy ever after Prince Charming, but a little bit of happy for now sounded damn good.

12

When they reached the stairs leading down to the beach, it was a conscious action on Laurie's behalf to move over and make room for Jake beside her. He stepped up without a moment's hesitation, their arms close enough that she could feel the golden hairs covering his skin brushing against hers. Taking a risk, she glanced up at him, shading her eyes from the glare of the sun to meet his gaze. 'Tell me,' she said, her voice a little husky with anticipation. 'About this ulterior motive of yours.'

Jake grinned and she wondered how she'd thought his features were anything other than perfect. 'I thought you could tell me about that family legend Kitty mentioned the other day, the one about one of your ancestors being a mermaid.'

As effectively as if he'd drenched her with a bucket of seawater, Jake drowned her foolish daydreams in a cold wash of practicality. Here she was tying herself in knots over whether or not the attraction she felt was mutual, and all he was interested in was picking her brains to help with his research! The shock of it made her stumble over the first step down, the heat of his hand on her elbow as he reached to steady her a humiliating brand it took all her presence of mind not to shake off. Offering a smile of thanks that tugged at suddenly dry lips, she eased from his hold, using the excuse of reaching for the iron railing beside her to put a little distance between them. 'It's just a silly story. I'm not sure how much help it will be to you.' She did her best to keep the disappointment out of her voice, hoping any waver he might hear would be put down to shock over almost falling.

'Indulge me, anyway? We can walk and talk at the same time.' Seemingly oblivious to the turmoil he'd stirred up inside her, he tucked the cake box into the crook of one arm, leaving the other free to circle behind her in a gesture so solicitous and caring it was enough to make her want to weep, or snap at him that she was more than capable of walking on her own. But that would be peevish, a reaction to a hurt delivered without knowledge.

The hand at her back was a chivalric gesture on his part, a touch proprietorial perhaps, but she didn't think he meant it to be so. Nothing about him suggested he thought her incapable of using the stairs on her own, even if she had given every impression of being about to tumble head over heels. It was more as if he'd been raised a certain way, a habit ingrained in him. Her dad would do the same without blinking, as would Nick, being cut close from their father's cloth, and she'd never dream of being offended by either of them doing it. Taking the time to push away any lingering disappointment, she let Jake escort her down the worn steps to the pebbles and shale below. She should be grateful, she supposed, that she'd realised his attentions were entirely benign before she'd had the chance to embarrass herself.

* * *

As she'd hoped when she'd first hatched the plan to offer samples to potential customers, there were plenty of signs of life on the beach. Couples strolled along the waterline, children clambered over the rocks to peer in the rockpools left by the receding tide. To their left, a couple of teens were tossing a frisbee between them. A few groups had even staked claims on the small strip of sand available. They'd have to retreat once the waves rolled back in, but their striped windbreaks and umbrellas added colour to the scene.

Deciding to start with the nearest family group to them, Laurie introduced herself, explaining briefly what they were doing while Jake offered them the box of treats. Once everyone had taken a piece, she wished them an enjoyable day and moved on, not wanting to put anyone off with a hard sales pitch. She had enough confidence in her baking to know the cakes would speak for themselves.

The next group were less friendly, the man they approached not even bothering to look up from his paperback as he shook his head in refusal. Laurie retreated at once, wondering if her plan might end up backfiring. 'Maybe this wasn't such a good idea,' she confided in Jake as they made their way between the sunbathers and the waterline. 'I don't want to annoy people.'

'Give it another couple of tries, and if we get rebuffed, we can knock it on the head,' he suggested. Thankfully, the next group they approached were delighted to be offered some samples and Laurie and Jake found themselves chatting to them for several minutes. They'd only taken a few steps further on when a couple approached them, curious to see what they were doing. Two pieces of rocky road later and

they were enthusiastically promising to drop in after they'd
finished their walk.

By the time they approached the far steps, more than half
the samples were gone and she'd received several other
promises of visits. The sunshine felt lovely on her face, and
after a quick check-in text with Nerissa, Laurie decided to
make the most of it. Heading for a large rock near the base of
the steps, she took a seat and gestured for Jake to sit beside
her. If anyone came down onto the beach, they were close
enough to attract their attention. Jake had been good enough
to give up his time to help her, and his natural charm had
made approaching people that bit easier. The least she could
do was repay that kindness with the background information
he'd asked her about.

'I don't really know where the mermaid story originates
from,' she said, reaching inside the box to help herself to a
tiny square of millionaire's shortbread. 'Nan was told about it
when she was a little girl, and she first told me when I was
five or six and upset about being teased over my name.'

'Did you get a lot of stick for it, then?' Jake took a piece of
brownie and popped it into his mouth. 'God, this really is the
best thing I've ever tasted.'

Casting a glance beneath her brows, Laurie watched his
eyes close in enthusiasm over the melt-in-the-mouth treat.
He might not fancy her, but at least he appreciated her
baking skills. To her relief, the pang of disappointment over
that thought didn't sting quite so much. Give it a day or two
and she'd be over this silly crush of hers, with Jake none
the wiser. Not wanting to be caught staring, she glanced
down at the stone beside her, letting her fingers trace idly
over the worn grooves and pockmarks in the rock. 'In a
class full of Emilys and Sophies, an exotic name like

Lorelai stuck out like a sore thumb. That's why I shortened it.'

Bracing an arm behind him, Jake tilted his head to one side as he regarded her. 'Do you regret feeling like you had to conform? It's too beautiful a name not to use.'

Helping herself to a bit of brownie, Laurie mulled it over. At the time, it'd been such a huge issue for her, and she'd been really upset with her parents for saddling her, especially when Nick had got away so lightly on the name front.

It was only after Nan had sat her down and explained the origin that she'd started to feel better about it, though not enough to have the confidence to reclaim her name. Now... well, she'd been Laurie for such a long time, it would be too weird to try to change it. 'Sometimes, I guess. I mean, Nerissa kept her name, although I'm not sure what else she might have changed it to.' She shrugged. 'I don't know, it's been so long I don't *feel* like a Lorelai.' She wrinkled her nose. 'Does that make sense?'

He shrugged a shoulder. 'I think it's a shame you feel that way, but I get it. I only use Jacob for professional or legal stuff.'

'I like Jacob.' She tilted her head to look up at him, considering. 'But you look like a Jake.'

He laughed. 'I'm not sure what that means, but okay, then.'

Lifting her feet to brace them on the rock, Laurie curled her arms around her knees. 'Jacob sounds a bit up himself, less approachable than Jake. Jake is more straightforward. You know where you stand with a Jake.'

'I definitely want to stick with Jake, then.' He nudged shoulders with her, sending a frisson of sensation through her she did her best to ignore. 'Back to the story.'

'Oh, yes, sorry...' *Focus, Laurie*. Shifting an infinitesimal distance further from him, she turned her concentration inwards. 'Back in the day, the Morgans were seafaring folk, though they gave up the sea a lot sooner than Mum's family. It was my great grandad who opened a shop where the Cave and the café are now. He used to sell dry goods and general supplies for the village. When the Point first became a bit of a tourist attraction the family started adding postcards and a few other bits and pieces. Over the years the demand for those grew until that's all we sell now.' Realising she'd digressed again, Laurie gave Jake a sheepish grin. 'I'm not a very good storyteller.'

'You're doing great, I love a bit of backstory.' He plucked a piece of rocky road from the box and offered it to her. 'Go on.'

Not sure if he was urging her to take the cake or continue with her story, she opted for both, nibbling one corner of the treat. 'So, as I was saying, everyone earned their living from the sea, and not just fishing. Dad's got an old bible with a family tree sketched out on the inside cover. I've got great-whatever uncles and cousins who joined the navy; others who were merchant seamen who went all over the globe on the earliest trade routes. One of those distant relatives, Davy Morgan, returned to the village after years away with a wife in tow. She never spoke to anyone; and would spend hours sitting at the window of their little cottage staring out at the sea. There were other odd things, like the way she refused to cut or brush her hair, letting it grow into a wild mess until it tumbled past her knees. Over the years, their family grew, but still she never uttered a word – not even to her children.

'Things started to go wrong in the village – boats sank, nets developed holes and catches were lost. Cows and goats stopped producing milk and the few crops people raised to supplement their diet began to fail. Rumours and whispers circulated about the strange woman Davy had married: that she was mad; that she was a witch; that she was cursed and that my many-times-great-grandad had brought that curse upon the village by bringing her home with him. Fed up with the gossip and wanting to protect his wife from the growing threats, he went to the pub one night and showed everyone a fine golden comb studded with pearls. He said it was a mermaid's comb, that he'd first seen it pinning back the locks of a beautiful woman swimming off the coast of one of the islands he'd sailed to on the other side of the world. Entranced by her beauty, he followed her progress along the beach until she disappeared into a cave.'

Pausing, her mind full of the azure seas and golden rippling sands she'd seen in brochures of the Caribbean, Laurie shifted on the rock. She'd been sitting in the same position for too long, and her leg had grown numb.

'Don't stop now!' Jake protested. 'You've just got to the good bit.'

She laughed. 'Sorry. Where was I?' She let the image of that fantasy beach fill her mind once more. 'Okay, the cave. Soon Davy heard the strains of a song drifting from the depths of the cave, like nothing he'd ever heard in his life. Captivated by the music, he crept over the rocks and stole into the entrance to find the woman sitting on an outcrop, naked apart from cascades of long ebony curls through which she drew the jewelled comb over and over, in a hypnotic rhythm to match her song.

'It was love at first sight for him, and he stepped out from his hiding place to speak to her. The moment she saw him, she shoved the comb in her hair and slipped into the water, her legs transforming into a scaled fishtail the minute they touched the sea. Distraught, he could only watch as she swam from the cave in a couple of swift flicks of her tail and disappeared beneath the waves. Desperate to follow her, he waded into the water, until a sudden squall whipped up the sea around him into towering waves and forks of lightning shot from pitch-black clouds that had blown in from nowhere. Soaked and shivering, Davy could only trudge along the beach and back to the tavern his shipmates had all but taken over. Though he drank and drank, nothing could drive the image of the woman from his mind.

'The next evening, instead of joining his friends he crept back into the cave and hid amongst the rocks. When he'd almost given up hope, his beautiful mermaid swam through the entrance and took up position on the rocks once more. Afraid to move even a muscle, Davy crouched in the darkness and watched, and waited, and yearned. Night after night he returned to his hiding place and listened as his love sang the song of his heart. Her routine was always the same – once she finished her song she secured the comb in her hair, and her legs would turn into a tail before she swam away. At first, he thought it was the touch of the water that caused her to shapeshift, but then he noticed sometimes she trailed her toes in the sea as she sang and they retained their human shape.

'Eventually, he decided the comb was the key to her transformation, and the next night he switched his usual hiding place to one right behind the rock she always sat on. As her song reached its sparkling crescendo, he reached out and snatched the comb from her hand. She fell silent the moment his hand touched hers, but as he'd suspected she would, she remained in human form. He talked to her, told her he wouldn't harm her, that he loved her and wanted to spend the rest of his life with her. All the while he talked, she kept her eyes fixed on the comb in his hand. Testing his theory further, he walked slowly out of the cave, and instead of swimming away, she followed him, remaining by his side even when he boarded a ship and sailed back across the ocean far away from the azure seas of her home.

'Without her comb, she couldn't transform back into her mermaid form, Davy told the villagers. He knew he should give it back to her, but he loved her too much. His beloved wife wasn't a witch, she was his prisoner kept from the sea by his own selfish obsession. As he trudged wearily from the pub, tears wetting his cheeks at the weakness within him, he failed to spot one of his daughters sitting in the shadows. She couldn't believe what she'd heard. After all those years believing her mother had never loved her or her brothers and sisters, and cursing her for her cruelty, she finally understood the truth. She followed her father home and watched as he prised up a floorboard beside his bed and hid the comb inside the cavity beneath it. When he left the house the next morning, she tried to get into his room, but the door was locked. She fetched her siblings, told them what had happened and together they smashed down the door. After retrieving it from its hiding place, they went to their mother's room and handed her the comb.

'Years of pain and anguish melted from her face, and she started to sing, a song so beautiful her children fell to their knees at her feet, weeping for joy at the sound of their mother's voice. From the first touch of the comb to her hair the tangles and knots loosened, and soon it shone like a black pearl. When she finished her song, she rose from her seat and kissed each of her children in turn before walking down the stairs and out of the house. They followed her to the beach where she dropped her robe and began to wade into the freezing-cold water. With one last smile at them, she fixed the comb into her hair and dived into the waves. The last they ever saw of her was a rainbow flash where the sunlight reflected off the scales of her tail. When their father returned home that evening, he was devastated to find his beloved wife had escaped him. Ignoring the words of anger and scorn his children poured down on him, Davy took up the seat she'd abandoned at the window and kept a lonely vigil for the rest of his days, convinced right up until the end she would return to him.'

13

Jake sat transfixed as the last echoes of the story settled upon him. He'd thought when Laurie started it was going to be a love story, not a tale of coercion and tragedy. 'You should put it in a book.'

Laurie tilted her head to one side, fixing him with a curious gaze. 'I thought that's what you were going to do, wasn't that the point of me telling you the story?'

Damn. He'd been so wrapped up in the moment, he'd completely forgotten his cover story. 'Well, yes, of course, but mine is more of a factual collection, a study of myths and their origins. I was thinking more along the lines of a fairy tale or a fantasy story.' He forced a smile, hoping his scrambling explanation didn't sound as inauthentic to her as it felt to him.

'Oh, I see what you mean.' Laurie curled her arms around her legs once more, resting her chin on her knees as she stared out across the beach. A strand of hair had escaped her ponytail and was dancing in the light breeze, the jet strands shimmering in the sunlight turning jewelled shades of purple, green and pink like those on a starling's wing. If there was a grain of truth in her family legend, he could see where she'd inherited the colouring from. There was an unfocused sheen to her eyes, as though she was looking inward rather than enjoying the view. 'It's a bit bleak for a fairy tale, though, don't you think?'

'Maybe a little, but isn't that true of most folktales and fables? Although we're more used to the Disney versions these days, the original stories often have very dark origins. I can still remember a book of Hans Christian Andersen fairy tales my parents gave me when I was little. They scared the hell out of me with their child-eating witches and what-have-you.'

'Yes, I suppose you're right. I just remember wanting to be Belle from *Beauty and the Beast* because she had the most amazing library I'd ever seen.' Laurie climbed down from the rock, brushing the sand off the back of her jeans in a way, which drew his attention to how perfectly the denim hugged her curves.

Not wanting to be caught admiring her figure, he glanced down. The box of treats on his lap was almost empty. Recalling how the two of them had absent-mindedly helped themselves during the story, he tilted the box towards Laurie with a sheepish grin. 'I think you need to sack me as your marketing assistant.'

She laughed and whatever dark thoughts the old story had stirred up banished in the bright burst of sound. 'Oh, well, consider it payment for services rendered.' She held out her hand for the near empty container. 'That's enough playing hooky for one day, I'd better be getting back.'

Not ready to yield her company just yet, Jake kept hold of it. 'I'll walk back with you.' When she looked as though she might refuse him, he grabbed for the nearest excuse. 'I haven't had a chance to explore your parents' shop yet. I saw a couple of books similar to what I'm working on that I want to check out. I don't want to end up duplicating what's already on the market.'

Catching her bottom lip between her teeth, she regarded him for a long moment before lifting one shoulder in a half shrug. 'Fair enough.'

Jake let her lead the way up the steps, wondering at the sudden distance between them. When they'd been sat together on the rocks, there'd been an easiness, almost an intimacy as he'd fed her treats from the box while she transported him back in time with her story. Perhaps he'd imagined it – a bit of wishful thinking on his part. Every time he thought they might be edging a step closer to getting to know each other, Laurie pulled an about-face and tried to push him away. His instinct told him she found him attractive, but then the shutters would come down and they were back to square one. He would just have to give it time. Besides, he had come here to do a job, and getting romantically entangled with one of the locals was probably not conducive to doing that – no matter how pretty she was.

Flashing neon lights caught his eye from the opposite side of the street. When he'd walked past the penny arcade it had been shrouded in darkness, but the windows shone now in a shimmer of pinks, oranges and reds. The word OPEN was spelled out across the front door in an ever-changing array of LED bulbs. He hadn't been in an arcade for years, but they'd always been a highlight when his grandparents had taken him to stay in one of the many holiday parks along the east coast. With barely a glance at the traffic and his head full of memories, Jake found himself drawn across the road like a moth to a gaudy flame. He could all but feel the sticky-sweatiness of his palm clutching a shiny coin pressed there by his Gramps and he found himself raising his hand to his face, as though he could catch the coppery ghost-scent on his skin even all these years later. Feeling nostalgic and a little bit sad, he tucked his hand in his pocket as he peered beyond the flashing window display to the arcade beyond. 'I haven't been in one of these in years,' he confessed to Laurie as she stepped up beside him. 'I used to be a dab hand at the coin drop.'

'The claw grab was always my favourite.' Laurie tapped a finger on the glass to indicate the big square machine in the middle. 'I spent nearly all my pocket money one summer trying to win that pink teddy in the far corner.' She huffed a laugh as he looked to where she indicated, his gaze settling on a rather bedraggled looking bear with fur a shade somewhere between candy floss and luminous marker. Beauty must've definitely been in the eye of the beholder, because the poor thing looked cross-eyed to boot.

'I can't believe it's still there,' Laurie continued. 'I could've probably paid for an equivalent of it ten times over, but I wanted that one.' There was a determined edge to her voice that suggested somewhere deep inside she *still* wanted it.

'You might be the only person in the world whose nemesis is a pink fluffy bear,' Jake teased, earning another laugh from her.

As they began to make their way back towards the café, Laurie continued telling him about the arcade. 'When the previous owner decided to retire, he got an offer from a franchise who wanted to take it over and modernise the place – fill it full of fruit machines rather than traditional games. Thankfully he refused and Pete Bray who owns the pub bought him out. Apart from updating the lights, he kept the rest of it intact.'

'Does it still do a lot of business?' Given the popularity of smart phones and the myriad games children had access to, he was a bit surprised something as manual as the machines filling the arcade would still hold attention.

'It gets pretty busy, especially if the weather's not great. I'm not sure Pete makes much in the way of profit, I've never really thought about it. We were just glad he decided to keep it open because a boarded-up shopfront in a prominent position like this would give visitors the wrong impression.'

Jake nodded. It didn't take much for an area to start to look rundown and unappealing – a few empty businesses, a bit of peeling paint here and there; rubbish clogging up the drains. He cast an eye along the parade of shops. Each and every one looked neat and tidy, with pretty striped awnings shading the windows of some and hanging baskets or decorative pots of plants lining the upper windowsills of others. Even the regularly spaced rubbish bins looked to have had a lick of shiny black gloss paint. Times might have been tough for the residents and businesses here in Mermaids Point, but they seemed determined to put a brave face on it.

He hoped it paid off for them, that the tourists who'd been drawn by the phenomenon of the mermaid continued to return. Too many of these small communities were dying off. He'd seen enough of that in his own region as a local reporter. Ever-increasing rents, the lure of out-of-town retail parks with ample parking and the power of online retail giants were pushing more and more small high streets to the brink, and beyond. As the jobs went, communities fractured and the trouble rose. Young people with few prospects and even less hope made easy pickings for the criminal fraternities keen to exploit them.

From what he'd seen so far, Mermaids Point had escaped a similar fate, but relying on tourism for the bulk of their income must make for a precarious life. A lot of the traditional seaside communities were struggling with a population imbalance – their younger generations driven out by lack of jobs and pressure on house prices from those looking for a second home by the sea. 'If your family didn't already have a business here, would you have found it hard to find work?'

Laurie flicked him a glance from under her thick fringe. 'You ask a lot of questions, don't you?'

She didn't sound defensive, more curious. 'It's in my nature, I guess, and definitely part of my job being an in—' he cut himself off before the words 'investigative reporter' slipped out. Damn, if he wasn't more careful he was going to blow his cover story. 'Being *interested* in what's around me is part and parcel of being a writer – it's all in the research.'

'I suppose it is,' she mused, apparently unfazed by his almost slip of the tongue. 'I've not met many people who see past the surface of things, I guess. All they care about is how things look – is the beach tidy, can they get a decent meal in the pub, are the napkins in the café folded correctly.'

The last part of her statement was from so far out of left field, it stopped Jake in his tracks. 'Are the napkins what?'

Laurie rolled her eyes. 'The Tripadvisor website is the bane of every business owner in a holiday village like ours. You wouldn't believe the things that people get worked up about.'

Given some of the letters to the editor he'd seen over the years at the paper, he could well believe it, but *napkins*? 'I didn't know there was a wrong way to fold napkins. I can honestly say that until this moment it's something I've never felt the need to have an opinion on.'

Laurie's laughter filled the air. 'It's a minefield. I stopped using paper ones because we were getting through them at a rate of knots. People are incapable of taking just one for a start. I used to have little dispensers on the tables, but even so I couldn't understand how we were getting through them so quickly until I watched one woman lift off the top, remove the entire stack and place them in her handbag. She didn't even try to hide it – like it was something she did every day. It was the same with those sauce sachets. Not only did they end up leaving a mess everywhere, but people took them by the handful. Once I switched to cloth napkins and started decanting individual servings of sauce and mayonnaise into miniature dishes, I saved a small fortune. It's better for the environment too and reduces litter. I keep a few disposable napkins under the counter – like for today when we were giving out the samples, but as a rule, I use the cloth ones.'

Jake nodded. It not only made business sense, but it gave the café a classier touch. When he said as much, Laurie grinned. 'It's not classy to fold them into squares, though, as my reviewer was at great pains to tell the world. *A little effort makes all the difference.*' He could tell by the way she spoke the words in a haughty tone she was quoting directly from the review.

'How else would you fold them?' Sure, he'd been in restaurants where they shaped them into fans or stood them up in the centre of the plate in those funny cones, but for a seafront café serving sandwiches and salads? Some people needed to get a life.

'You'd be surprised. I've got plenty of YouTube videos

bookmarked demonstrating a hundred and one ways to do it – I'll send you the links if you like?' she teased.

'I'll pass, thanks. So, apart from napkin controversies and petty theft of consumables, do you enjoy what you do?'

Laurie's face lit up, the joy in her expression a warmth he wanted to hold his hands to. 'I love it. When I first pitched the idea to Mum and Dad they took a bit of convincing, but I put together a proper business plan and spoke to the bank manager about a loan to cover the refurbishment costs. I wanted to show them it wasn't some fly-by-night idea, but a proper plan to build a future here. Of course, they wouldn't let me pay for the conversion works, and won't accept any rent from me for the shop or at home.' She shook her head, the frustration evident in her tone. 'I've set up a savings account, though, and I put something by every month so when they're ready to retire I've got something to give them. Nick pays in what he's saving in rent by living at home, too, though I don't suppose that'll be for too much longer.'

'He's planning on moving out?' Jake couldn't fathom living with his parents at their age. Hell, he'd struck out on his own as soon as he could, refusing to tow the rigid line his father had laid out for his future. Journalism wasn't a proper job in his father's eyes, and his mum had never argued a word in Jake's favour, only wanting him to be a good boy and keep the peace. Nigel Smith ruled the roost in the little two-up, two-down Jake had been raised in. A mean man; not cruel – at least in the physical sense – but mean and small and tightly-wound. Only one opinion had mattered to him – his own. As Jake had grown, he'd pulled the reins of control ever tighter around his son until the walls of the house shook from the constant raising of voices and slamming of doors.

Jake hadn't slammed the door on the day he'd left to go to

university. He'd pulled shut the white double-glazed door behind him with a quiet snick, knowing in his heart he wouldn't walk through it again. He sent his mum cards on Christmas and birthdays, but he'd taken his father at his word when he'd told him that if he walked out there'd be no place for him any more. If his mum had had an email address, he might have made more of an effort to keep in touch, but she didn't have anything beyond the most basic mobile phone. Not wanting her attention on anything or anyone other than him, his dad had done a grand job at keeping her isolated from the outside world. Jake couldn't say he really missed them. When his friends at uni had rushed off at the end of term to enjoy family holidays and Christmases, it'd hurt being the only one who stayed behind. But that hurt had always been tempered with the knowledge that what waited at home was nothing like the present and laughter-filled fun he heard about when his mates came back loaded down with car-boots full of gifts, food and bundles of clean washing. The thing he'd yearned for in those lonely hours was a dream, a fantasy played out in movies and on TV shows.

Not everyone was like him, though, and from the bits and pieces he'd glimpsed so far, the home life of the Morgans couldn't be further from what he'd grown up with. There was genuine affection between Laurie and her family, so perhaps living at home wasn't a burden for them.

'Nick's got his eye on our uncle's boathouse down by the docks. It was a warehouse back in the day and the offices upstairs haven't been used in years. He wants to move in once the summer season is over and refurbish it as he goes along. There won't be much else for him to do over the winter evenings.' Her lips pursed, the happiness in her eyes dimming. 'I hope Uncle Tony agrees, or else I fear we might lose him. He's become really restless lately, and though I'd never try to hold him back, I'll do whatever I can to persuade him to stay.'

'You could offer to give him back his contribution to the savings account.' Jake snapped his mouth shut as soon as the words escaped. It wasn't any of his bloody business. 'Sorry, I shouldn't have said anything.'

'No, it's fine. It hadn't even occurred to me to make the offer to him, but it's definitely something to consider. It's good to have someone to talk these things through with, someone who doesn't have a vested interest.' She paused as they reached the entrance to the café. 'I really need to get in there, I've left Nerissa on her own long enough.'

'I'm happy to help.' Jake hesitated, then decided to push his luck. 'We can talk more about it later if you like. You could come for dinner at the cottage. Might make a nice change for you to have someone else do the cooking.' He shrugged. 'If you like, or not, whatever.' *Smooth, Jake, so smooth.*

'Oh. Well, yes, that would be nice. Shall we say seven o'clock?'

Swallowing down a sigh of relief at her acceptance, Jake nodded. 'Seven will be perfect. I'll see you then.'

With a quick smile, Laurie spun on her heel and disappeared into the café, the little bell over the door tinkling in her wake.

Grinning madly to himself, Jake made it four steps further along the pavement before reality struck. He had no idea what he was going to make them, had nothing in his fridge other than a couple of cold slices of pizza and some bottles of beer. The veg box delivery he'd arranged wasn't arriving until Monday, and though he'd got plenty of staples in the cupboards he hadn't planned on entertaining. At least Carolyn had been in to change the sheets that morning – not that he had any real designs on getting Laurie to slip between them, at least not tonight, but she might want a tour around the place and he wanted to make the best impression possible. Had he cleaned the sink that morning after shaving? Or picked up the pair of socks he'd stripped off last night while watching TV in the sitting room? The sinking feeling in his stomach said he knew the answer already. Worried about what other signs of bachelor-slobbery he needed to remedy, Jake abandoned any thoughts of checking out the books in the Morgans' shop. Turning on his heel, he retraced his steps, picking up the pace once he was safely past the café.

14

Laurie surveyed her reflection in the full-length mirror hung on the back of her bedroom door before yanking off the pink floral t-shirt with a growl of frustration and tossing it on the bed where it landed on an ever-growing pile of discarded clothes. The hair she'd taken her time blow-drying into soft waves was starting to frizz from being tossed around, and her face was taking on an unpleasant sheen.

Sinking down on the edge of the bed, she regarded her underwear-clad reflection. 'It's only dinner, why are you making such a big deal about it?' When her mirror image had no advice to offer, she poked out her tongue then bounced back to her feet to study the clothing scattered across her bed. A floaty skirt trailed over the side of the mattress, the bottom section pooled on the floor already starting to crease. Tugging it out from the pile she clipped it back on a hangar and returned it to the wardrobe. One day she might actually wear the flipping thing, but although she loved the material she'd never been invited to an occasion dressy enough to wear it. She needed a nice balance – something that showed she'd made an effort without looking as though she was trying too hard. If Jake had gone to loads of trouble, she didn't want to pitch up in basic jeans and a t-shirt, but if he had something casual in mind then she didn't want to be overdressed, either. God, it was a minefield.

A tap sounded from the bedroom door. 'Just a sec,' Laurie called, shoving her arms into a thin cotton dressing gown and belting it at the waist before opening the door.

Her mum stood there with a pair of tall glasses beaded with condensation, one of which she pressed upon Laurie. 'Hello, love. It's almost half-six, you know?'

'Is it? Bloody hell, I'm going to be late!' Laurie was prevented from turning back to the bed by a gentle hand on her arm.

'Calm down, darling. Nick's going out in a few minutes and it's no bother for him to run you up to the top of the hill. Sit and have your drink.' Sylvia gestured her towards the little stool that matched her pretty white-pine dressing table.

Doing as she was told, Laurie raised her glass to stare suspiciously at the sprigs of mint floating in amongst the ice cubes. 'What's this?'

'A mojito. Your dad's been experimenting with that cocktail book your brother bought him for Christmas. As you and Nick are both out tonight, we thought we'd have a little party.' Sylvia raised her glass and took a long drink. 'Well, that's certainly... refreshing.'

Laurie took a more tentative sip of her own and almost choked. 'Blimey, Mum, there's enough rum in this to send a sailor reeling.' She set her drink down on the dressing table. Turning up at Jake's half-cut was not a good idea.

'It might be a bit strong,' her mum conceded, taking another good swig. 'But it's delicious.'

She had a point, there. The bite of mint and lime cut through the sweetness of the sugar and rum very nicely. Another little sip wouldn't do any harm. Laurie reached for her glass once more. *Mmm*. It really was tasty.

'Right then, what's going on here?' Her mum gestured to the rumpled pile of clothing on the bed. 'Wardrobe crisis?'

Putting her drink down again, and this time making sure she pushed the too-tempting cocktail out of reach, Laurie rose and joined Sylvia beside the bed. 'Silly, isn't it?'

'Not at all.' Her mum gave her shoulder a gentle nudge. 'It's been a while since you've been out on a date, it's not surprising if there's a few nerves fluttering.'

'It's not a date, as such, just dinner.' Laurie plucked the floral t-shirt from the pile and held it up. 'What about this?'

'When an attractive single man invites you to dinner, it's most definitely a date.' Sylvia tugged the t-shirt from Laurie's hands and tossed it back on the bed. 'Too casual.' After setting her drink down on the dressing table, Sylvia rummaged through the pile a moment. 'This always looks lovely on you,' she said, holding up a pale gold silk blouse to Laurie's chest and squinting at her with what might have been a critical eye, or the heady effects of three quarters of a very strong mojito. 'Yes, definitely. Now, where are those nice jeans you wore at New Year? The ones with the sparkles on the back pockets.' Sylvia was already bending over to rifle through the bottom of the chest of drawers. 'These ones.' She thrust them into Laurie's hands as she squeezed between her and the bed and made a beeline for the wardrobe. 'And where's that pretty chain belt?'

Hangars screeched along the rail as her mum shoved a handful of clothes to one side to give a better view of the shelving at the back where Laurie stored her belts, shoes and other accessories. 'There it is.' She picked up the delicate loops of interwoven gold chain and leather with one hand and hooked the fingers of the other through a pair of straw wedges. 'And these will finish everything off nicely.' She draped the belt over the jeans still hanging over Laurie's arm and dropped the sandals at her feet. 'Shake a tail feather, darling! I'll tell your brother you'll be down in five minutes, and I'd better help you finish this off.' She swept her almost empty glass and Laurie's half-full one from the dressing table. 'Another one of these and your father might be in with a shout tonight.'

'Oh God, Mum, behave!' The bedroom door was already closing on Sylvia's unrepentant laughter.

Feeling lighter and more composed than she had since Jake had dropped his unexpected invitation, Laurie dressed in the outfit her mum had put together for her. A quick inspection in front of the mirror lifted her spirits even more – or maybe that was the mojito kicking in – whatever. The blouse hit the right note between casual and dressy and matched perfectly with the first hints of a summer tan which would deepen over the next few weeks if the good weather stuck around. Crossing to the accessory shelves in the back of her wardrobe, Laurie found a pair of gold combs and her favourite slender hoop earrings. It felt good to wear her hair down after having it tied back all day, but the combs helped to pin the sides back, opening up her face and displaying the earrings at the same time. 'You'll do,' she whispered to her reflection before pulling a little face. *Stuff that*. 'You look really good,' she attested, pushing her shoulders back and lifting her chin to face herself square on. Grabbing the little purse with an emergency £20 note and her door key zipped inside, she tucked it into a small shoulder bag together with her phone and her favourite sunglasses then hurried downstairs just as Nick bellowed her name from below.

* * *

Nick steered the little Nissan Micra the family used for local trips around the familiar winding streets one-handed. His other arm rested on his open window, the breeze ruffling the dark curls on his head into the impossible tangle that had become his trademark look since Aidan Turner had popularised wild curls in the TV revival of *Poldark*. Laurie had to admit it suited him better than his previously favoured crew-cut. The severe cut had given his face a harsh look wholly unsuited to her brother's chilled personality. Jake, on the other hand, had the kind of strong features more suited to the close-cropped look. As she recalled an image of him on the beach earlier, hand shading his eyes from the sun, a frown of concentration half-hidden behind the frame of his plain glasses as he listened to her telling him about the mermaid legend, her tummy did a little flip of excitement.

'So, where are you off to tonight?' she asked Nick, more as a distraction than anything else. He was out more than in and no doubt on his way to meet his latest love interest.

'Just a bit of work for a client, nothing special.'

Nothing special? Loosening the shoulder strap of her seat-belt, Laurie half-turned to regard her brother. His eyes remained resolutely fixed on the road ahead, even though there was very little traffic and his casual pose from before had been replaced by a two-handed grip on the steering wheel. 'Bit late to be setting out, isn't it?'

He shrugged, still refusing to even glance her way. 'Sh—

my client is a keen photographer, wants to catch some sunset views around the islands.'

Laurie wondered at the odd way Nick had started and stopped, as though correcting what he'd originally been about to say. Tempting as it was to pry, she knew from experience that if Nick didn't want to talk about something, she might as well try getting answers from a stone. Glancing instead out the window, she noted a few fluffy, cumulus clouds forming against the still-blue backdrop of the sky. They got some spectacular sunsets when the weather conditions were right. 'You've picked a good evening for it.'

'Yeah, should be good.' He steered the car around the roundabout at the top of the hill then pulled up once he was clear of the junction. 'This do you?'

It would be no more than a couple of minutes' walk to Walkers' Farm, even in her wedges. 'Perfect, thank you.'

'Look, I'm not sure what time I'll be finished. Will you be all right to make your own way home?'

She laughed. 'I'm not sixteen any more, big brother, you don't have to worry about me. I'll be fine.'

Reaching out, Nick tweaked her nose, an old gesture of affection. 'I'll always worry about you, Squirt, it's my job.' As she let herself out of the car, he leaned across to speak to her out of the window. 'Tell Jake I can take him out tomorrow if he wants. Give him my number and tell him to message me and we can take it from there.'

No doubt that would conveniently remind him he was about to have dinner with Nick's little sister at the same time. Laurie didn't need to say anything, her raised eyebrow was enough to make her brother grin. 'Just looking out for you!' With that, he turned the Micra around in the road and headed back towards the village and the dock just beyond.

Still smiling at his antics, Laurie picked her way along the path to the farm, trying to ignore the nerves that had come roaring back to life.

* * *

The door to the cottage was propped open, and the smells of frying garlic and herbs wafted out to greet her, along with the pulsing beat of Bastille's 'Pompeii'. It was one of Laurie's favourite songs and hearing it settled something inside her. With a quick rap on the doorframe to announce her arrival, she stepped inside.

'Oh, hello!' Jake flashed her a dazzling smile over his shoulder from his position in front of the oven. She was pleased to see he was wearing jeans too, in a shade of pale grey that matched the darker steel shade of his short-sleeved cotton shirt. Feeling she'd hit the same smart casual note as him helped her relax even further. 'Talk about perfect timing,' he continued. 'Just let me finish this off, and I'll be with you. There's a bottle of Prosecco in the fridge door, help yourself.' He nodded her in the right direction before turning his attention back to the oven.

Laurie hesitated. She had such a useless grip that her dad had bought her a special opener to help with everything from jars to bottles. Her old-lady lever he called it, but it wasn't much use to her sitting in the kitchen drawer at the café. Opening the fridge, she was relieved to see the bottle had already been opened and a hinged metal stopper was attached to the neck. The rest of the fridge was well-stocked, heightening her expectations of the meal to come. A plate of antipasti covered in a protective layer of cling film sat next to a bowl of mixed salad leaves and a vine of ripe cherry tomatoes. The shelf below was stuffed with a selection of cheeses wrapped in the wax paper favoured by the local deli on Market Street, and she fervently hoped they were going to be part of their meal later. Half a dozen bottles of beer jostled for space on the upper shelf with a couple of Tupperware boxes. A pair of glass flutes waited on the counter beside the fridge so she filled them both and set one where Jake would be able to reach it, but away from his immediate work area. 'Cheers,' she said, tapping her glass against his before retreating to a position further along where she could watch him cook without getting in the way.

'Cheers.' Intent on the sizzling pan in front of him, Jake did little more than flick her a quick grin before turning back to his task. Laurie didn't mind, it gave her a chance to nose around the place a bit without making it too obvious.

Across from her position sat a large, scrubbed pine table surrounded by four ladder-back chairs with mismatched cushions. A black office chair, which she assumed Jake used when writing, had been pushed against the wall to one side. Two sets of stoneware crockery had been stacked on the table with matching cutlery. A closed laptop and several stacks of paper covered the opposite end and she resisted the urge to wander over and take a closer look. Turning her attention back to Jake, she watched as he shook and stirred the frying pan with the confident moves of someone familiar with a kitchen. A tea towel was draped over his right shoulder and he raised his fingers to wipe them on the dangling end of it. It was an old chef's trick, and she wondered where he'd learned it. As she watched, he lifted a saucer covered in neat little piles of herbs and tipped them into the pan. A quick stir and he added a generous glassful of red wine, sending fragrant steam hissing into the air. Jake turned his head away from the

pan before the steam could mist up his glasses, another practiced gesture that told her he was used to being in front of the
oven.

The scent of the sauce hit her nostrils, making her
stomach gurgle in appreciation of the meal to come. 'God, I'm
sorry.' She pressed her free hand to her middle to try and
quell the embarrassing noise.

Jake laughed, a sound as rich as the red wine sauce in the
pan. 'I'm glad you brought your appetite. One more minute
and we can sit down, I promise.' Using a fork he added a
couple of chicken breasts to the sauce before lifting the cast
iron pan and sliding the whole thing into the lower section of
the oven. With a flick of his wrist, he turned off the gas
burner, wiped his hands on the tea towel then hooked it over
the handle of the oven. 'Right, we can leave that to do its own
thing for a bit. I thought we could sit on the back patio with a
drink. We can eat out there, too, if you like, but it might get
chilly.'

Eating outside appealed to Laurie, but she knew how
quickly the temperature could change so close to the sea.
'Let's wait and see what it's like when the food's ready, shall
we?' She suggested. 'It won't take a minute to lay the table,
whatever we decide.'

'Sounds good.' While Jake took the plate of antipasti from
the fridge, Laurie gathered up his glass before letting him
lead the way through the kitchen and into a neat lounge with
a large open fireplace and a pair of comfortable looking
chocolate-brown sofas. A flatscreen TV dominated a low
table in the corner.

They wove around the far sofa and exited via a pair of
French windows onto a neat patio set in a small garden
fenced on both sides for privacy, but open at the end to a

gorgeous view across the end of the Point and the seascape beyond. Jake led her to where a white wrought-iron table and two chairs with beige cushions sat in the middle of the patio and indicated the right-hand chair to her. Setting down the glasses, Laurie took her seat while Jake fiddled with the cling film covering the food. The patio was a perfect sun trap, and she couldn't resist closing her eyes and lifting her face to the lingering heat of the evening sun for a moment.

'I can put up the umbrella if you like.' Jake extended an arm towards the unfurled sun parasol rising from a hole in the centre of the table.

'No, it's fine. I've got sunglasses with me.' She unhooked her shoulder bag, retrieved her glasses and slipped them on before looping the strap of the bag over the back of her chair. 'That's better.'

'I should've thought to grab mine, be right back.' Jake disappeared into the cottage, returning moments later wearing a pair of sunglasses with tortoiseshell frames. He'd brought his phone with him too, which he placed on the table. The volume of the music coming from it was much lower than it had been in the kitchen so although it would fill any silence between them, it wouldn't intrude on their conversation. He placed a small plate in front of her, the plain surface covered with a flowery paper napkin she couldn't imagine him choosing for himself. 'They were all I could find in the drawer,' he said with a grin, confirming her suspicions. 'Hopefully they won't affect my rating too negatively.'

She frowned for a moment, before catching the throw-back to their early conversation about her weird Tripadvisor review. 'I won't knock off more than half a star, I promise.'

'Harsh, but fair. I'll have to work extra hard for the rest of the evening to make sure everything else is perfect.' He was smiling as he offered her the antipasti.

Laurie chose a selection of her favourite titbits from the plate, including stuffed olives, a hunk of fresh parmesan cheese, and wafer-thin prosciutto speared onto sticks with artichoke hearts and pieces of sundried tomato. 'Lovely, thank you.'

Jake helped himself, set the plate down then raised his glass towards her. 'Cheers, again. It's really nice to have you here.'

Alternating sips of crisp Prosecco with the bite-sized treats on her plate, she watched the setting sun turn the sea into a shimmering dance of golden light. If the rest of the evening followed what was already a promising start, Laurie didn't think Jake would have any problems getting a top scoring review from her.

15

The glorious sea view from his little patio might be one many people would've envied him for, but right then the only thing Jake was interested in looking at was the beautiful woman beside him. Though the dark lenses of her glasses shielded her eyes, there was no mistaking the note of pleasure in the little sigh she made as she nibbled the ham, artichoke and tomato pieces off the skewer. Discovering the deli earlier had been a stroke of luck, and not one he'd expected to find in the small coastal village. 'How's your antipasti?' he asked, more because he wanted Laurie's attention on him than for anything else.

She glanced towards him, raising her hand to shield her from the setting sun before changing the angle of her chair to avoid the worst of the glare. 'Delicious, thanks. You got one of Luca's mixed specials, I'm guessing?'

'Yeah. There was just so much choice. I think he took pity on me in the end – either that or got fed up of me trying to make up my mind – and put together a selection. I must say, I was a bit surprised to find a place like that here.' Realising how that must sound, he gave an embarrassed laugh. 'Sorry, that sounds a bit snobby, I just meant it's a bit of a remote part of the country for an Italian family to have settled.'

'Don't worry, I knew what you meant. Luca's grandfather, Gio, was captured in the Second World War and brought to England. I had no idea we even had prisoner of war camps here until he came and did a talk about it when we were at school. He worked on several farms around the county. By the time the war had ended he'd fallen in love with the daughter of one of the farmers he worked for and when her father offered to secure him a work permit, he decided to stay.'

She broke off to take another mouthful of Prosecco, and he watched, fascinated, as her gaze turned back across the water. Though his journalist brain had stood to attention at her first mention of the war, the rest of him was happy to sit and wait, and watch. Laurie was a natural born storyteller, both the tone of her voice and the cadence of her words something he could listen to for hours. An image of the two of them sprang to mind, a blanket spread out on the beach beneath the shade of a sun umbrella, his head resting in her lap as she read from a book. It was so vivid it felt like a premonition or a promise of what could be – and he wanted it. Surprised by the sudden rush of emotion he reached for his own drink, letting the cold wine cool his passion a little. But it wasn't only passion, he conceded to himself, as he took another long mouthful. Passion he could deal with. That would just ignite the spark he sensed between them and stoke the flames to a quick, hot burnout that would pass as quickly as it came. It would be the easy choice, the convenient choice, the sensible choice for someone who didn't want or need to become enmeshed in anything more complicated. Right then and there, though, Jake was feeling anything other than sensible. Which should probably worry him a lot more than it was. 'What brought them here to the Point?'

Laurie twisted to face him once more, bringing one foot up to rest on the seat of her chair, her chin all but propped on her knee. She'd kicked off her sandal, exposing her pink-polished toes. 'Her family used to take their holidays here, and she'd always loved the place. They moved here in the fifties and opened the deli and it's been handed down from father to son to grandson.' Her expression clouded. 'When Gio died a couple of years ago, the whole village turned out to pay tribute to him. He was such a character.'

Her sudden sadness was more than he could bear. Reaching out he stroked the front of her raised calf, wanting to offer some comfort. 'I didn't mean to make you sad.'

The corner of her mouth tilted up. 'It's okay. He was just one of those people who seemed to take up more space than most, so when he went it left that much bigger a hole. He spent the first six months after I opened the café trying to teach me to make a proper cappuccino.'

'And did he succeed?'

'Eventually.' She laughed. 'It was worth all the hassle pleasing him because he gave me his mother's recipe for biscotti and I've used it ever since. I think it was an excuse for him to come in every day and support a new local business. Same as my knitting ladies. They turned up the first week I opened, having always taken it in turns to host the group. I think they enjoy having a nosey out the window at what's going on, but still, it's a kindness I never forget.'

What must it be like to live in such a close-knit community that every birth and death was celebrated and mourned as though they were a relation? Jake knew his neighbours to say hello to, and take in the odd parcel, but that was about it. The couple next door had a boy at university who caused havoc on home visits because parking was so tight outside, and the woman two doors down had a cat that had kept trying to climb in his window until he'd got so fed up he'd invested in some magnetic screens that let the air in while keeping his inquisitive visitor out. As Mac had told him when he'd first started out at the *Comet*, journalists didn't get involved – they reported the news, they didn't make it. Somewhere along the line that advice had worked its way into every corner of Jake's life. 'Does it ever bother you, everyone knowing your business?'

Her lips quirked, not quite a smile, something more rueful. 'It used to when I was younger. I couldn't do anything without it getting back to Mum or Dad by the end of the day.' Her expression clouded once more, her gaze dropping to the fingers twisting her wine glass this way and that. He didn't think he'd met anyone as transparent or unguarded as Laurie. The way she wore every emotion on her face was both appealing and unsettling. He'd never have lasted a day in his job without being able to mask his true feelings behind a neutral expression.

'I met Matt the summer I turned seventeen.'

Jake froze at the soft words, the confessional tone of them. When she didn't say anything further, he had to squash down his instinct to prompt her. If Laurie wanted to open up to him, then it had to be in her own time. 'You finished with this?' He indicated her empty plate and when she nodded, he cleared the table of everything but his glass and returned to the kitchen. He took his time, covering the remains of the antipasti, stowing the dirty plates in the dishwasher and checking on the chicken in the oven. Pleased with how it looked, he turned the heat down low, retrieved the bottle of fizz from the fridge and wandered back out to the patio.

Laurie had moved to the end of the garden and was staring out over the waves. Her glass stood on the table beside his and he filled them both before setting the bottle in a shady spot beneath his seat. She glanced around at the sound of the chink of glass on stone but didn't move.

'I've turned the oven down so there's no rush for dinner.' Jake lifted her drink, offering to bring it over to her but she shook her head, letting her gaze drift back to the sea once more.

The music on his phone switched to one of the bass-heavy tracks he used to motivate himself through his morning run. It was a classic, one of his absolute favourites, but too intrusive for this moment. A quick scroll and he found the chill-out instrumental list he played at night when he was winding down for the day. Slow, dreamy synth over-laid with a hypnotic repetitive guitar line and a shimmer of bells. There was something simultaneously relaxing and anticipatory about the music. He and Laurie were on the cusp of something, he could feel it deep within his bones. The urge to reach, to try to grasp it thrummed through him like the pulse of the guitar driving the music towards its conclusion, but she'd put this distance between them for a reason. All he could do was wait and see if she would come to him.

Tilting his head back, he watched a seagull high above him, soaring and dipping as it rode the evening thermals, and let the music wash over him. If he was that way inclined he might see it as a sign, to live in the moment like the bird above him and be carried along wherever the wind chose to take him. More likely, it was looking for a perfect white sheet flapping on the breeze that it could take a huge crap on, or for some unsuspecting fool to step out of the chippy with a bundle of hot chips to steal. Jake chuckled to himself; he'd never be a zen master, it seemed.

Minutes passed, the contents of one glass disappeared while the other turned flat and warm in the sun and still Laurie stood with her back to him. New-found patience wearing a little thin, Jake gathered the glasses and returned to the kitchen. If he didn't serve dinner soon, the chicken would be overdone. He'd just transferred the pan from the oven to the stove top when he felt a gentle touch on his back and Laurie leaned past him. 'That smells wonderful. Shall I take the plates and the salad outside?'

Grateful she'd come back to him even a little bit, Jake murmured his thanks and they worked in harmony for the next few minutes as he threw a handful of fresh pasta into a pot of boiling water while she prepared the salad. By the time he'd drained the pasta, sliced the chicken breasts and transferred them to a couple of serving dishes, Laurie had ferried everything else out onto the patio and was pouring them both a glass of white wine. She'd also put the umbrella up and tilted it to block the rays of the setting sun.

'This looks fantastic,' she said, pulling her chair up closer to the table.

'Help yourself, I hope you like it.' Jake pushed the hot dishes a little closer to her plate and transferred some salad to a smaller bowl while she took what she wanted.

'After being in the kitchen all day, I'm always grateful to have someone else do the cooking. Everyone pitches in at home, so I only have to make dinner once or maybe twice a week.'

To most people, the idea of being surrounded by cakes, pastries and other delicious treats would be their idea of heaven, but he supposed the reality was far different. It was the same with his work. People assumed journalism was one exciting scoop after another. They didn't think about anything beyond the headlines. When he'd been a junior reporter, writing filler articles about local dog shows and kids' sports leagues was as close as he got to the news – maybe a hot debate over the proposed installation of a skateboard ramp if he was really lucky. He'd been obsessed with what he'd considered real news. He'd scoured the websites of all the major daily papers, and his TV was almost permanently tuned to one of the twenty-four-hour news channels. He'd even started files on his favourite journalists, delving into how they'd started, searching out old articles from their times on the subs desk at various local papers, trying to find the key to their success. It hadn't been a healthy way to live, and it was only once he'd been able to switch his focus to the kind of in-depth reporting he did now that he'd found a way to step back from the constant barrage of breaking news.

'Too much of a good thing, hey?' he asked her with a touch of sympathy.

'Something like that. As I said, I'm lucky because everyone takes their turn at home. Dad's the best cook in the family, although not all of his experimental recipes can be called a success.' A wry grin crossed her lips. 'Beef and banana curry isn't going to feature on the café's menu anytime soon. What about you, where did you learn to cook?'

It was an innocent enough question, but it struck him to the core how different their upbringings were. His dad had never lifted a finger in the kitchen, believing homemaking to be a woman's job. And he'd done his best to instil the same ridiculous, outdated notion in his son's head. Chores were set as a punishment, never because there was some value to be gained from learning how to cook or clean or run a home. Wanting only to relieve some of the pressure his mother had been under, Jake misbehaved more often than was his natural inclination to ensure he could help around the house. His mum had stuck to the basic meals his father preferred and had been more concerned with ensuring everything was cooked exactly right than in encouraging any burgeoning interest Jake might have had in learning.

'It was the second year of university. I moved out of halls into a shared house. One of my housemates was a trainee chef, and she took me under her wing a bit, taught me all I know.'

And not just in the kitchen. Jules had been two years his senior and a lifetime more experienced than him. She'd helped him see beyond the limitations his parents had set for him, and though their parting had been difficult at the time, they kept in touch through social media and had followed each other's careers with nothing but encouragement and admiration. Jules had sent him a framed reproduction of the front page from his first major article which still hung pride of place above his desk at home. He'd sent her a bottle of champagne when she'd been promoted to sous chef; danced with her at her wedding with only a touch of regret because anyone with eyes could see she and her husband, Zac, were made for each other.

Laurie forked up a mouthful of chicken and tasted it. 'My compliments to you *and* her, then, because this is delicious.'

Jake accepted the comment with a smile. 'Don't get any fancy ideas that I'm up here dining in style every night. Cooking for one isn't very appealing; thankfully Mrs Walker's offered to fill my freezer with leftovers once a week. So I won't have to do much more than boil a bit of rice or pasta while I'm reheating something in the microwave.'

'It's good someone is taking care of you.'

'I'm not exactly helpless, Laurie. I've been taking care of myself since I was eighteen.'

'Sorry, I was only teasing.'

He watched as she chased a piece of chicken around her plate, seeing the colour rise in her cheeks and hating himself just a little bit. Not just because he'd snapped at her, but because he couldn't let the last edges of the wounds left by his parents heal. It'd been nearly ten years, more than enough time to stop picking at it. 'No, it's me that should be apologising.' Reaching out he stilled her hand holding the fork. 'Don't let this spoil things, please.'

She took a deep breath, then released her fork to turn her hand until they were palm to palm. 'It's not your fault. I stirred up a few memories earlier, and I'm not quite sure what to do with them.'

He rubbed his thumb across the back of her hand in a soothing gesture. 'You can talk about them if it would help, or we could just sit quietly.'

'You're very good at silences, aren't you?' The look she cast him from beneath her lashes could mean a hundred and one things.

'Or just very good at not talking about the things that bother me,' he countered with a wry smile.

16

It was the kind of remark that, if most people had said it, would be an invitation to explore further, but she was starting to learn that Jake Smith wasn't most people. If she had a picture dictionary, there'd be a photo of him underneath the word 'guarded'. Oh, there was a chink or two in his armour, but the moment she thought she might have wormed her way beneath it, he pushed her away just long enough to seal up the hole. He did it so gently, so skilfully that she didn't realise what he was doing until it was too late. It would be more infuriating if he wasn't so charming. She squeezed his hand, giving him a hint of her nails, telling him in the silence he so loved to retreat into that she was onto his game. His only response was to reach for his wine glass, that tell-tale half-smile of his playing around the corners of his lips.

Damn him. If he wasn't going to talk, then she would. She'd never been one to let things fester, having been encouraged from an early age to talk things through by her parents. Not that this was something she could talk to them about, not without hurting them all over again. Pushing aside her plate of cooling food, she reached for her own glass and took a mouthful before setting it back down. It would be too easy to try to drown out the memories with alcohol, even though she knew from experience that it didn't work. 'I met Matt the summer I turned seventeen.' She echoed the inadvertent words from earlier, which had stirred everything up. Her stomach fluttered as his image sprang to mind, as crystal clear as the first time she'd caught him smiling at her across the crowded pub.

'We were too young to drink, but Pete didn't mind us being in the pub as long as we didn't take the mick. If we wanted to get drunk then there were plenty of parties down on the beach where people passed bottles of cheap cider bought in the offie by one of the older kids. Me and my friends were happy enough to sit there with a glass of sparkling water and pretend it was a G&T or that our Diet Coke had vodka or Bacardi in. No one knew any different, and it was just nice to feel a bit more grown-up than we actually were.'

'Hard to get away with it when everyone knows your folks, too, I bet.'

She laughed at his spot-on observation. 'There was always someone ready to grass us up, that's for sure. I can still remember my dad storming down to the beach in nothing more than his dressing gown and a pair of boxers when he found out Ivy and I had lied and said we were staying at each other's houses.' She raised her hand to her face as though she could shield herself from the embarrassment engrained in that memory.

'Ouch.' Jake wrinkled his nose in sympathy.

'God, we were only fifteen and too stupid and naïve to

understand how much trouble we might have got ourselves into.' Laurie shook her head. 'Two years later, I was still bloody naïve but unfortunately that bit too old to be told what to do.' An unexpected lump in her throat quieted her for a moment, and when she spoke again she could hear the huskiness of it. 'Matt was twenty-one. He and his friends had rented a cottage for the summer to celebrate completing their finals – a last hoorah before they went their separate ways. There were two couples and three singles. I think because there were women in the group it made it easier to trust him.' She curled her feet up under her, scrunching a little deeper into the chair.

'They were all so sophisticated, or so it seemed to me who'd never been further than fifty miles in any direction from my doorstep, but they never made me feel stupid. We watched films with subtitles and discussed them long into the night while getting drunk on cheap wine. A couple of them smoked, and not just cigarettes, but when I didn't want to try anything there was no pressure. I spent more and more time with them as the summer went on. Ivy and I fell out when she said something nasty about Matt flirting with other girls when I wasn't around.' Laurie pressed her forehead against her knees, remembering the harsh accusations of jealousy she'd flung at her best friend. Her *former* best friend because they'd never been able to make their way back to how things had been after that.

'I spent hardly any time at home. Mum and Dad expected me to help in the shop – it was their busiest time of year. Nick was working out on the boats with our uncle so there was only me. Matt told me they were exploiting me, that if they weren't paying me a proper wage then it was unfair. Never mind I was living rent-free beneath their roof and the money they paid me was mine to spend as I pleased.' Laurie pressed a hand to the heat suffusing her throat as though she could stave off the blush rising to prickle her face. 'When Dad said he couldn't promise me any more, but would see about a bonus at the end of the summer if things went well, I stormed out, full of what felt like righteous indignation.'

She grabbed at her glass and gulped a mouthful down, trying to wash away the image of her father's hurt expression. 'I was horrible. A complete and utter spoiled brat. I said all these awful things, and even as they were coming out of my mouth they sounded like the words of a stranger. I thought I was so grown-up and demonstrating my independence, but the thoughts in my head weren't my own, they were Matt's. I was a puppet, a plaything, an experiment to stave off the boredom. He was the first man I said "I love you" to. The first man who took me into his bed. I cried so hard the day he left, I made myself sick. "I'll call you" was the last thing he said to me.'

Laurie stared down at the bottom of her somehow empty glass until a gentle hand pried it from her fingers. Claiming that hand too, Jake placed both of hers between his and chafed them softly. Warmth spread from his touch, chasing away some of the cold squeezing at her heart. Lifting her gaze, she found him watching her through the half-gloom of the setting sun. Though fixed in grim lines, she sensed no judgement in his expression and it gave her the courage to finish her sorry little tale. 'He made so many promises about how I could go and visit him just as soon as he got himself sorted out, only he didn't have an address to give me because there were a couple of flats he was looking at and hadn't made a final decision.'

'Christ.'

'That's not even the half of it.' She laughed without an ounce of humour, still too hurt for the shocked girl whose world had turned from the kind of fiery all-consuming passion only first love could bring to ashes in the blink of an eye. 'Turns out he'd got himself a pay-as-you-go SIM card. I wouldn't be surprised if he tossed it out the car window before he'd even cleared the outskirts of the village. When I didn't get an answer to any of my texts, I checked his social media to find he'd unfriended and blocked me. Ghosted, that's what they call it, and I understand why. He vanished from my life so completely, it was like he'd never been there at all, like I'd made him up in some terrible fever dream. Only there was no waking up from it. I turned my very small world completely upside down, hurting the most important people in the process and I had nothing to show for it.'

'And everybody knew.'

There he went again, striking right to the heart of it. The pain of feeling like Matt had ripped out her heart and stomped all over it was bad enough but carrying the shame of knowing the rest of the village had seen her played for a fool had been almost too much to bear at times. 'Yup.'

'What did you do?'

'I crawled under my duvet and cried. Would've stayed that way, too, had Dad not intervened. He came into my room the next morning, put a cup of tea down on my bedside table and told me he expected me to be behind the counter in the shop by nine o'clock. When I told him I couldn't face anyone, he told me it would be horrible, that people would gossip about me, that some might even be rude enough to say something to my face. He also told me that the longer I left it, the worse it was going to be. A covered wound never heals, he said, it just festers.'

'Your dad's a very smart man.'

'He is. I wish I hadn't hurt him and Mum so much before I learned it.'

Jake squeezed her fingers. 'I'll bet if you asked them about it now it's a much bigger deal for you than it ever was for them. Kids push boundaries, it's a part of growing up. So is making mistakes...'

She knew he was right, intellectually at least, but the guilt still came back to bite her at the most unexpected times. 'You're very good at this.'

When he wrinkled his brow at her, clearly confused, she laughed. 'Listening, I mean. I thought it would be difficult to tell you, to admit this thing I'm ashamed of but you never once made me feel like you were judging me.'

He dropped her hands and stood, the move so sudden as to be startling. 'I'm the last person to judge anyone about anything.'

She watched in silence as he cleared and scraped their dirty plates, wondering what on earth she'd said to shift the mood. The intimacy and trust she'd felt building shattered by his stiff shoulders, the loud scrape of fork on china. 'Here, I'll help you.' She made to stand, but he waved her off.

'Sit. It's fine. I'll just dump these in the kitchen, put some coffee on and I'll be back.'

'Oh. Okay.' There wasn't much else she could say, not unless she was willing to challenge him about his change in mood and she was still a bit too raw around the edges from talking about Matt. As she sat in the rapidly fading light listening to Jake clatter around in the kitchen, the awkwardness of the moment grew to an uncomfortable degree. Maybe it would be better if she just cut her losses and left. She'd spent the last half an hour explaining why she didn't date visitors any more while on a date with one! While she didn't think Jake would try to treat her like Matt had, and she knew enough about herself now to cut him off if he did, really, what was the point? They'd have a few weeks of fun, sure, but was that enough at this stage in her life? And for all she could tell herself that's all it would be, she'd still be opening herself up to a world of heartache because she liked Jake. A lot. She could see herself falling for him, was more than a little along the path already if she was being brutally honest with herself. When the summer ended, could she let him go with a kiss and a wave and get back on with her life? It didn't take a genius to work out the answer to that.

His back was turned when she entered the kitchen, the material of his shirt pulled tight over the muscles in his shoulders as he reached for a pair of glazed pottery mugs from a high shelf above the bubbling coffee machine. Edging towards the door, she spared a quick regretful glance at the cheese board he'd prepared, a fresh baguette waiting to be sliced next to it. She'd barely eaten the delicious chicken he'd cooked for them, and now she was leaving him with a small mountain of cheese to tackle. 'No coffee for me.' She offered him an apologetic smile as he swung around to face her, the mugs clasped against his chest. 'I've got an early start in the morning.' Nothing. Not a twitch, just those eyes of his drilling into hers as though he could read every silly thought in her head. She cleared her throat. 'Thanks for dinner, it... it was lovely.'

She fumbled behind her for the door handle, missed and before she could try for it again he was across the room, the door pressed into her back, his hands still gripping the mugs, the only thing keeping their bodies apart.

'Don't.'

17

He wasn't sure if he was begging her not to leave, or telling himself not to push her, a bit of both, maybe. All he knew was if he let her walk out the door he would be letting go of the first spot of brightness that had come into his life in a very long time. It was his fault she was trying to leave, his inability to drop his own shields or give her even a fraction of the honesty and vulnerability she'd shared with him. There'd also been a creeping edge of worry that he'd been inadvertently using his journalistic skills against her, that he'd slipped into interview mode when they were talking, using the right prompts to keep her secrets spilling. Unconscious or not, it'd been enough to make him feel like he'd manipulated her into telling him something she might otherwise have kept private.

Being this close to her emphasised the difference in their heights, the inappropriateness of him looming over her, but he couldn't make himself step back. He wanted only to get closer, to dash the damn stupid mugs to the floor so he could wrap his arms around her and hold her to him. He gripped them tighter instead, his knuckles turning white with the effort of not giving in to that basest part of his nature that didn't give a shit about anything other than what it wanted. Her eyes were saucer-wide, her cheeks flushed and breath coming in little pants like he'd already acted on the driving need inside him and kissed the air from her lungs.

Time stretched, the silence broken only by the last hiss and gurgle of the coffee machine. *Coffee.* He could persuade her to stay for coffee. Instead of that simple invitation, what came out of his parted lips startled them both. 'I hated my parents growing up.'

He might have regretted those impetuous words, but she cupped the back of his neck and drew him down until their lips were all but touching. 'Tell me,' she whispered, their mouths brushing in a not-quite kiss. 'Please.'

This was it. Time to either back off and play it cool or take another step towards emotional intimacy. Like one of those choose your own adventure books he'd loved as kid. Take a step onto the wobbly rope bridge, which might give way beneath him or walk the long way around. The safe, sensible option would be not to open the book at all, to tuck it back on the shelf amongst all the other unread moments in his life. He was tired of being sensible. 'Okay.'

Reaching down, she eased the mugs gently from his painful grip and he stepped back enough to give her room to slip around him. He watched for a moment or two as she bustled around placing the mugs, the freshly brewed coffee and a small jug of milk on a tray. 'Give me a hand?' The sweet smile she sent him over her shoulder got his feet moving and he picked up where he'd left off, slicing the baguette and tossing the pieces into a basket. 'Let's go next door where it's more comfortable.'

'Good idea.' Still a little anxious about what the rest of the evening might lead to, he picked up the bread and cheese and followed her into the lounge. The breeze coming in from the garden was fresher now the sun had set, but he didn't want to shut out the distant crash of the waves over the rocks at the base of the Point. He put down the food, then reached for a fleecy throw draped over the back of the sofa. Shaking it out, he laid it around Laurie's shoulders then took his place beside her on the sofa.

Smiling, she tucked the soft material around herself then shuffled closer until her bent knee rested on top of one of his thighs, as though she was staking a claim, pushing into his space just enough to let him know she expected him to come through on their deal, to talk for once, instead of listening.

'My father was a hard man.' He paused, mouth going dry. Was he really going to lift the lid on this Pandora's box?

Laurie poured them both a coffee, added the perfect amount of milk to his and pressed it into his hands before cutting a selection of the cheese into bite-sized pieces she shared between two plates. Settling herself against the back of the sofa, she raised a square of brie and studied him over the top of it. 'Violent?' The question eased the tightness in his chest, let him know she was prepared to accept his story, no matter how bad it might be.

He shook his head. 'Not physically abusive, no. But mean. Controlling, particularly of my mother. She was never strong. I don't remember a single time when she answered him back or didn't try to do whatever she thought he wanted.' Jake rubbed a weary hand over his face. 'It was exhausting watching her try so hard, day after day, only to have her efforts knocked back because that man never had a kind word for her.' *That man.* It hadn't occurred to him until then, but that was how he thought of him, when he spared his father a thought at all.

Laurie placed the plate he'd ignored in his lap, added a chunk of bread to it before taking one for herself and sat back again. 'What about you?'

Jake shrugged. 'I was just this annoyance. A useless thing that took up too much of my mother's precious time. Time owed to him because he worked to feed and clothe us, to keep a roof over our ungrateful heads.' Jake found himself slipping into the sharp-edged tone his father used, the razor of accusation that had sliced away his younger self's confidence and need for love. Unlike his mother, Jake had at least realised at some point that it didn't matter what he did. There was no pleasing the man, so he'd stopped trying.

'I can't imagine how hard that must've been for you.'

'Once I decided to steer clear of him as much as possible, it wasn't so bad. I stuck to the kitchen and my bedroom. He worked long hours so left most mornings before I had to get up and Mum made sure I had my tea and was out of the way before he got home. I learned to recognise the sound of his van over the other cars on the street and would switch the TV over to the news channel he liked. The first time he came home and the telly was on, he yelled at my mum but she covered for me and told him she'd turned it on ready for him. He was arrogant and self-centred enough to believe it, so that became our little secret.' One of many over the years. Perhaps he should've tried harder as he got older, stood up to the man when it was clear his mum wouldn't, or couldn't, but there hadn't seemed any point.

'Don't make waves.' He laughed, an ugly bitter sound. 'That's what she told me over and over again. And so I became her co-conspirator. Another enabler to the years of abuse at his hand because it was easier than fighting. I toed the line and watched her diminish until she was barely a shadow, and then I left.'

The guilt he'd tried so hard to block rose up in him like a tsunami, threatening to wash him away under its force. He barely noticed when Laurie shoved their plates aside and took his hand, lost as he was in the horror of those dark places he should never have dug into. This was why he didn't talk about things, because it hurt too fucking much, and he'd sworn when he'd shut the door to his parents' house that he'd never let either of them hurt him again. She tugged his hand, pulling him out of the past and back into the moment. 'I'm here, it's all right.'

'Laurie?' He wasn't quite sure what he was asking, but when she shifted around to rise on her knees he leaned forward to meet her. For long, sweet minutes there was nothing to think about other than learning the shape of her mouth, the taste of her skin, the softness of her as her body shifted and slid against his. It wasn't enough, he needed to be closer, needed the light of her to drive away the lingering darkness. Hands a shade too rough, he muttered a curse as one of the delicate buttons on her pretty blouse went flying. With a half-laugh, half-gasp, she sat up and took over the task, each flick of her clever fingers revealing scalloped lace cupping perfect curves, the tempting dip of her waist. Shedding the blouse, she lifted one leg over his to straddle his lap. She stilled when his hands flexed, holding her in place so he could drink her in.

God, she was beautiful. Sultry and sexy, with just a hint of shyness in the way she lowered her lashes. It would be so easy to move things from the sofa to his bed and forget about everything other than this lovely woman in his arms. *Not like this.*

'Wh... what?'

As confusion wiped away some of the desire in her expression, Jake realised he'd voiced the fleeting thought aloud. *Shit.* He reached for her hands as she raised them in reflex to shield her upper body, held them wide apart and let his appreciation for the beauty he saw shine bright in his eyes. 'You are the most gorgeous woman I have ever seen.' When she flicked her gaze from his he released one hand to cup her cheek and made her look at him again. 'And I very much want to take things between us further.'

When he didn't continue, she nibbled her kiss-swollen lower lip as that hint of uncertainty returned to shadow her eyes. Using his thumb, he soothed the red mark before touching her chin, so she met his eyes.

'Let's not rush things for the wrong reasons when we've got the whole summer to get to know each other better.' He let one hand slide down a fraction, unable to resist tracing the delicate dip between shoulder and collar bone before forcing himself to reach behind her for the tangle of silk pooled on the cushion next to them. With the greatest of care, he helped her put her blouse back on, muttering an apology over the missing button.

With a sigh that sounded tinged with more than a little regret, Laurie scooped her hair free from where some of it had caught down the back of her top and smoothed the ruffled strands. When her weight shifted, he thought for one awful moment she was going to clamber off him but she wriggled around until she could lie on her side, her legs cocooned between his, her cheek resting on his upper chest. 'That was very noble of you.'

It sounded so much like a grumble of complaint that Jake couldn't help but laugh. Raising his head slightly, he kissed the top of hers before sliding an arm around her waist and holding her a little tighter against him. 'I'm sorry. I promise the next time I take your top off to behave very badly indeed.'

'You'd better.'

18

Laurie woke the next morning feeling a little uncertain about where things stood between her and Jake. It'd been well past midnight by the time he'd walked her home, leaving her on the doorstep with a promise to call and a sweet kiss without any of his earlier passion. She'd tossed and turned until her alarm went off, running over the events of the evening, wondering if she'd messed things up. Why on earth had she brought up all that stuff with Matt, for goodness' sake? Dragging her sleepy body into the shower, Laurie let the hot water sluice over her. As she watched the soap bubbles disappear down the plug, she wished she could wash away her doubts as easily.

Laurie did her best to go about her morning routine, deflecting her mum's questions with a few noncommittal platitudes about how nice the meal he'd made had been – not that they'd eaten very much of it. She skipped out on breakfast with the excuse she had baking to do and would eat at the café, needing a bit of time on her own to sort through the muddle in her head.

The first batch of muffins was in the oven and she was buttering a couple of slices of fruit loaf when she heard a knock at the front door. The window shades were still down, so she pulled one aside to peer out and found Jake grinning at her. Unable to stop an answering smile, tummy suddenly dancing with butterflies, she flipped the latch and let him in, locking the door behind him. 'You're an early bird.'

'I woke up just before seven so I went for a walk on the beach. It's so beautiful this time of the morning when no one else is about. I was up on the rocks at the far end when I saw you heading this way so thought I'd give you time to get the coffee going and see if I could blag a cup.' He cast an eager glance over her shoulder, his face falling when he spotted the tea towel she'd hung over the machine after cleaning it down the night before, was still in place.

'I open a little later on Sundays, so I haven't finished setting up yet. There's a kettle in the kitchen if you don't mind instant.' Needing reassurance things were still good between them, she reached a tentative hand to brush the back of his.

His fingers closed around hers, drawing her close until she had to tilt her head back to meet his eyes. She'd never thought of herself as the kind of woman that needed to be sheltered, but she liked the way her body fitted into his. Liked that she could slide her arms around his waist and nestle her head beneath his chin so she did just that, a little sigh of contentment escaping when he folded his arms around her and held her close. 'This is nice,' she snuggled in to press her nose against the skin of his neck, the clean woodsy scent of his aftershave filling her senses.

'I could get used to it,' he agreed, tightening his arms briefly before letting them fall slack so he could draw back and gaze down at her. 'That's what I wanted to talk to you about, actually.' He put a hand in his pocket and drew out a collection of pretty pebbles. 'And I wanted to give you these.'

Cupping her hands, she let him tip the stones onto her palms. One pebble was a uniform grey and might be considered dull if it wasn't for the perfect smoothness of it. A second was the polar opposite, a creamy jumble of lumps and bumps striated with vivid streaks of orange and brown. Others were flecks of coloured glass, bits of discarded bottles worn smooth by wind and water. He'd added a couple of shells too, the ridges on their backs like the ripples of the waves on the shore. The last pebble was mottled shades of pale pink and she gasped in delight when Jake flicked it over with his thumb to reveal the imprint of a fossilised starfish. 'They're beautiful, thank you.'

Jake tucked a strand of hair that had fallen from her messy ponytail behind her ear, his touch turning into a caress down her neck which sent delicious shivers through her. 'I thought you could put them on one of your shelves.' He gestured to the assorted lengths of wood Nick had helped her mount on the wall behind the counter, which she'd filled with an assortment of plants, little bits of driftwood she'd found and even a child's bright red bucket and spade.

The little collection of pebbles would fit in perfectly, and only she would know the significance of them. 'I've got just the spot for them.' Heading behind the counter, she deposited them on the corner of a shelf closest to the door into the kitchen where they would catch her eye every time she passed them. She led the way through to the back, where she rinsed her hands under the tap. 'Take a seat.' She gestured Jake towards one of the stools next to the wooden table in the centre of the room.

'I thought about bringing you flowers, but that seemed a

bit public and I didn't want you facing any awkward questions.' She paused, kettle in hand to look over at him, not quite sure what he was trying to say. 'After what you told me about that idiot, Matt, I wanted to give you the option to keep things between us on the down-low. If you want to, I mean.'

Because he would be leaving her too at some point. It was too late to worry about that now, she'd made her choice last night to make the most of the summer. Besides, Jake was a good man, an honest man who wasn't trying to string her along with false promises. They were two adults choosing to spend the limited amount of time they had together. She wouldn't be ashamed of that. 'And if I want to shout it from the rooftops?'

Jake threw back his head and laughed, the sound filling the room. 'Then I'll happily hold the ladder. Come here.' He turned sideways on the stool, patting his knee. Abandoning the kettle, Laurie perched on his lap, her own laughter bubbling out when he adjusted her position with a proprietorial grip. 'We haven't said good morning properly yet,' he said, voice growing husky.

'No, we haven't.' Laurie slid her arms around his neck, lifting her face to meet his in a long, lazy kiss. His hands were never still, stroking the length of her ponytail one moment, cupping her neck the next to find the perfect angle he wanted. It was blissful and tender. She pressed her palms into his back, holding him to her.

Bzzzzt!

The timer she'd set for the muffins startled Laurie so much she might have tumbled from Jake's lap had he not steadied her with quick hands. 'You're too distracting,' she laughed, pressing another quick kiss to the corner of his mouth before wriggling free.

'Hurry up and get back here, so I can distract you some more,' he countered, sending her an unrepentant grin.

By the time she'd lifted the muffins from the oven and set them out to cool, he'd boiled the kettle and finished buttering the fruit loaf she'd started preparing, helping himself to one of the slices in the process. They settled opposite each other this time, Laurie needing to keep her wits about her if she was going to open up on time. Though he'd given her a knowing smile when she put the table between them, Jake made no protest. After they'd eaten, he cleared their plates and mugs to the sink and washed up without being asked, leaving her free to stir up another batch of cakes ready for the oven.

She was in the process of spooning the sponge mixture that would form the base of a pair of lemon drizzle loaf cakes into their tins when Jake lifted her ponytail and smacked a kiss on the back of her neck, making her jump. 'I'll leave you to it,' he said, placing a second kiss on her cheek when she turned towards him. 'I've got some more research to do this morning, but I'll pop in later.'

'Okay. Oh, hey, I almost forgot, Nick said to give him a call about that trip you want to do out to the islands. His number is in my phone.' She gestured with her elbow towards where she'd dropped her phone on the counter next to her hand-bag. 'He's listed under my contacts.'

'You don't mind?'

She shook her head, holding up her hands, which were a mess of butter smears and flour. 'Saves me having to clean up first. I don't think it's locked.' She'd got so fed up with it switching to the locking screen every few seconds, she'd set it so it only locked when she pressed the power button. It wasn't like she had anything to hide.

'I'll put my number in there, too, while I'm at it, shall I?'

'Oh, yes please. And take mine.' She turned her attention back to the task in hand while he fiddled around with the handset.

'All done,' he said a few moments later. 'I'd best be off, then. Don't make plans for this evening.' He was gone before she had chance to respond, the bell over the front door tinkling moments later to signal his departure.

Don't make plans. Ha! She was pretty sure she'd be making plans about all sorts of delicious things for the rest of the day and was even more sure that was exactly his intention when he'd said it. 'Tricksy man,' she muttered to herself as she lifted the loaf tins into the oven, the grin plastered across her face wide enough to make the Cheshire Cat envious.

19

Tuesday dawned bright and clear. It had taken him a few days to find a spot in his busy schedule, but Jake had finally managed to arrange for Nick to take him out on a tour around the islands. Having made a quick pit stop at Laurie's on his way to the dock to collect a couple of takeaway coffees, a bag of pastries and a kiss sweet enough to carry him through the day until he saw her later, he approached Nick's boat at the allotted meeting time. There was no sign of him, and uncertain of the protocol in boarding a vessel without permission Jake paused on the quayside and called out. 'Hello? Nick? You there, mate?'

'Just a sec.' Nick poked his head out from a small square hole in the deck not much wider than his shoulders, wiping his hands with a stained cloth.

'Problem?' Jake nodded at Nick's dirty hands.

'No, no, everything's fine, I was just adding a bit of grease to the anchor winch.' Tossing the cloth into the semi-darkness behind him, Nick climbed the short stepladder and secured the cover, sealing the deck. He cast a grin at the tray of drinks. 'One of those for me?'

'Double-shot cappuccino with a dash of hazelnut syrup. Your favourite, I believe.' Jake offered the tray with a knowing grin as Nick approached him along the railed gangplank. 'Permission to come aboard, Captain?'

'Granted.' Nick took the tray then stepped back to let Jake pass him. 'Been snooping, have we?'

The question startled Jake until he realised it was a joke. 'Just got a bit of insider info from Laurie to keep on your good side.' He couldn't help a twinge of discomfort at how close Nick had come to the truth. His lack of honesty with Laurie about his real motivation for being in Mermaids Point had begun to play on his conscience. He was going to have to find a way to explain things to her, and sooner rather than later.

'There are some storage cabinets in the cockpit if you want to stow your bag. I'll show you.' Nick led Jake across the viewing platform, ducking his head slightly as he entered the cabin area at the front of the boat.

Rows of neat cupboards were built into the bulkhead on either side, but Jake's attention was drawn to the sophisticated display screens surrounding the ship's wheel. He whistled, a low sound of appreciation. He knew the square root of nothing about navigation, but he recognised decent equipment when he saw it. 'Nice.'

'Know much about boats?' When Jake shook his head, Nick gave him a quick crash course in what everything did, most of which went over his head. Nick's surety and familiarity demonstrated he was in safe hands, and that was all that mattered.

Shrugging out of his backpack, he opened the top to

remove his camera, leaving his waterproof jacket, notebook and lunch inside, then tucked it into one of the storage cupboards. When he rose from his crouch he found himself staggering a couple of steps, the floor not quite where he'd expected it to be. 'There's more motion than I thought there'd be,' he admitted, clutching at the rail running around the edge of the cockpit.

Nick chuckled. 'Tidal waters will do that. Here, stick this on.' He tossed an orange lifejacket to Jake before pulling a matching one over his head and showing Jake how to secure the ties at the side of his waist. 'I've got a map here of the islands,' he said, unfurling the rolled document and securing it to a stand with a couple of bulldog clips at each corner. 'I was thinking we could make one big circuit and then I'll take you closer to a couple of the more interesting islands.'

'Sounds good. Will we be able to anchor near the Seven Sisters? I'd like to take a few pictures.' Jake tapped the scattering of rocks at the far end of the string of islands.

'Sure we can. If we get lucky there might be some seals basking on the rocks. Probably no mermaids, though.' He threw a wink at Jake. 'Come on, let's get the ramp shifted and we can get going.'

With Jake lifting from inside the boat and Nick guiding it with the wheels on its base, the ramp was soon clear of the boat and secured on the quayside. As soon as it was out of the way, Jake could see just how close they were moored to the dock, with only a set of cushioned floats hanging over the side of the boat to keep it from scraping against the dark stone. Nick hopped back onboard with effortless grace, and while he doubted he would be quite that surefooted, Jake was pretty sure he'd have been able to make the same step down without too much effort. 'You didn't need to put the ramp out for me.'

Nick punched him lightly on the arm. 'Don't let your ego get the better of you while you're on my boat. The ramp goes out for everyone, no exceptions. Safety first; safety always.'

Feeling a little chastened, Jake apologised. 'You're right, I'm sorry. Why don't you tell me exactly what I should and shouldn't do?'

Nick spent the next few minutes giving him a tour of the exterior of the boat. 'You can sit or stand anywhere here on the open deck, but don't attempt to stand on anything that might give you a higher vantage point. If you want a clearer view then you can come up here.' Nick led the way up a sturdy metal stairway to a small viewing platform above the cockpit. 'If you want to come up here make sure you let me know first. Use the railing when you are making your way to and from the seating area and stay in your seat at all times when we're moving.' Tilting his head back he shaded his eyes as he surveyed the morning sky. 'It'll be hot later, but I've got a canopy that's easy to put up if we need it.' He glanced back at Jake. 'Did you put sunscreen on?'

He shook his head. 'No, but I've got some in my bag.'

'Best put some on now, and keep it topped up. The reflection off the water increases the chance of sunburn, and people don't always notice it if the wind's blowing. A hat wouldn't go amiss, either.' He tapped a finger against the wide-brimmed fisherman's hat on his head. It might have been any colour from green to brown when new but had faded to a pale grey mottled with saltwater stains.

'I thought of that too,' Jake said with a grin. 'I'll dig it out along with the sunscreen when we go down.' He hadn't wanted to risk his new Fedora blowing away so had picked up a cheap cap from one of the display racks outside the newsagents.

Returning to the cockpit, Jake applied a liberal layer of sunscreen and put on the baseball cap and his sunglasses. Once he'd finished, he moved to the far corner of the cockpit where Nick had indicated he could stand and be sure he wouldn't be in the way. Having paused to cast off the lines securing them to the dock, Nick ran through the last of his predeparture checks. Checking over his shoulder, he gave Jake a nod of approval for the position he'd adopted with both hands braced on either side of him on the handrail then returned his attention to the front. A quick twist of the key and the boat's engine roared to life and they were off.

It wasn't as noisy as he'd been expecting, but they still had to raise their voices to be heard. 'Hold on,' Nick called over his shoulder. 'We're about to pass beyond the break-water so the motion will increase a bit more now.'

Setting his back deeper into the corner, Jake braced his feet wider apart to spread his weight better. The first of the waves thudded against the prow, the impact juddering through the soles of his feet.

'Okay?' Nick shouted without turning around.

'All good.'

'Great. Not long now and I'll be able to change course.' Nick throttled up the engine in a slow steady increase of pace Jake could feel as his shoulders pressed back. They rocked and rolled for a minute or two more before they cleared the last of the bigger waves and their ride smoothed out. Nick spun the wheel, steering them out to the right and towards the first of the islands and slowed their pace once more to a pleasant chug.

'Come up here now if you like.' Nick raised a hand to point to the front rail next to him. 'It'll be pretty smooth sailing from here on out.' Jake released his grip, flexed his fingers to ease the ache where he'd been holding on a bit tighter than was strictly necessary, and worked his way forward, keeping his left hand gliding along the rail until he was in position.

As they closed in on the first island – a towering escarpment of jagged rocks tall enough to cast them into shadow – a raucous chorus of squawks and cries filled the air. Throttling right down, Nick turned off the engine. 'We're far enough away here it won't matter if we drift a bit. Come on, you'll want to see this.' Grabbing a pair of binoculars from the console, he led them out onto the viewing deck.

Tilting his head back, Jake could see the upper part of the rocks was stained white. In addition to the constant cries of the seabirds whirling and turning overhead, other calls echoed from the rockface.

Nick trained his binoculars on the island, fiddled with them a bit then handed them to Jake. 'Check it out.'

Tucking his sunglasses up above the visor of his cap, Jake raised the binoculars and squinted through the lenses. It was just a blur of white until Nick nudged his hands, urging him to look higher. Grey and white birds covered every inch of the rock, from yellow beaks poking out from hidden cracks and crevices to daredevils clinging to almost invisible perches. The white he'd seen was a mass of guano trailing over the dark rocks like the world's most unpleasant waterfall. 'That's a lot of shit.'

Nick laughed. 'Just be thankful we're upwind, because you've never smelt anything like it, I can promise you that. I bring volunteers out here from the local wildlife trust, even been on a couple of the occupied islands myself from time to time when they've been short on numbers and need a hand with their data gathering, and it's enough to make your eyes water.'

A gust of wind hit them at that moment from a different direction, sending a choking cloud of ammonia and fish scent straight up Jake's nose. Clapping a hand over his mouth, he spun away, all but retching from the vile assault on his senses. Shifting to the other side of the boat he gulped in a few lungfuls of clean salty air until his stomach settled once more.

'I did warn you.' Nick clapped a hand on his shoulder, not an ounce of sympathy to be found in his grinning gaze. 'Come on, I'll shift us a bit further out and we'll keep going, I just wanted to give you a quick glimpse of what it's like.'

Jake stayed outside this time, taking a seat on one of the long benches that lined the edge of the viewing deck. Turning his head towards the sea, he closed his eyes against the stinging edge of salt spray tossed up by their motion. It was gorgeous being out on the water and as Nick steered them clear of the island's shadow the warmth of the sun's rays bathed him in a wash of golden light he could see through his closed lids. He'd never considered himself one of those people who connected much with nature, but these past few weeks were making him realise how much he missed out on living in an urban environment.

The sheer pleasure of being able to step out onto the patio of the little cottage and enjoy his first cup of coffee of the day looking out over the end of the Point had given him a new-found love for the sea. He'd always enjoyed going to the beach on holiday, but that had been to laze around and nap off a hangover before he and his mates hit the bars and clubs, and he'd have happily stayed on a lounger by the pool of whatever hotel they were staying in.

Now the beach *was* the destination. A microcosm to be

explored, a new discovery to be found lurking in the rock-pools, the chance to smile, maybe say hello to people when he was out on his morning stroll. And now this riot of sensation and motion out on the water was already something he could imagine becoming addicted to.

What would it be like to be out here when the weather turned? Would it make him sick? Scared? Or exhilarated as the forces of nature swirled around and under him? The sudden knowledge he wouldn't be here long enough to find out sent a ripple of disappointment through him. What would it be like to watch the seasons turn? Would he still enjoy strolling along the beach when it was wet and windy? It might be worth it if it meant coming home to the warm welcome of the real fireplace in his cottage; the even warmer welcome of Laurie's sweet smile as she rubbed the salt from her hair with a thick towel. He could almost feel her curled up on the sofa beside him while the rain lashed the windows outside, cosy and snug as they watched a film and mopped up soup he'd made from thick bowls with slabs of fresh bread from the deli. Raising a fist, he knocked it against his forehead as though he could drive the images from his brain. It was pointless to think of such things. He was here to do a job, to enjoy the summer and get back to his own life with a pocket full of happy memories and hopefully a half-decent story to tell. He was supposed to be working, not sightseeing like a bloody tourist.

20

Making his way back into the cockpit, Jake pointed to the island they were passing on their right. 'Does it have a name?'

Nick nodded. 'Most of them do, apart from the ones that are just big rocks. That's Little Gowston.' He pointed to a larger island some distance beyond it. 'To no one's surprise that's Great Gowston.' He grinned. 'All half a mile of it from tip to toe. We'll get a better view of that on the way back. There's some ruins at one end, home to a monk or hermit according to local legend. There was an archaeological dig out there back in the eighties that dated first occupation to the early medieval period and through for about four hundred years or so. My dad's got a book about it in the shop with photos and illustrations that show how the architecture changed. I couldn't see much difference in one pile of rocks from another, if I'm honest.'

They shared a laugh. 'Something to show the tourists, though,' Jake said, feeling a bit excited himself about catching a glimpse later. How or why anyone would choose to live out in the middle of nowhere was beyond him. Especially in the days before the kind of modern conveniences he took for granted.

'The first island, the one with all the birds, is Tarwick,' Nick continued. 'And together with Dunstone and Ninforth, which are the last pair of islands closest to the Seven Sisters, it forms a wildlife sanctuary. Most of the birds that nest here are regular visitors, but we occasionally get a rare nesting pair and then we get an influx of avid bird watchers.'

'How many of the islands can you actually set foot on?'

Nick shrugged a shoulder. 'If you've got a small enough boat and enough experience you can land on pretty much any of them. There's not much to see on most of them, though there's plenty of inlets and caves that were used by smugglers way back when. They would land the stuff on the islands and then transfer it to the caves beneath the Point.'

'There's caves beneath the Point?' Jake perked up. 'Whereabouts?'

'The whole coastline is riddled with them. Your cottage stands right on top of some. We don't publicise their presence because it's treacherous when the tide comes in. After a series of accidents and near-misses the council erected a fence and posted warning signs. Thankfully, it deters most people who walk towards that end of the beach. We haven't had any mishaps since.' Nick raised his knuckles and rapped them on his forehead. 'Touch wood.'

Jake pictured his daily walk down the cliff path from his cottage. When he got to the bottom he always turned left towards the village and the main stretch of the beach. On his return trips to the cottage he followed the same route, the steps leading from the beach a natural exit point to access the cliff path. From what he could remember of the area beyond the steps it was covered in scrubby grasses and rocks and never looked very inviting. 'I can't say I've noticed a fence.'

'I'm not surprised, really. The decision was made to let that end of the beach grow wild and the council posted a few warning signs in the hopes that would be enough to deter people. You have to walk quite a bit further than the steps to reach the fence. A few dog walkers use the area, but when picking a spot for sunbathing, people tend to avoid it. We used to have a great laugh playing and exploring all along there when we were kids, but we also knew and respected the tide times. You don't grow up this close to the sea and not understand the dangers as much as the beauty of it. Some of the visitors don't get it, which is why we often end up rescuing some idiot in an inflatable raft who's been caught on the current and swept out to sea, or a group of inexperienced kayakers who get too tired to make it back to shore.'

Nick's expression clouded. 'The final straw was when a family went exploring and got cut off when the father slipped and hurt his leg. They retreated into one of the caves, not realising some flood entirely when the tide comes in. It was touch and go whether the lifeboat crew would get them out in time and the kids were hypothermic from being in the cold water so long.' He raised his eyes to meet Jake's, an unfamiliar glint of steel in them. 'They came so close to tragedy, and not just for them. Something like that could destroy the reputation of a place like ours. The fence went up within a matter of weeks after that.'

There was nothing of the laughing man Jake had started to come to know in that look. Instead, he understood that Nick was a man with a deep and abiding love for his home, and his community. A man who knew who he was, understood both the land and the people he came from, and had pride in that heritage.

An ugly sensation gripped at Jake's gut and it took him a moment to identify it as envy. He had nothing; no roots, no family history he could call upon to ground himself with. He'd lost all chance of that when he'd left home. Unlike the man in front of him, he didn't have generations he could look back upon with pride, because he had no idea who his people were. He'd never met any relations on his father's side and those brief happy summers at his maternal grandparents' had ended before he'd been old enough to wonder about who they were as people; to ask for their stories.

He'd considered once or twice digging into his family tree, but what would've been the point? They'd just be names on bits of paper. He had no memories passed down to him, no anecdotes or stories that would bring them to life. The loss of those unknown names rolled over him in a wave that had Jake clutching for the railing even though the deck beneath his feet barely moved.

He had nothing and nobody he wanted to call family. He was alone in the world, and always had been. The only person he had any connection to was Laurie, and what did she really know about him? She thought he was an author, someone who made up stories for a living. The only stories he'd made up were the ones he'd told her about himself.

What would she think if he told her the truth? Would she accept it, or slam the door in his face? He wouldn't blame her if she did. His gut tightened. It was one thing to obfuscate the truth when researching for a story, but to deliberately deceive someone he was beginning to care about? A wave rocked the boat and the cockpit suddenly felt a little too small. Using the handrail to guide himself, Jake escaped out onto the viewing deck and sucked in a few deep breaths.

'You all right, mate?' The question was accompanied by a soft touch on his shoulder, and there was no way Jake could avoid glancing up at Nick, though it was the last thing he wanted to do.

'Just needed some air,' he replied, though he doubted the sickness curdling his stomach had anything to do with the motion of the boat. 'I'll be fine in a minute.'

Nick thrust a cold can of Coke into his hand before giving him another sympathetic pat on the shoulder. 'This might help. Keep your eyes on the horizon. We can head back if you want?'

They hadn't even made it as far as the rocks where the mermaid sighting had been recorded, but Jake didn't care. He needed to be off this boat and get back... to what? Jake popped the tab on the can and swallowed several mouthfuls. The icy bubbles were almost harsh as they poured down his throat and spread a chill through his belly. The cold liquid quelled the roiling in his middle. Perhaps it was time to stop hiding from the past and to start thinking about the future. He was seeing Laurie later, he could tell her the truth about why he was really in Mermaids Point. She would either accept him, or she wouldn't. The rest of it? He blew out a long sigh. He had a lot of decisions to make, but one step at a time.

* * *

As they approached the harbour, Jake was feeling much more in control of himself, and not a little abashed at his behaviour. Nick seemed to be taking it all in his stride, clearly used to passengers who lost their sea legs. Jake hadn't been able to work out an alternative explanation that didn't lead to further lies or sharing stuff with Nick that Laurie had the right to hear first, and directly from Jake. He'd collected his backpack from the storage cupboard and retreated back to his corner position at the rear of the cockpit to make sure he wasn't any hindrance as Nick steered them into the mouth of the small harbour.

'What the hell?' Nick throttled back as they entered the sheltered area before pointing to a clipboard hanging on a hook nailed to the side of the cabin wall. 'I'm sure we don't have anything else booked today, but can you just double-check?'

Jake took the clipboard down and scanned the top document. It was a calendar-style layout with a double column for each day of the week showing the two boats Nick and his uncle operated. 'It shows Tony out all day with a fishing party, and my name blocking out your morning schedule. You've got nothing showing for this afternoon.'

Nick nodded. 'I wasn't sure how long we'd be out for.' He pointed through the front window to a group of people gathered on the quayside next to the small white hut they used as a booking office. 'I wonder what that lot are waiting for, then.'

Jake checked the clipboard again. 'You've got a wildlife group tomorrow, maybe they've got their dates mixed up.'

'Maybe.' Nick didn't sound too happy about the prospect.

Jake's phone began vibrating in his pocket, the notification alert pinging repeatedly a moment later. At the same time, Nick's phone started doing the same. Shoving the clipboard onto the sloping panel in front of him, Jake grabbed his phone and stared in disbelief at the mass of alerts and messages filling the lock screen. A second mermaid video had been posted and was already going viral, given how many of his search alerts it had triggered. He'd been almost on the spot and allowed himself to get distracted with stupid family stuff instead of focusing on his job.

Annoyed with himself, he tilted the phone to show Nick. 'The bloody mermaid's been spotted again, and we missed it!'

'You've got to be kidding me?' Shutting down the engine completely, Nick let the boat bob up and down a good hundred metres from the dock as he pulled his own phone out and began scrolling. 'I don't bloody believe it,' he muttered, sounding almost as frustrated as Jake felt.

'Should we go back?' He didn't hold out much hope of seeing the mermaid herself, but they might stand a chance of spotting whoever was behind it, or at least the boat they'd used to get out there.

'No point. It wasn't filmed out on any of the islands.'

The absolute certainty in that statement set the cogs in Jake's brain turning. He suspected someone local was behind the stunts, and it was clear from their discussions during their abortive visit to the islands that Nick knew his way around every nook and cranny. Sometimes two and two just equalled four. 'How can you be so sure?' Jake tried to keep the question casual, not wanting to tip off his rising suspicion.

Nick showed Jake the screen on his phone, the latest video clip paused to show the mermaid seated on a rocky outcrop at the edge of what looked like a large cave, arms raised high above her head. 'See the cave behind her?' He tapped the darker area at the back of the image. 'That's one of the ones beneath the Point I was telling you about earlier.'

He clicked play. As the action started again, Jake did his best to ignore the antics of the woman on the rocks and focus instead on the background. The quality of the clip wasn't great, as though it had been recorded on a phone at maximum zoom. It was clear from the angle that whoever was filming the scene was at a higher elevation than the mermaid. As the clip ended the camera panned up, revealing a steep expanse of rock face above the cave and the merest glimpse of sky beyond before cutting off abruptly. Jake raised his head to meet Nick's coldly furious gaze. 'You're sure it's beneath the Point?'

'I don't know anywhere else around here that has a cave that size. Bloody idiots are lucky no one slipped and broke their neck,' Nick snapped.

The genuine anger in his tone had Jake second-guessing his theory over the other man's involvement. 'I thought you said access to that part of the beach is blocked off?'

Nick scrubbed a hand around the back of his neck. 'Not completely. It was a compromise between creating something that blended into the existing landscape and deterring people from the area. There are a couple of signs up warning of the danger.' The furrow between his brows deepened. 'Maybe that's why they chose it, assuming no one else would be around to catch them.'

'You haven't bought into the myth, then?' Jake asked in a teasing tone, trying to lighten the other man's foul mood.

Nick snorted out a laugh. 'Not so much.' He sighed. 'Like everyone else around here, I was grateful for the shot in the arm the first sighting gave us, but if this ends up with people putting their lives at risk then we'll be worse off than ever.'

'What are you going to do about that lot?' Jake nodded over his shoulder towards the people on the dock.

'Take them out, weave a few tall tales and let them take a load of selfies. Most of them won't know one rock or cave from another. Let's hope we can keep it that way.' With that,

Nick reached for the radio positioned just above head height and relayed a short, terse warning to his uncle about what was going on. Restarting the engine, he reached for the throttle then paused to look Jake square in the eye. 'I'm trusting you with what I've told you just now.'

Jake swallowed, not sure what he could say without making a promise he might not be able to keep. 'I won't breathe a word about the location of this latest sighting.' He could work with that; he still had a lot of digging around to do to try and get to the bottom of things. He also hadn't promised he wouldn't write about it, nor that he wouldn't go poking around the rocks himself. Sketchy, but sometimes that was the nature of his job. Ignoring the nasty taste in the back of his throat, Jake shouldered his backpack and retreated to his corner while Nick guided them expertly back to the dock.

21

By the time Laurie had ushered out the last of her customers on Friday evening, she was ready for nothing more than a hot bath and to fall face down on her bed. It had been chaos for the past few days, the latest mermaid sighting drawing the crowds back in droves. Along with curious members of the public, several news crews had descended on the village, blocking pavements and generally making a nuisance of themselves. And the worst was yet to come with the weekend just around the corner.

She'd hardly seen hide nor hair of Jake since he'd headed off on Tuesday to go sailing with Nick. With the café so busy, there was no quiet corner for him to work from, nor had he wanted to occupy a table other customers would use and take the revenue from her. She appreciated the thoughtfulness of the gesture, but she missed being able to look up at any time and catch his eye.

He'd popped in yesterday morning to grab a takeaway coffee and a kiss or two, but there'd been a distance about him, like he was going through the motions. When she'd asked him if everything was okay, he'd waved it off, saying he was busy with his writing and finding it hard to focus on anything else. The words had sounded right, but there was something about his behaviour she couldn't quite put her finger on. The intimacy she'd hoped would continue to grow from that evening at the cottage had stalled somehow. She needed to try harder, to eke out some proper time to spend with him and see if she could get to the bottom of things. Maybe when she was less tired.

A knock on the door behind her sent a curse from her lips. She was already staying open an hour later than she would normally, but it didn't stop customers ignoring the CLOSED sign and trying their luck. She was tempted not to answer, but the lights were still on and would be visible around the edges of the blinds. 'Sorry, we're closed,' she called out. 'They do meals at the pub, or there's a fish and chip shop on the high street.' With any luck that would be enough to send whoever it was on their way.

'If you want to go out, that's fine.' A familiar deep voice sent a happy shiver through her. 'But I thought you might prefer something home-cooked.'

Laurie flipped the lock and yanked open the door so fast the bell above jangled like it might fall off its bracket. Jake stood on the doorstep, one hand tucked into the front pocket of a pair of dark grey jeans he'd teamed with a moss green t-shirt, the other clutching the handles of a red overnight bag that looked suspiciously familiar. 'What have you got there?'

He raised one shoulder in a nonchalant shrug, a cheeky gleam in his eye. 'Just a few bits and pieces your mum put together. I just collected it from next door.'

'My *mum*?' She might have expected him to have roped Nick in with whatever his plans were, but to approach her mum was a bit much. Her cheeks flushed as the further implications of his actions swept through her tired brain. She had a very open, very honest relationship with her parents, and they treated her as the adult she was, but there were things they didn't need to know about when it came to her private life.

Jake gave her a sweet smile. 'I thought she'd know your favourite things better than anyone else. It's just a few bits of toiletries and some comfy clothes to change into for the evening.' Expression growing serious, he reached out to brush his fingers through her limp, messy fringe. 'You look worn to the bone, sweetheart. I just wanted to give you a break for a few hours, pamper you a bit before you face the weekend crowds.'

She studied his face, trying to read between his words but could see nothing beyond what looked to be genuine concern. 'This isn't a nefarious plot to get me into your bed?'

His eyes widened, the innocent expression just a touch too on point as he pressed his free hand to his heart. 'As if I would.'

Crossing her arms, she raised an eyebrow, fighting against the urge to grin. God, he was too irresistible for his own good.

'The only plans I have for this evening are to run you a hot bath with your favourite rose oil, let you soak for a bit before I come in and wash and dry your hair for you...' Stepping closer, he eased his arm around her waist and drew her close.

God, the thought of those strong fingers currently splayed across her back moving up to massage her aching scalp was enough to send her eyes rolling back in her head.

He bent closer, lowering his voice to whisper in her ear. 'Then I'm going to feed you goat's cheese, pine nut and spinach lasagne.' His lips moved against her skin and she could feel him grinning at the mention of one of her favourite dishes. There was something incredibly seductive about knowing he'd gone out of his way to tailor everything to her needs. 'And afterwards, I'll let you watch whatever you want on TV while I rub your feet with peppermint foot balm.'

She had to swallow down a moan of delight to speak. 'Is that all?' Her attempt at casual came out far too breathy for her liking.

Instead of replying, Jake began to feather kisses over the shell of her ear, across her temple then down her cheek until his mouth brushed the corner of hers. 'Then, I'll walk you home.' Teasing her lower lip between his, he pressed a soft kiss against her mouth. She was all but trembling now.

Clearly aware of the effect he was having on her, he raised his head to capture her gaze with a scorching look that told her she wasn't the only one feeling the heat between them. 'Or not, whichever you prefer.'

Oh, she knew what she preferred, and if she wasn't hot and grubby from rushing around all day she might just tug him inside the café and forego all the delicious treats he had planned for her. But rolling around on the cold tiles was definitely not how she'd pictured their first time together. Speaking of which... 'I need to tidy up, first.' Not just herself, but the café too.

'Leave it.' He stole another kiss, all heat and sweet temptation. 'We'll come down early and sort everything out before you have to open.'

She cast another quick glance around. Apart from a couple of cups and plates, everything else was already in the dishwasher. She'd tidied the back kitchen and wiped the counter and the unoccupied tables down, hoping her lingering guests would take the hint. The floor needed mopping, along with a handful of other bits and pieces she liked to do to get a head start, nothing that wouldn't keep.

'Hold that thought.' Grabbing the dirty crockery, she raced out the back, stuffed them in the dishwasher, switched it on and was back in front of Jake with her handbag over her shoulder in record time.

* * *

Forty minutes later, Laurie lay in a steaming bath full of essential oils with enough foam to cover her from the tips of her toes to her chin. Jake had folded a hand towel over to act as a pillow and lit an array of candles that cast the shadowy room in golden flickers of light. He'd left his phone on the top of the toilet cistern, a chill-out playlist he'd found on Spotify drifting from the speaker. It was a tiny cocoon of girly heaven, and not something she'd ever have expected from a man as practical as him. The heat from the water seeped into her bones, easing away the physical aches as the scents of rose and lavender combined with the gentle lighting and soothing music to melt the stress of the day. Her eyelids fluttered closed. If Jake Smith wanted to seduce her, he was going the right way about it.

A soft knock stirred Laurie to awareness; she hadn't quite dropped off to sleep but she had definitely been drifting on the drowsy edge of it. Jake opened the door and grinned at the sight of her smothered to her ears in foam and contentment. 'Everything all right?'

'Everything's perfect. You might have to feed me my dinner in here, though, because I'm never moving again.'

He laughed, clearly pleased she was enjoying his treat so much. 'You'll be wrinkled like a prune if you stay in there too much longer.'

'Don't care,' she muttered, but raised the fingers on one submerged hand to check them. The skin was starting to pucker and swell. 'Five more minutes?'

'Take as long as you like. Do you want me to wash your hair for you?' He took a step over the threshold, then stopped.

It would be a new level of intimacy for them. Her supine position in the tub altered her perspective of him, making him look that much bigger, that much more masculine in the softness of their surroundings. He was dressed, she was naked beneath the shield of iridescent bubbles. A hint of shyness had her ready to refuse, but she pushed it away. 'Yes, please.'

Keeping the bubbles in place as best as she could, Laurie sat up and scooted forward in the tub until she was next to where the shower head rested on a holder behind the central taps. She reached one hand up to release the elastic band holding up her hair, but Jake's fingers were already there, and she let her arm drop back beneath the water, surrendering herself to his ministrations.

He didn't speak much; the odd murmured question about the temperature of the water, or an instruction to tilt her head back a bit more, his entire focus bent to his task. The pressure of his fingers was harder than she might have used herself, but oh, it felt so good, especially when he slid soapy hands down to massage the knots of muscle between the vertebrae in her neck.

A sigh of pleasure escaped her lips and he laughed softly before pressing a lingering, wet kiss to her shoulder. 'Good?'

'Uhnn,' she responded, unable to think beyond the pleasurable sensations spreading from the heated imprint his mouth had left.

His pleased chuckle vibrated against her ear. 'Let's rinse you off.'

'Yes,' she said, ready for this to be over. Not because she didn't want his hands in her hair any more, but because she was ready to feel them in other places now.

As though sensing her urgency, or perhaps driven by the needs of his own body, Jake rinsed her hair with a swift practicality devoid of any of his earlier gentleness. He wasn't rough with her, but it was all about getting the job done and she found her heart speeding faster. The moment he shut the water off she pulled out the plug and was rising from the tub ready to step into his arms as he yanked a bath sheet from the rack. Warm towelling enfolded her and he all but lifted her out of the tub. 'Dry yourself off,' he said, voice terse as though he couldn't trust himself to do it for her. 'I'll go and turn the oven down.'

She scrubbed the fabric over her skin, uncaring of the bits she missed. The hand towel she'd used earlier as a pillow had slipped to the floor and she snatched it up to blot the worst of the water from her hair. 'Leave it.' Jake was back, tugging at her hand, leading her out of the bathroom and across the hallway to his bedroom.

A small lamp on the bedside table cast a semi-circle of light onto part of the bed, a beacon to guide them in the otherwise darkened room. The moment he stopped and turned towards her, Laurie's hands were on him, tugging at the bottom of his t-shirt to free it from the waistband of his jeans, needing it off. He ripped the fabric over his head, tossing it behind him to be swallowed by the darkness before ducking down to capture her mouth.

The kiss was rough; all heat and demand and the crushing of lips on teeth as he spun them around and pressed her down onto the bed. The bath towel rucked up between them, forming an uncomfortable lump. Jake muttered a filthy curse into her mouth, making her laugh, driving the need inside her higher. His weight lifted off her and the offending towel was ripped away with enough force to make her bounce on the mattress.

Jake stood over her, his face shadowed from the circle of light illuminating her naked body. 'Christ, you're beautiful.'

The fervour of his tone matched the heat building inside her. 'I need you,' she confessed. 'Right now, right this very second. I need you inside me, Jake.'

He ripped at the button of his fly, shoved down his jeans and underwear, pausing only for a moment to mutter another curse as he encountered the obstacle of his trainers before he was – *finally!* – naked. Laurie held up her arms, welcoming him to her as he climbed back onto the bed and settled his weight over her. 'Laurie.' Her name on his lips was a desperate plea, an echo of her need.

'Yes. I'm here, Jake.' And then there were no more words between them, everything they were feeling expressed in long tender touches and hard, driving heat until the world fell away and there was nothing but him and her.

* * *

They might have stayed in bed all night had Laurie's stomach not started rumbling. Ignoring her protestations, Jake had herded her into the shower. Dressed now in the comfy yoga pants and t-shirt her mum had tucked into the bag, Laurie sat at the kitchen table, trying to get a comb through her tangled hair.

'I made a mess of you.' Crossing over from where he'd been checking on the food in the oven, Jake took the comb.

'I can do it,' she protested, without much force because she was already addicted to his touch.

'Shh, it was on my list, remember.'

Laurie settled in the seat, braced for the first tug against her scalp, but it never came. Starting near the ends, Jake worked his way through the knots they'd created while tangled together in his bed. Just like in the bathroom earlier, he bent all his focus to the job in hand until, finally satisfied, he handed her the comb. Though she could do nothing about the uneven waves it had dried into, it felt slick and silky when she ran a palm over it before twisting the mass up into a loose bun on top of her head. 'Thank you.'

'My pleasure.' Jake pressed a kiss to the exposed skin of her neck, triggering an echo of sensation from when he'd done the same thing earlier as they'd rocked together in a slow, lazy rhythm lacking nothing of the intensity of their first frantic bout of lovemaking. When she whimpered, he laughed and tugged gently at the knot of her hair. 'Food first.'

She might have protested, but the smell filling the kitchen as the lasagne warmed in the oven was all things divine. Tilting her head back she met his gaze. 'Deal.'

Jake leaned forward to brush a kiss to the tip of her nose. 'Do you want a glass of wine?'

It was tempting, but she had a long day ahead of her tomorrow. 'A glass of water will be fine.'

He gave her shoulders a quick squeeze then headed to the

fridge to pull out a large bottle of sparkling water which he held up to her. 'This okay?'

'Perfect.'

Twenty minutes later, she was stuffed to the gunnels. She really hadn't needed a second helping of lasagne, but it had tasted too good to refuse and she had been running on empty for the past week, snatching meals that were quick rather than necessarily nutritious. The whole evening had been wonderful, and not just because she'd enjoyed some of the best sex of her life, though it would be up the top of her memories' highlights reel. Dirty plates and glasses littered the table, and though her belly told her to stay put and be lazy, her conscience forced her to her feet.

'You don't need to do that,' Jake protested, half-rising from his seat. 'I'm taking care of you this evening.'

'Oh, shush.' Placing a hand on his shoulder, she pushed him back into the chair then circled around to enclose him in a hug. 'You've done more than enough already, this is my way of saying thank you.'

Jake raised a hand to cover hers where they were clasped together at the centre of his chest. 'You don't mind me kidnapping you, then?'

Laurie laughed. 'Not at all, in fact, you have a free invitation to do it again, anytime.'

It didn't take her long to tidy up and load the dishwasher. Though she told him to stay put, Jake seemed to be one of those people who couldn't sit around when there were things he could be doing so he pottered around making them tea. With a damp cloth, Laurie wiped over the end of the kitchen table they'd been using. Noticing a bit of dust covered the unused part, she cleaned the rest, stacking a few loose papers together, lifting Jake's closed laptop with care to wipe beneath it. 'How's the writing coming on?' Because he hadn't been frequenting the café it'd been a while since she'd had chance to ask.

'Okay.'

'*Okay*?' She raised an eyebrow as she passed him on the way back to the sink where she rinsed the cloth beneath the hot tap. 'That's it?'

When she glanced over at him again, he'd turned his back and was fiddling around with the cups, checking the teabags she'd seen him put in them not two minutes before. 'What do you want me to say about it?'

Wow, defensive, much? Feeling like she'd put her foot in it but with no idea why, Laurie started wiping down the sink and surrounding work surface. She'd already done it once, but there were a few splashes from the tap, and it gave her time to think. They'd not really talked much about his process, so maybe he was struggling with a bit of writer's block or something. Maybe that was the real reason he'd stopped working in the café, and he was just using how busy it was as an excuse.

She stood at the sink, refolding the cloth as she mulled it over. Should she ask him about it? Would it help if she offered to talk it out with him, maybe find a solution to whatever the problem was? Or would that make it worse? He didn't strike her as the kind of person who found it easy to talk about his troubles. The conversation they'd had about his parents had been painful, and not just because it had made her heartsick to hear about how horrible things had been. Jake had physically struggled with the words, stopping and starting. She might have grown up in Swiss Family Blabbermouth, but he'd been neglected and ignored. With no one showing an interest in him as a child, a reticence to share would have become second nature. If he only ever had himself to rely on, it might not occur to him to reach out if there was a problem.

Dropping the cloth into the sink, she moved up behind him and slid her arms around his waist, pressing a gentle kiss between his stiff shoulders. 'I didn't mean to pry, if you don't want to talk about your writing, that's fine.'

Jake turned in her hold, his arms encircling her to draw her close against his chest. 'It's not a problem you can help me with, I just need to sort it out for myself.'

Tilting her head back so she could meet his eyes, she offered him a smile. 'I won't push, but if you need to talk, you know I'm here for you.'

He pressed his forehead to hers. 'I know. Give me a couple more days to figure things out, and then I'll tell you all about it. I promise.' He straightened up, dropping his arms and she did the same. As he turned back to finish making their tea she glimpsed a shadow flickering through his gaze, and for the briefest moment it felt like she was watching a stranger.

When he turned a moment later to press a mug into her hands it was *her* Jake looking back at her with his trademark quirky smile that promised all sorts of wicked and wonderful things. It must've been a trick of the light, she decided, taking the hand he offered and following him back towards the bedroom. Nothing more.

22

By the time Monday morning rolled around, Jake was ready to pack it all in and go home. Sick to death of staring at the blank screen in front of him, he slammed down the lid on his laptop and slouched out into the garden. A bit of fresh air might help clear his head. His mobile started ringing and he pulled it from his pocket and checked the screen. Mac. Again. Jake flicked the reject button. He had been avoiding his editor's calls for the past few days now, replying with vague texts promising an update soon. The wily old man would know the instant they spoke he was holding something back. He also knew what Mac's opinion would be about getting romantically involved with someone who might have a connection to the story. Though Nick had seemed clueless about the most recent video, Jake hadn't yet crossed him off the list of potential hoaxers. It was all a big mess.

Walking to the end of the garden, Jake climbed over the slatted wooden fence and strolled to within a dozen feet of the edge of the Point and sank down on the grass, feet stretched out in front of him, elbows planted behind to prop him up enough to see the view. It wasn't even ten o'clock and the sun was already scorching its way through the thin material of his t-shirt. By the time it reached the full heat of the day, the beach would be packed with lobster-red bodies.

He didn't want to think about the beach, nor the reason why it might be more crowded than usual. He was making no headway on his investigation, and the second 'sighting' of the mermaid had moved the story from social media and into the mainstream. He'd been stopped over the weekend by a Sky news crew trying to capture soundbites for one of those feel-good pieces they wedged in between their rolling stream of doom and gloom. He'd shaken his head and moved on without responding and the reporter had let him go without a fight.

When he'd watched the piece later that evening, he'd understood why – everyone else in Mermaids Point had an opinion on their unusual visitor, and those that didn't still wanted their thirty seconds of fame. Every comment had been the same, strong on speculation, thin on facts. He hadn't seen Laurie or her folks among the talking heads, but Pete Bray had given a cheerful interview about the mermaid bringing good luck to the village and had managed to get the name of the pub in the shot behind him.

Good on him for getting a bit of free advertising, but if the rest of the media didn't push off soon, Jake wouldn't have a story left to sell. With any luck some actor or singer would make an idiot of themselves on Twitter or Instagram and the ever-hungry media monster would sate itself on their misery for a couple of days.

Or, even better, one of the other reporters hanging around would get to the bottom of everything and the whole thing would go away.

If there was no more story to tell, maybe he could change tack and try and write a book instead. Maybe he should jack it in regardless and do that anyway. Then his reason for being in the bay wouldn't be a lie and he could forget about trying to find a way to tell Laurie the truth.

He'd thought about it a couple of times, but the timing hadn't been right. She was working so hard, it seemed almost cruel to ruin what little spare time she had with a long discussion about his real reason for turning up in Mermaids Point. Discussion? Who was he trying to kid? If the boot was on the other foot, he'd be furious with Laurie for keeping something like that from him. He'd had a brief window when they'd started showing interest in each other to come clean, where he could've explained away his deception without too much fuss, but they were way past that now. From the moment she told him about that bastard ex-boyfriend of hers it'd probably been too late. Now he was the bastard, and he had no idea how he was going to fix things.

Jake flopped on his back, watching the fluffy white clouds drift overhead. There wasn't a way to fix it, not a way in which he got to keep Laurie in his life at least. He sighed. Even if by some miracle she forgave him for holding back the truth, he was chasing a pipe dream. Stay in Mermaids Point and write a bloody book? And live on what? Mac was expecting him back in a couple more weeks, with a decent story to not only publish, but sell on to the nationals. The TV hype increased the saleability of an exposé piece, heaping more pressure on Jake to come up with something. From the unread emails in his inbox, his piece on the trafficked women was generating the right sort of interest. If he could break another national story, it could be his ticket into Fleet Street.

His phone rang again. *Laurie.* Perhaps he should just bite

the bullet and tell her the truth right now. Blowing out a slow breath to release the tension in his gut at the thought he answered. 'I was just thinking about you.'

'Oh, really?' Her husky laugh did all sorts of very pleasant things to him. 'Well, hold that thought until later – assuming you're still free this evening?'

'Let me check my diary, I've been inundated with requests for my scintillating company lately.'

'Maybe you'd better take up one of those then, because I'm only interested in your body.'

Her cheeky retort delighted him. Lying back on the grass, he let the smile she brought to his lips fill his whole body with joy. 'I'm not much of a conversationalist, as you know, so I'm happy for you to use and abuse me however you please, Lorelai Morgan. I'm a big fan of what you did in the shower on Saturday morning, for example.'

'Stop it, you're making me blush!' she gasped between giggles. 'God, Jake! How am I supposed to serve my customers with my face as red as a tomato? Wicked man.'

He could picture her now, rosy cheeked with a mix of humour and shy desire as she glanced up at him through her lashes. 'You could close for the morning and I could come and help you with some emergency stock taking.'

'I couldn't,' she said, with enough regret to satisfy him that she found the suggestion tempting. 'Apart from anything else, I share said stock room with Mum and Dad.'

The idea of Andrew Morgan marching in and catching Jake checking his daughter's 'stock' dashed his ardour as effectively as a bucket of cold water. 'Yeah, let's not do that.'

Laurie laughed. 'Thought that'd change your mind. Look, as fun as this is, I really must go and do some work.'

'You called me, remember.'

'Oh. Yes, I did, didn't I? Mum wants to know if you'd like to come to dinner next Sunday. Dad does a big roast with all the trimmings and then we normally watch a film – but you wouldn't have to stay for that bit... unless you wanted to.'

Jake thought about his own family's miserable version of Sunday dinner. His dad with a tray on his lap, yelling at the football on the television, Jake and his mum mostly silent at the kitchen table. There'd been no point in trying to talk because she never relaxed enough to pay attention. Her ears were tuned to the noise from the front room as she waited for the next bellowed summons for more potatoes, another beer, even for the curtain to be adjusted when the sun shone on the screen.

'Jake?'

His attention snapped back to the present. 'Sorry, I mean, yes, that sounds nice, thanks.'

'If you're sure? It's not a big deal, but Dad likes to get his meat order in with the butcher at the beginning of the week so wanted to know numbers. Nerissa will be there, too, I think.' Laurie sounded a little hesitant, and he realised he'd made her uncomfortable by waiting too long to answer before.

'I'd love to come, I promise. Thank your parents for the invitation.'

She puffed a little sigh of relief into the phone. 'Okay, great. Look, they'll probably bombard you with a million and one questions about your book and stuff, so don't be afraid to tell them to mind their own business if it gets too much.'

This was it. The perfect invitation to come clean. 'About that...'

'Hang on.' She must've covered the phone with her hand because her next words were muffled. 'I'll be right there.'

When she spoke again a moment later she sounded flustered. 'Sorry, can we talk about this later? I've got customers. Come and meet me after work and we can go for a drink in the pub if you fancy it?'

'Sure.' There was nothing else he could say because she'd already hung up. Later, he promised himself. He'd talk to her about it later. A quick drink in the pub and then he'd take her for a quiet walk on the beach and do his best to explain things then.

* * *

The week passed, and somehow Jake was still no closer to telling her. First Nick and a couple of friends had gate-crashed their drink in the pub and they'd ended up staying until closing. Tuesday had been a day of small disasters – a blocked sink at the café causing headaches and an emergency plumbing bill for Laurie, and a software update on Jake's laptop that crashed twice before finally completing some five hours after it had started. By the time they met for the walk they'd postponed the previous evening, neither of them were in the mood to do anything other than stroll in silence as they soaked up the quiet peace of the setting sun. Wednesday evening they'd made no plans, but Laurie had surprised him on his doorstep with a bottle of wine, a Chinese takeaway and an invitation he couldn't refuse. And so on it had gone, never the right time, never the right moment until here he was walking up the hill towards her parents' house on Sunday evening clutching two bottles of wine he'd bought in the deli and an armful of flowers.

As he stepped up to the front door, it swung open and Jake almost dropped his burdens as Nick came barrelling out, stopping just short of bumping into him. 'Oh, hi!' Nick stretched out his hands to steady the bottles as they clanked together. 'Here, give me those. Honestly, mate, you're a mind reader or something because I was on my way to the off licence. Dad's convinced himself we don't have enough booze for the evening, even though we could float a battleship on the contents of the drinks cabinet. Come in, come in, don't worry about your shoes.'

Jake found himself propelled into the hall by a friendly push from Nick where he came face-to-face with a smiling Mrs Morgan. Laurie had told him they didn't dress up for dinner, but he was glad he'd put on a decent shirt and worn chinos instead of jeans as Sylvia was looking quite glam in a wraparound navy polka dot dress. 'Hello, Mrs Morgan, these are for you.' Jake juggled the three bouquets in his hands before handing her the one he'd selected for her with a mix of sunflowers, cream roses and dark greenery.

'Well, aren't you a darling? And it's Sylvia, please.' Stretching up, she planted a kiss on his cheek. 'And you bought wine too?' she said when Nick held up the bottles in his hands. 'Well, you can come again!' Laughing, she led him in the direction of the kitchen from where a combination of music, voices and the unmistakable smell of roast beef drifted. 'Look who's here!'

Laurie, her father, and Nerissa turned as one from where they were gathered around the oven, faces wreathed in smiles. 'Perfect timing.' Laurie crossed towards him, a sliver of beef in her hand. When she offered it to his lips, he opened to accept, letting his eyes close briefly at the delicious taste of the meat. 'What do you think?' she asked.

'Perfect.' Jake glanced down to admire the short, floaty red dress she'd teamed with black leggings. 'Very nice.'

A hint of pink touched her cheeks. 'Is one of those for me?' She nodded at the flowers in his hands.

'Of course.' He handed her a bouquet with a dozen velvet-soft roses in a shade of red so dark the edges of the petals looked dipped in black ink. A cliché, perhaps, but if the glow on Laurie's face was anything to go by, she didn't mind at all.

'And these are for you.' Sliding his free arm around Laurie's waist, he offered the final bouquet, a mix of colourful tulips, to Nerissa.

'Well, isn't that a lovely surprise?' Nerissa touched his arm before accepting them. 'I can't remember the last time anyone gave me flowers.' A shadow of something flitted across her expression before she shook her head and gave him a bright smile. 'Thank you, I'll go and put them with my things in the hall so I don't forget them later.'

Watching her go, Jake frowned. 'Did I do something wrong?' he whispered to Laurie.

'Not at all.' She curled her arm around him, giving him a squeeze. 'She lost someone, but it was a long time ago. Give her a minute and she'll be fine.'

Before he could second-guess his decision about the flowers, Laurie's dad called to him. 'Nothing for me?' The mock-pout on his face had them all laughing.

Nick held up the wine he was still clutching. 'Only two bottles of your favourite Cabernet, Dad. Someone got some insider info.' He winked at Jake.

'I might have asked Luca at the deli for a bit of advice,' he admitted with a shrug. 'Got to play the advantage where you find it.'

'Too true, son! Too true!' Andrew Morgan turned his attention back to the beef. 'Right, let me get this back in for a few more minutes. Everyone go through to the lounge, and I'll be there in a jiffy.'

Son. Though it'd be said in the most casual way, the word touched something deep inside Jake. He watched as Nick put the wine on the table before nipping over to snatch a piece of meat that had been cut off the end of the joint and stuffing it into his mouth.

'Hey, I was saving that.' Andrew swiped at his son with the cloth he'd been using to put the hot tray into the oven.

'For me, right?' Nick blinked an innocent look at his dad.

'Spoiled brat,' Andrew said, shaking his head even as he laughed and slung a friendly arm around Nick's shoulders.

'Silly pair.' Sylvia cast them both an exasperated look before turning to Jake. 'Come on through, dear, we've got Bucks Fizz and nibbles next door.'

* * *

As he watched Nick and Laurie clear the plates a couple of hours later, Jake couldn't remember the last time he'd laughed so much – or felt so relaxed. Dinner with the Morgan family wasn't anything he needed to have been worried about. This wasn't a test he needed to pass; no one was waiting for him to make a mistake. They hadn't found him lacking, even when he'd accidentally put his foot in it the way he feared he might have done with the flowers for Nerissa. And he knew he had, regardless of what Laurie said. Though she'd joined in the conversation when prompted, there was a quiet sadness to her in the moments when she sat back and let the noise and chatter swirl on without her. Andrew and Sylvia were deep in conversation about whether to move onto dessert or cheese next, so Jake leaned forward on his elbows and tried to catch Nerissa's eye. 'I don't know about you, but I'm not sure I could eat another thing,' he said when she focused away from whatever memories haunted her and gave him a small smile.

'Give it a few minutes and I'm sure you'll get your second wind.' She cast a fond look towards her brother and his wife. 'No one leaves their table hungry, that's for sure.'

Jake pressed a hand to his full stomach. 'I'll need half an hour at least. I missed you the past few mornings,' he continued, referring to their usual meeting on his morning walks.

'Doc's had a rough week, so I've been sticking close to the surgery,' she said, brow furrowing. 'He's had a chest infection, and I was worried it might develop into something worse given his age. He seems to be on the mend now, but I'd still like him to get a check-up.' She cast up her hands in a gesture of frustration. 'Of course, he won't listen to a word I say, because I'm not the one with medical training.'

'Doctors make the worst patients, isn't that what they say?'

She rolled her eyes. 'That's for sure.'

Finished with the debate over dessert, Sylvia joined their conversation. 'Is he any closer to making a decision about retiring?'

'I think so.' Nerissa folded her arms on the table in front of her and rested her weight on them. 'Though he won't admit it, I think this latest bout of illness has unnerved him. He's been looking at the details of the retirement flats, the ones on Crown Road. And with Michael in his ear every five minutes, I'm sure it won't be too much longer before he makes the decision to sell.'

'And about bloody time, too,' Andrew grumbled, rising to his feet. 'Past time he was gone.'

'But if he goes, what happens to me?' Nerissa sighed. 'There's no guarantee whoever replaces him will want a receptionist, never mind a live-in housekeeper. Sometimes it's better the devil you know.'

Andrew paused behind her chair to rest a hand on her shoulder. 'It'll work out, love. Things always do.'

'I hope you're right.'

* * *

As Nerissa predicted, Jake managed to find room for both dessert and cheese. Feeling more than a bit uncomfortable, he was glad for the opportunity to stand up when Nick commandeered him to unload and reload the dishwasher while he made a final round of coffees. 'How's the writing going?' Nick asked as he handed him a china platter and pointed at one of the cupboards behind Jake. 'Bottom shelf in there.'

Jake's stomach turned a bit queasy, and not because he'd over-indulged. For a couple of hours there he'd been able to cast his deception to the back of his mind. 'Not bad. Still mostly in the research phases. I like to get a proper feel for a place before I write about it, you know?'

Nick nodded as he held out a stack of dinner plates. 'I get it. Hopefully the trip out to the islands helped a bit with that. I can take you out again if you like. Anytime you want, just ask.'

The friendly gesture only served to make him feel worse, but Jake forced a smile. 'Thanks. Shame I can't get a look at the caves under the Point. From what you and Laurie have both told me, they were an important part of the history of the village.'

'I can take you for a look-see if you want. We'd have to do it via the water, but if you don't mind a swim I can anchor off at low tide.' He paused. 'You can swim, right? It's not far, but I won't take you if there's any risk you'd get into difficulties.'

'I'm a decent swimmer,' Jake promised him. 'But I don't want to put you to any trouble.'

Nick shrugged. 'It's no trouble. I wouldn't mind taking a look myself, make sure those idiots didn't leave anything behind after pulling that stupid mermaid stunt. We can go tomorrow, unless you've got other plans?'

The suddenness of it took Jake back. 'Won't you have day trips to run tomorrow?'

'I've got a group who want a sunset sail, but nothing in the morning. Meet me on the dock just after nine.'

'Well, if you're sure?' Getting a look at the caves would be helpful with his investigation and the sooner he could explore them, the better. Once Nick found out he had an ulterior motive for being in the village, Jake didn't expect he or any of the rest of the family would want to have anything to do with him – even in the unlikely event he could talk Laurie into seeing past his deception of them all.

'Let's get these coffees made,' Nick said, moving towards the kettle. 'I think Mum's got a box of Bendicks mints tucked away in the sideboard. I'm sure we can persuade her to get them out.'

The idea of walking back into the dining room, of taking a place he didn't deserve at their table was too much. 'No more coffee for me.'

'You sure?'

Jake nodded. 'I won't sleep a wink if I have any more caffeine. I think I'll call it a night.'

'More mints for me then!' Nick stuck out a hand. 'I'll see you in the morning.'

They shook. 'Sure, thanks for a great evening.'

'You're not going, are you?' Laurie entered the kitchen with a handful of empty wine glasses, which she placed on the worktop above the dishwasher. 'It's not that late.'

Crossing to her, Jake took her hand and led her out into the hall. 'I've already over-indulged and your dad said something about port, which I'm not sure I can face.'

Laurie wrinkled her nose. 'Once he gets going, he's hard to stop. You've had a nice time, though?'

He pulled her close, loving the way her arms slid to encircle his waist as she tucked her face into his neck. They fit together so well, he felt like he could hold her forever. 'I've had a wonderful evening. Your family is amazing.'

She raised her head to meet his gaze, a wry smile on her lips. 'They have their moments. Come on, I'll see you out.'

Though he tried to call his goodbyes from the hall, the whole family trooped out to the doorstep to wave him off, preventing the kind of private goodbye he and Laurie might have preferred. Probably just as well, he thought, as he gave them a final wave over his shoulder. The need to come clean weighed heavier still. *No more excuses*. He'd talk to her tomorrow night – come what may.

23

A sleepless night and the weight of his guilty conscience had Jake out of bed and on the beach before the sun was up. Although media interest in Mermaids Point had waned once more, the village was buzzing with sightseers and holiday makers. Plenty of those curious visitors would want a close-up view of where the mermaid sightings had happened, no doubt. As much as he wanted to satisfy his curiosity about the caves beneath the Point, it made Jake feel even more of a shit that he was taking up time Nick could be using to make money. But he'd been adamant last night he could find time for a personal tour, and in the end it had been impossible to refuse without being rude. He'd spent some of his sleepless hours wondering how much of a grilling he was in for. As an only child, he'd never had anyone else looking out for him – or anyone else to look out for other than his mother, but he knew from the behaviour of his friends at university that older brothers liked to have a say over their younger sisters' boyfriend choices. Though Nick didn't know it, he had plenty of reasons to be protective.

Far too early for the meeting time they'd arranged, Jake decided to do a bit of exploring from the land first. Instead of his usual route, he turned right at the bottom of the steps and made his way across the scrubby grass and away from the main beach. These morning walks had become something of a ritual for Jake. He loved the peace and quiet of it, the bright promise of a new day as the sun peeped its first rays over the horizon. He'd never considered himself a romantic but being with Laurie brought out a softness in him. There was no peace for him this morning, no anticipation of the day to come. If things went as badly with Laurie later as he feared, this might be the last time he watched the sun rising over the Point.

Utterly depressed at the thought, he trudged on across the rock-strewn terrain. Here and there were signs of secret parties like the ones Laurie had mentioned to him. A dark circle of burnt wood and ashes, a handful of empty beer cans and plastic bottles of cheap cider. If he'd had a bag with him he would've collected the rubbish, but he couldn't carry it all. He also didn't fancy starting the day stinking of stale booze so resolved to come back later and clean up the mess. Shaking his head, he moved on, wondering what possessed people to spoil the very beauty that drew them to somewhere like Mermaids Point in the first place.

Five minutes later, he reached the fence Nick had told him about. The sturdy, slatted planks reminded him of the one lining the back garden of the cottage, though this one was several feet higher. Thin mesh had been nailed to the wooden rails, enough to deter anyone who might try to climb it, without blocking the view of the waves crashing over the rocks beyond. Yellow and black signs spaced at regular intervals warned of falling rocks and high tides beyond.

Disappointed he couldn't see much more from this vantage point, Jake wandered the length of the fence, snapping photos with his phone as he went. In the far corner he noticed a part of the mesh didn't lie quite flat. Crouching, he noticed a couple of the nail holes had damage around them. He took several close-up shots. It wasn't definite proof of trespass, but it was another potential breadcrumb on the trail. If he could gather evidential images that one of the caves beneath the Point matched the images on the video, he'd be able to suggest this as a potential access route. His earlier guilt vanished beneath a buzz of adrenaline. He was on the right track, he could feel it. Tucking his hands in his pockets, he began to make his way back. A flash of ebony hair near the shoreline caught his attention followed by a familiar bark. Raising his hand in greeting, Jake shifted his trajectory to intercept the woman. Laurie's aunt, Nerissa, was another early riser, it seemed.

He'd encountered her often since their first meeting. Though she'd never mentioned Laurie directly, he'd been on the receiving end of a few appraising glances from her aunt since they'd gone semi-public with news of their relationship. He'd felt the weight of those looks, the silent expectation he would do right by Laurie. Not wanting to give the local gossips any extra fodder, he behaved himself whenever he dropped into the café during business hours, but they'd been for a drink together in the pub and could be seen strolling the beach hand-in-hand after Laurie finished work most evenings. Regret stabbed him. If they'd kept things quieter it would be less difficult for Laurie to explain things after he left. Her embarrassment at being on the receiving end of the wagging tongues when she was younger had left a scar. The very least he should've done was to shield her from more of the same, but at the time he'd been so caught up in the fantasy of what might be, he hadn't stopped to consider the reality.

Bounding up, Toby, the golden retriever, dropped a tennis ball at his feet then backed up a couple of steps, fluffy tail wagging madly in expectation. It was hard to feel sorry for himself when faced with such enthusiasm and simple joy. 'Good morning, Toby,' Jake greeted the dog as he scooped up the ball and tossed it down the beach. Barking in delight, the retriever dashed past him in pursuit of his prize, sending a fine spray of seawater splashing in his wake.

'That'll teach you to go too near the water,' Nerissa chided with a grin as she watched him brush at the salty spray spattering his jeans.

'You'd have thought I'd have learned my lesson by now,' Jake agreed, abandoning his task. He'd be out on Nick's boat soon enough and was bound to get splashed a time or two more. 'How are you doing, Nerissa?'

Her smile seemed genuine enough, but there was no hiding the dark circles beneath her eyes. 'I'm fine.' She wrinkled her nose. 'Sort of.'

A swell of sympathy rose in his chest, recalling some of the family's conversation the previous evening about the local doctor's plans to retire and the quandary Laurie's aunt was in as a result. 'Still no news about a replacement for Doc?'

She shook her head. 'Nope. And I'm stuck in limbo until he manages to sell the practice. I'm keeping my fingers crossed whoever comes in will at least want a receptionist, but the odds on them wanting a live-in housekeeper, too?' She shook her head. 'At this rate, I'll end up living in Andrew and Sylvia's attic. The poor spinster.' He could tell from her tone it was meant to be a joke, but neither of them laughed.

Not sure what to say, Jake settled for silence, hoping his presence was enough to offer a little support. The sun inched higher on the horizon, turning the sea to a shimmer of fiery gold. It lasted just a few seconds, a snapshot of perfection caused by the scientific alignment of a distant ball of gas and a weird spinning rock. If that wasn't a miracle, Jake wasn't sure what else was.

Toby came splashing up to them, ball in mouth, tail still flapping like a signal. He dropped the ball at Jake's feet, but instead of nudging him to throw it once more, the dog stuck his nose in Nerissa's hand and whined.

'I'm all right, boy.' Crouching, Nerissa curled her arms around Toby's neck and scratched her fingers through his salt-encrusted fur. 'I've got you, and that's all I need.' Straightening up, she patted Jake on the arm. 'Well, I'd better get going or Doc will be grumbling about his breakfast. You have a good day, sweet boy, thank you for the company, and for the beautiful flowers you gave me last night.'

'Anytime, Nerissa. And try not to worry, I'm sure things will work out.'

She raised a finger and pointed to the sky. 'From your lips to the universe's ears.'

Jake watched Nerissa make her way towards the steps leading up to the road. With the sun's rays blurring her outline and her long hair loose and blowing wildly in the breeze she looked for a moment like some unworldly creature not quite of this earth – as if she might turn at any moment and slip beneath the waves like that long ago ancestor Laurie had told him about. Shaking his head, he kept on walking. Mermaids Point was turning his brain to mush.

As he reached the top of the steps at the opposite end of

the beach, his phone beeped and he checked the screen to find a message from Laurie:

Breakfast's ready xx

It was followed by a pair of emojis showing a steaming coffee cup and a croissant. A bittersweet feeling rose in his chest. She was the last person he wanted to see right now with his mind still in turmoil about how he was going to tell her everything, but at the same time he needed one more precious moment before he set them on the path of no return. Already turning towards the café, he tapped a quick reply:

Mind reader, I'm about 10 steps from the door.

She was waiting for him on the threshold, hair in that familiar tangled knot on top of her head that his fingers always itched to take down. Flour dusted the front of the navy-blue apron she'd put on to protect her t-shirt and jeans. No make-up yet, not that she wore much during the day, but he liked how comfortable she was in her own skin around him. He'd noticed the little bag she kept on a shelf in the staff bathroom located next to the storeroom when she'd let him in there the other day, an eyeliner pencil sticking out of the open zip, a lipstick resting on the shelf beside it. 'Good morning, beautiful.'

'Good morning, yourself.' Reaching out she grabbed a handful of the sweater Nick had warned him to wear against the chill of the wind out on the water and tugged him into the café and down for a kiss. She tasted like buttery pastry with a hint of dark chocolate and he murmured in appreciation. God, she was sexy and sweet, and everything he'd never known he wanted until it was too late.

Turning her in his arms he toed the open door shut and pressed her back against it, slotting his body against hers in the perfect melding of muscle and soft curves, and kissed her again.

'That's the kind of welcome I could get used to,' she gasped when they finally came up for air.

She looked so pretty, all rosy cheeks and bright eyes and he wished he could steal her away for a few hours, to show her how much she meant to him, how much he had come to love her over these past weeks. He'd never told her and would likely never get the chance now.

Regret and tenderness battled within him. Curbing his passion with ruthless control, he softened the heat he'd stoked between them. After pressing a tender kiss to her lips, he traced a teasing line of kisses across her cheek to the little spot beneath her ear that always made her giggle and sigh in equal measure.

As he reached to brush a loose strand from her forehead, the dial of his watch caught the light, and he muttered a curse under his breath. He was due to meet Nick in just over half an hour, and Laurie needed time to set up before opening for the day. When she raised on tiptoe intent on another kiss, he placed a regretful finger on her lips. 'We're out of time, sweetheart.' In more ways than one.

She dropped back on her heels with a playful pout before giving him a smile fit to break his heart. 'Later, then?' She curled one hand around his nape. 'I'm closing after lunch today because I must do a stock take and some batch cooking for the week and that's impossible with customers around. It's a bit of a gamble, but the weekenders will have gone home last night so it should be less busy. I can knock off early and pick up a fresh pizza from the deli on my way to yours.'

The expectation in her eyes was almost more than he could bear. The need to confess everything, to spill his guts and be done with it, surged forward but he wrestled it down. Tonight would be soon enough to drive a wrecking ball through both their lives.

* * *

He was a few minutes late leaving Laurie's, having taken the time to put the chairs down, wipe over the tables and set out the little vases of flowers and menus before he left. It felt like the least he could do and yet nowhere near enough, but it was all he'd had in the moment.

Clutching a paper bag stuffed with pain au chocolat and almond croissants and balancing a carry-out tray with two huge takeaway cappuccinos Laurie had insisted he bring with him, Jake crested the rise next to the car park and looked down over the dock. He spotted Nick on the quay, one foot resting on the thick metal bollard that his boat's mooring lines were tied around. A small figure faced him, unidentifiable in an oversized sweatshirt with the hood pulled up to shadow their features.

Something about their body language made Jake pull up short, even back up a couple of paces so they wouldn't notice him. Nick was shaking his head, arms crossed over his chest in a way that made it clear he wasn't happy with whatever the other person was saying. The hooded figure gestured animatedly before spinning on their heel and marching away. They only made it a few steps before Nick called out something Jake was too far away to hear. The figure wheeled back towards him, pulled something out of their pocket and shoved it into Nick's hands before running off as though worried he might change his mind to whatever he'd agreed to.

Nick watched the hooded figure retreat before shaking his head and shoving the small bundle into the back pocket of his jeans. A few hurried steps along the gangplank and he was back on board the boat, making straight for the cockpit. A moment later the phone in Jake's pocket vibrated. Crouching, he set the tray with the drinks down on the ground and retrieved his phone. He stared at the message preview on the screen.

Sorry, mate, something's come up and I need to cancel. I'll let you know a new date ASAP. Cheers, N.

Jake glanced from his phone down to the now deserted dock, trying to process what he'd witnessed. It could be anything – a kid delivering a message, because from the shape and size of the figure they'd looked to him like a teenager, or a day tripper arguing over a future booking. The second seemed more likely because the bundle that had changed hands tickled something in the back of Jake's brain. It looked like the kind of hand-off he'd seen dozens of times before, though usually in a dark alley or the doorway of one of the shops acting as a front for illegal activities. Though he couldn't be sure from this distance, it'd looked an awful lot like Nick had accepted a bundle of notes.

A sick feeling churned in his gut. As part of a county lines drugs investigation he'd been involved in the previous year, he'd discovered supply routes into the country were often through one of the myriad bays and coves that littered the

British coastline. Small ports with little to no customs presence, where charter boats very similar to the kind Nick and his uncle operated could sail out to meet larger vessels under cover of darkness and board smuggled cargo.

He'd interviewed a guy once on the promise of anonymity. A decent enough bloke – if you could ignore the poison he was helping to put onto the streets – a former fisherman who'd fallen on hard times and been driven by the need to keep the bailiffs from the door. He'd been told it would just be a couple of trips, which had of course been a lie, and then he was trapped, not only by threats of violence to him, but to his kids and his wife. He'd been almost grateful when the coastguard had caught him and had exchanged a shorter jail sentence in return for cooperation. He'd lost everything he'd tried so hard to hold onto, his home, his family, his pride. Though his arrest had broken a few links in the local chain, the main organisers had escaped and no doubt shifted their operation a few miles up the coast where another desperate fool was willing to risk everything for the promise of quick cash.

'You're letting your imagination run wild,' he muttered to himself. There was no indication Nick was involved in anything untoward, quite the opposite. Was he so desperate to find a reason beyond his own stupid selfishness for why things with Laurie were likely to fall apart at any minute that he was ready to cast her brother as a villain? How twisted was he by his bloody job that his mind immediately saw the very worst in someone as honourable and generous as Nick had so far proven to be? Feeling wretched for jumping to conclusions, Jake put away his phone and reached for the abandoned tray of coffees and the bag of slightly squashed pastries he'd dropped without realising.

About to stand, he froze at the sound of an engine below him.

A black four-by-four rumbled down the access road at the opposite end of the dock area and pulled up on the quay next to the boat. It was a top of the line Range Rover, the latest model if the number plate was anything to go by. Mind snapping instantly back into reporter mode, Jake checked the path behind him was empty, then shuffled to his right into the taller grass.

He still had a good vantage point over the dock, but anyone glancing up was unlikely to see him. It felt weird to be spying, but something about the car didn't feel right and all his worst suspicions roared back to life. The windows had been heavily tinted to obscure the occupants, and it just sat there, engine idling, no one making a move to exit the vehicle. Hunkering down, he retrieved his phone and snapped off a few quick shots of the car as he waited to see what happened next.

Nick reappeared in the cockpit entrance and stared at the Range Rover for a long moment before striding across the deck and along the railed gangplank onto the quayside. Instead of approaching the driver's window he made straight for the rear of the vehicle. The back doors both opened. The same hooded figure Jake had seen before climbed out of the far side while a tall, broad-chested man exited closest to Nick, a baseball cap shielding his face. Something was definitely up.

The guilty feelings of a few moments before melted away as Jake's instincts took over. His heartbeat increased as the familiar adrenaline of being on the cusp of a good story kicked in. This was what he lived for, what he'd been missing all these weeks. Lifting his phone, he snapped off another round of pictures, zooming in to capture details he could study later if needed.

While Nick and the other man opened the boot and began removing boxes, the hooded figure made a dash for the boat and ducked quickly inside the cockpit. After slamming the boot closed, the man in the cap slapped a hand against the back window as though indicating they were done. The Range Rover pulled away, doing a slow circle on the dock and was disappearing back the way it had come before the two men had finished hefting a couple of boxes each onto the viewing deck of the boat.

Jake watched as they detached the gangplank, thumb still clicking on the capture button of his phone. With a couple of practiced moves Nick had the boat untied. As he approached the cockpit, the hooded figure appeared. Whatever transpired between them, it didn't look to be a happy exchange from the way Nick pushed past to duck into the cockpit while the mystery person stomped to the very rear of the boat, arms folded across their chest.

The guy in the baseball cap sank down on one of the benches and began rummaging in the box nearest to him. Hoping to snatch a shot of what was inside, Jake rose up on his elbows, lifting his phone higher, but the boat was already pulling away from the dock.

As though sensing his presence, the figure at the rear snapped their head up and towards him. Hoping he was far enough away not to be seen, Jake threw himself flat in the grass. He lay there for a long moment, making sure the boat was well clear before rolling onto his back to stare up at the sky. He'd only caught a glimpse in that split second but something about the shape of her face – and he was sure now it was a woman, not a teenager – was familiar.

Jake stood, dusted himself off and gathered the drinks and the bag of pastries. He had no idea what he'd just witnessed, but the instinct that made him such a good reporter told him it was something dodgy. Not illegal, perhaps, but not *right* either. He tossed everything into a rubbish bin next to the car park as he passed, wondering what his next move was going to be.

As he made his way down the hill, he swerved from the street down onto the beach, not wanting to pass the door of the café and risk Laurie catching sight of him. He had too many unanswered questions to sort through before he saw her later.

Weaving his way through the families and groups already beginning to gather for a day of sun-worshipping, clarity struck. He'd never made much progress with the mermaid investigation because he simply didn't care about it one way or the other. It was obvious to him it was a stunt, more than likely cooked up by some locals in a bid to attract visitors to their struggling seaside village. Well, they'd achieved that, Jake thought, glancing around the busy beach.

He spotted a quiet spot in the shade of the wall and sat for a moment, just holding his phone. Nothing about the mermaid story had given him even the faintest buzz, certainly nothing close to the excitement fizzing in his veins right now. Whatever was going on with Nick just now was *something*, every instinct he'd developed over the years told Jake that.

Although Mac had wanted him to take some time off, he was still expecting a story out of it, and Jake had no idea what to write. His grip flexed around his phone, the urge to go back over the photos he'd taken almost a physical itch in his fingers. The mermaid thing was a bust – but what Jake held in his hand right now could be the key to something much bigger. He'd already betrayed Laurie's trust by withholding the truth from her. How much worse would it be if the truth of who he was could lead to trouble, not only for Nick, but for the rest of the Morgan family, too?

Better to check it out, just to be on the safe side. Like he'd told himself earlier, he was probably jumping to conclusions and there was a perfectly innocent explanation. Knowing he was lying to himself in an attempt to assuage what pitiful bit of his conscience remained, Jake began scrolling through the photos he'd taken. A lot of the later ones were out of focus, his attention more on watching the action unfold in real time, but he'd got a few decent shots of the people stowing the cargo at least.

He looked further back, concentrating on the ones he'd taken when they'd been unloading the boot. A lot were in profile, but he'd captured a good one of the guy in the baseball cap looking straight ahead. Jake couldn't quite make out the logo on his cap, but there were words next to it. He zoomed the photo in and out to no avail. Jumping up, he shoved his phone in his pocket and strode for the steps at the other end of the beach. He had some image sharpening software on his laptop back at the cottage. It might be nothing, but the feeling in his gut told him otherwise.

24

Laurie hurried along the path towards the cottage, anticipation filling her belly with every step that took her closer. As well as the ham and mushroom pizza, she'd picked up a loaf of garlic bread and Luca's homemade dipping sauce which would be perfect for the crusts. Though Jake hadn't explicitly invited her to stay, Laurie had called in at home and stuffed her wash kit and a fresh change of clothes into the rucksack she now carried on her back. Though it had only been one night since they'd been together, she'd missed the feel of waking in his arms, the heat of him curled over her back as he took up more than his share of the bed.

She'd texted to say she was on her way, and as she crossed the yard she saw Jake had left the kitchen door open in anticipation of her arrival. A smile crossed her lips. Maybe he was as eager to see her as she was him. If that spectacular, toe-curling kiss he'd laid on her this morning was anything to go by, they had a night to remember in front of them. He'd scrambled her brains with that kiss so much her stock take had taken nearly twice as long as it should've done because she'd kept stopping to daydream about it.

'I'm here,' she called as she walked into the kitchen, surprised to find it unoccupied. Opening the fridge, she slid the food onto an empty shelf then turned to survey the still empty room. Papers were strewn from one end of the table to the other. In the centre of the mess sat Jake's laptop, the image of a stunningly beautiful woman plastered across the screen.

Recognising her at once, Laurie moved closer. Aurora Storm had been a huge star a few years ago, topping the charts with two hit albums before vanishing from the limelight. Her music was catchy, the kind of thing people sang along to when it came on the radio without realising they'd memorised the words. Her incredible beauty as much as her talent as singer had boosted her popularity to stratospheric levels until it seemed like not a day passed without a paparazzi shot of her on the front pages of the tabloids, or on the cover of the glossy gossip magazines.

She'd been all over the TV too. In the jungle eating disgusting bugs and posing just right beneath the waterfall shower on *I'm a Celebrity* the first year; tripping the light fantastic in the *Strictly* ballroom the next. Now Laurie thought back, that had been the last big thing Aurora had done. She'd made it to the quarter, or maybe the semi-finals and then basically disappeared with no explanation. Laurie had never been interested in her enough to think much of it, and it surprised her Jake would have her picture as his screensaver. Laurie gave the image a wry look. Or maybe not such a surprise given how much perma-tanned cleavage was showing.

Shrugging it off, she wandered through to drop her rucksack in the bedroom, calling Jake's name again. When there was still no answer, she followed the breeze blowing from the open patio windows in the lounge and spotted him standing at the far end of the garden. A bottle of beer dangled loosely from the fingers of one hand, his attention fixed on the far horizon.

'There you are,' she said, stepping out onto the patio.

He turned to face her, no hint of the smile she'd grown accustomed to seeing. 'Hey, Laurie.' He sounded awful, looked worse, his mouth a grim line.

'Is everything okay?' She asked, already knowing it wasn't even as the question left her lips.

'No.' He took a swig from the bottle before letting it swing loose once more. 'Everything is most definitely not okay.'

The sarcastic bite of his words was so unlike him. The memory of that half-seen expression she'd caught the other night when he'd been making tea flashed into her mind. This was the stranger she'd glimpsed, and feared, though at the time she hadn't put voice to the emotion. Clutching her arms around her chest to ward off a sudden chill that had nothing to do with the setting sun, she forced herself to cross the patio. When he made no move to approach her, her steps faltered before reaching the edge of the lawn. 'Tell me what's wrong.'

He laughed, a bitter sound. 'Me, Laurie. I'm what's wrong.'

She eyed the bottle in his hand, wondering how many he'd had. 'Are you drunk?'

Lifting the bottle, he stared at it for a long moment. 'I wish I was, but no.'

'You know you can talk to me, right?' Closing the gap between them she reached for his free hand. He didn't respond, his fingers stiff between hers. She squeezed gently, trying to ignore the little zing of fear in her heart. 'Whatever this is we can fix it. Together.'

Long moments passed, and though it went against her nature, Laurie schooled herself to silence. If she pushed too hard, he'd only steel his defences further. Side by side they stared out over the end of the Point, together but a million miles apart. The rays of the setting sun sparkled on the water, a view that had never failed to ground Laurie until tonight.

She was beginning to give up hope when Jake's fingers curled around her own. The next minute he was tugging her to him, drawing her into his arms and pulling her tight against his chest.

Grateful she was getting through to him, Laurie clasped her hands at the base of his back and held on. 'I'm here.'

'I'm sorry,' Jake muttered into her hair. 'I'm taking things out on you when you're the only one who's done nothing wrong.'

Though he still wasn't making much sense, the familiar feel of his body warm against her, the tenderness of the hand he buried deep in her hair told her she hadn't lost him. 'Talk to me,' she whispered against his chest. 'Let me help you.'

Cupping her cheeks, he lifted her face to meet his for a brief, sweet kiss and then released her. 'Come on into the kitchen.'

Still confused, but a little reassured that Jake seemed almost back to his usual self, she followed. He poured her a glass of wine without asking, opened a fresh beer for himself. She sipped, the dry bite of the alcohol settling her a little.

'Have a seat.' Jake nodded to the vacant chair in front of his laptop. He didn't move to join her, taking up post opposite instead, his back to the kitchen cupboards. He stared at the bottle in his hand before putting it on the work surface beside him and pushing it a few inches away. Folding his arms across his chest, he scuffed one foot against the tiled floor before lifting his eyes to meet hers. 'I haven't been honest with you.'

Panic struck in a blow so swift it all but stole her breath. Laurie's thoughts raced out of control, her deepest fears wrapping themselves up in a bundle of ugly, unhappy memories. *Oh, God, this can't be happening again.* 'Is there someone else?' She spun to face the screen behind her, meeting the mocking smile of gorgeous Aurora Storm. It couldn't be, could it? But why else would he have a picture of her plastered all over his laptop? 'Her?'

She clamped her lips shut, hating the waver in her voice, hearing too much of the distraught girl whose dreams of love had been shattered before she'd been old enough to handle it. She wasn't that scared little girl any more. Well, maybe echoes of her remained, but if Jake was going to break her heart, she wouldn't give him the satisfaction of seeing it. As calmly as she could possibly manage, she gave voice to her fears. 'Are you in love with Aurora Storm?'

'*What?* No!' Jake rushed across to drop to his knees in front of her. 'No, no, sweetheart. I don't love anyone else, only you.'

Only you. Relief washed over her, though she would have preferred to hear him say it for the first time under better circumstances than this. Still reeling from the constant leap from one emotion to another, Laurie closed her eyes and took a deep breath. Whatever was at the bottom of Jake's odd behaviour, it wasn't the one thing she wouldn't be able to forgive him for. Anything else could be worked through, given time. She cupped his face. 'I love you, too.'

He turned his head, pressing a kiss into her palm before lifting her hand away and placing it back in her lap. 'Well, you shouldn't. Not when I've lied to you about everything.'

Clenching her fingers together, Laurie swallowed back a bubble of panic before it could rise again. It was hyperbole on his part; he couldn't have lied about *everything*. 'So, now's your chance to tell me the truth.'

Jake sat back on his haunches. 'I'm not a writer, well, not in the way I've led you to believe. There is no book.'

'No book?' She repeated, dumbfounded.

'I'm an investigative journalist. I write for the *Eastern Comet*, based out of Norwich, though some of my pieces get syndicated in the national press.'

'Oh.' She had no idea what to make of his revelation, or why it seemed like such a huge deal to him. She wasn't thrilled he'd lied to her, but it felt more like a truth stretched to its limits than an out and out betrayal. 'And you came here working on a story?' What on earth would an investigative journalist want with sleepy old Mermaids Point? She glanced back over her shoulder. 'About *her*?'

He shook his head. 'No. Well, not initially. I spend a lot of my time digging around in the dark parts of life. The last big story I did took a bit of a toll on me.'

It was on the tip of her tongue to ask him about it, but the bleak look in his eyes told her she was better off not knowing.

'My boss sent me here for a break,' Jake continued. 'And a bit of a chance to recharge my batteries and to look into the mermaid sighting while I was here.'

She couldn't help but laugh. 'You're a mermaid hunter? Oh, God, Jake, is that what all this nonsense is about?' Laurie laughed and laughed until she had to clutch her stomach against the ache. It wasn't that funny, but the sheer absurdity of it got caught up with her earlier panic and doubt until she had to blink back tears.

Jake didn't join in, didn't look in the least bit amused or relieved at her reaction. If anything, his expression grew even more grim. He pushed to his feet, leant over her to reach his laptop and clicked on the trackpad. The image of Aurora Storm disappeared, a different one filling the screen.

Laurie's laughter died in her throat. The image was a bit blurry, but she knew that face almost as well as her own. 'That's Nick.'

'It is,' Jake agreed. Retreating to the other side of the kitchen he picked up his beer and downed a long mouthful.

Now a drink seemed like a good idea. She gripped her wine glass and forced herself to sip when she felt like draining the contents. 'Why have you been taking photos of Nick? *When* have you been taking photos of him?'

'This morning. I was on my way to meet him when he texted to cancel our trip.'

'So, you spied on him?' Something didn't add up.

'He was acting weirdly,' Jake shrugged, his tone defensive.

'In what way?' Laurie couldn't keep a note of accusation out of her voice.

'I saw him arguing with someone, and then he took something.' Jake swigged another drink from his bottle before continuing. 'It looked like a hand-off, all right?' he snapped.

'A hand-off?' God, she needed to stop parroting back everything he said, but nothing was making any sense to her. 'What does that mean?'

'You know what a hand-off is. A dodgy transaction. Cash. Drugs. Whatever.' He waved the beer bottle in a gesture of frustration at her ignorance.

He sounded so matter of fact, like encountering people

breaking the law was an everyday occurrence. Perhaps it was to him, but even so, the very idea of it was ridiculous. 'You thought my brother was dealing *drugs*? You have met him, right? That *was* you sitting next to him at our dinner table the other night, laughing and joking like you're his new best friend? I didn't imagine that?' It was so far beyond belief she couldn't help the sarcastic tone. Sure, he'd pulled a few pranks in his younger days, but Nick was the straightest person she knew, apart from their dad, perhaps.

'What was I supposed to think?'

She couldn't believe how cross he sounded, not when it was *her brother* he was accusing. 'Almost anything other than that! God, if you were that bothered about it, why didn't you go and speak to him at the time? You were right there.' She pointed an accusing finger at the evidence plastered across his laptop screen.

'You were right there,' she repeated, another realisation dawning. 'You thought Nick might be involved in something, maybe even in trouble and you just stood by and watched...' An unpleasant feeling twisted her stomach. 'What if something bad had happened? Would you have intervened?'

His shuttered expression told her everything she needed to know.

'You wouldn't have, would you?' She shook her head, wondering who the hell she'd let herself get involved with.

'Nothing happened. He was fine.' An excuse, not an answer.

Laurie turned her back on him, not wanting to hear any more. She tipped her glass to her mouth, noticed how little was left in it and placed it on the table, pushing it out of reach. She needed a clear head. Needed to think.

Using the trackpad, she scrolled through the picture roll

on the screen. The only thing that looked even remotely out of place to her was the fancy Range Rover. It wasn't the sort of car often seen in the area. Local farmers rattled around in muddy Land Rovers, or pick-ups with their flatbeds filled with miscellaneous tools, rolls of fence wire, and bags of animal feed. No one who lived here would risk trying to navigate the narrow streets in a beast like that either. Tourists tended to favour estate cars or practical people carriers to ferry themselves, their kids and the tons of paraphernalia a family needed for a holiday by the sea.

She scrolled further, hunting for what, she had no idea. An answer, perhaps? Something that though it might not help her to forgive Jake, would at least explain his thought process.

Taking her time, she studied each individual image, trying to piece together the story. There could be anything in those boxes, and while Nick didn't look happy, there was nothing about his body language to suggest he felt threatened or in any kind of danger. He looked a bit pissed off in a couple of the close-ups, but she knew him like she knew her own bones and he appeared in control beneath the sullen frown.

Flicking her thumb over the trackpad, she rolled right through to the end then back to the beginning, trying to work out what she was missing. 'I don't see anything like the hand-off you described,' she said, eyes still fixed on the screen.

Jake dragged one of the other kitchen chairs next to hers and sat. 'That was before I started taking photos,' he said, with none of his previous defensive anger. 'It... it's hard to explain other than to say that it *looked* wrong. It's what I'm trained to do, to look for the things that don't fit; things other people might not even notice.'

He placed a hand on her thigh, but she shifted her leg out of the away, not in the mood to let him try and placate her. 'I'll admit I jumped to some pretty awful conclusions without giving Nick the benefit of the doubt.'

'I don't understand how you can have spent half the summer here in Mermaids Point, and not see who we are.' That's what hurt, almost as much as the personal slight against Nick. Jake had been here all this time and he didn't understand the first thing about the community that meant everything to her. How could she possibly have thought he would ever fit in here for the long term? She might not have said anything to him, but she'd hoped, oh God, had she hoped.

'The only kind of trouble we get around here is when someone parks on a double-yellow and causes a traffic jam; or a drunk gives Dave a hard time after last orders.' And those cases were few and far between. The Point wasn't the kind of resort to attract stag and hen weekends. 'This community, my community, looks out for each other. If there was even a hint of the sort of problems you're intimating, we'd have rooted them out and dealt with it.'

Dropping his hand, Jake sighed. 'I talked myself out of it, Laurie. I swear, I was ready to walk away and forget all about it, but then the car showed up and it hit all my buttons.'

Leaning across, he enlarged a picture of the Range Rover. 'It's brand new.' He tapped a finger on the number plate. 'Top of the line. Not the sort of thing most people around here can afford to drive. And look at how dark the windows are. That's not a level of tint you need to keep the sun out. That's the kind intended to keep prying eyes from seeing who or what's inside.'

Laurie had to agree. She'd mentally flagged it as the one

thing out of place. She tried to view the image from his perspective. 'If you saw one of these parked up somewhere else would you look twice?'

He shrugged. 'Depends on the location. Plenty of city execs drive them, so if I was in a more urban area it probably wouldn't stand out as much. They're ten a penny in London.'

'So, the car arrives...' she prompted, wondering if he went through the rest of the story things would start to make more sense.

'Yeah, and as I said, it didn't fit what I was seeing so I watched for a minute. Nick clearly wasn't happy, and he wasn't the only one.' He enlarged a photo of her brother and the person in the hood standing near the cockpit of the boat. 'Look at the body language; they're fighting about something.'

It looked that way to her too. 'That's still a massive leap to accuse Nick of being involved with something as vile as the drugs trade.'

'I didn't accuse him of anything.'

'You *thought* it, though.' Which was as unforgiveable in her eyes.

'I thought he was mixed up in something, I'll admit to that.' Jake shoved a hand through his hair. 'Because he is, although it's not anything like I suspected.'

He brought up two more images. The first was the one she'd seen on arriving – Aurora Storm in all her glitz and glory. Beside it was a blown-up version of the final image on the camera roll – the person in the grey hoodie standing at the back of Nick's boat as it pulled out of the harbour. It was a bit blurred, but there was no mistaking the resemblance. 'You think my brother was sailing around with Aurora Storm onboard?' she asked, not ready to believe what her eyes seemed to be telling her.

'I do.'

He pulled up another image, this time of the guy in the baseball cap who'd also been on the boat. 'I managed to get a clear image of the logo on his hat.' He clicked on his internet browser and brought up the website for something called Siren Productions. The background was black, with a blue and green stylised mermaid graphic next to the name of the company in bold white letters. The mermaid's tail swirled beneath the word Siren as if to underline it.

'It's not much more than a holding page,' Jake continued. 'The contact section directs enquiries to a PO box and an admin email address. No phone number.'

The pieces finally clicked into place. 'You think this is connected to the mermaid sightings.'

'I haven't been able to prove it, but I've got enough to make an educated guess in that direction. I looked them up on Companies House, and the registered director is Dennis Rouse.'

Laurie sent him a questioning look; the name meant nothing to her.

'Dennis Rouse runs DR Talent Agency, and guess who one of his biggest clients was until she disappeared off the face of the earth?'

'Aurora Storm.' Laurie took control of the trackpad, flicking back to the two photos, still not quite sure she believed it. 'So, what do you think she's up to? If she's the one staging the mermaid sightings, what's it for?'

He shrugged. 'I don't know, but it doesn't really matter. There's enough breadcrumbs to put together a story. Celebrity stuff isn't my usual area of expertise but, given the way she dropped out of the limelight, anything with even a whiff of connection to her will be a hit with the tabloids. I've sketched an article outline and sent it over to my editor to see what he thinks.'

Jake was right. This was exactly the sort of thing the press loved to splash all over their front pages. The village would be crawling with news crews again the moment the story broke. Something else occurred to her, something that sent her stomach churning. He'd already sent the story, before speaking to her about it. 'What about Nick? Did you at least keep him out of it?'

When he didn't respond, Laurie swung around in her seat to face him. 'Jake?'

His mouth was set in a determined line. 'The name of the boat is clearly visible in the photo. It wouldn't take five minutes for ownership to be traced back to Nick, so there wasn't any point.'

'You could crop it out.'

Jake shook his head. 'It won't work. I need to show her on the water, it ties her in with everything.'

'Nick isn't going to know what's hit him,' she said, faintly.

One of the reporters who'd been filming over the weekend had been a pain in the backside, barging into the café and sticking her microphone under people's noses asking for their thoughts about the mermaid. Laurie had managed to get her to leave, but only as far as the pavement. As though wanting to spite her for turfing her out, the reporter had set up shop right outside the café, annoying everyone trying to enter or leave. Once the press connected the boat to Nick, it would only be a matter of time before they linked him to the rest of the family. And with a celebrity added to the mix, she doubted they'd settle for 'no comment' and leave them in peace. 'It'll be a nightmare.'

'If we spin it right it'll be good business for you and your parents.' Jake didn't sound like he believed that for a minute.

'For you! I can't believe you'd do this to us.' God, she wished that were true, but there was a ruthlessness about him that made it all too clear he'd put his drive for a good story before everything. Even her.

Jake leaned forwards, elbows propped on his knees, hands extended as if appealing to her to be reasonable. 'If Nick gives me an interview, I can put his side of the story out there from the start.'

'And if he doesn't?' Laurie hunched her arms around herself, thinking about the photo Jake had of Nick and Aurora arguing. If that got out in the public domain, who knew what people would make of it? How could Jake do this? God, she wished he had been cheating on her, because this betrayal felt even worse. This wasn't something he'd done in a fit of passion. He'd sat at this table with a clear mind – if not an entirely clear conscience – and written the story in full knowledge of the consequences. Hurt beyond measure, she lashed out.

'Just because your family isn't worth anything, doesn't give you the right to try to ruin mine!' It was a cruel blow, and one she regretted the moment it was dealt.

She watched as it struck home; saw Jake flinch as if she'd raised her hand and slapped him. Shock and pain chased each other across his features before the mask slammed down, and the stranger she'd glimpsed the other night sat before her. 'It's a good story.' Cold, he sounded so cold.

'It's gossip and speculation, and you know it!' she retorted.

'Do you know how much a story like this sells for? I've got bills to pay, just like you, Laurie. And if I play my cards right, it could be enough money to—' he cut off whatever he was about to say.

'To what?'

'I thought with enough money behind me, I could look at other options. It could be my last story, if you wanted it to be.'

His last... 'Are you crazy? Did you honestly believe I would sit by and let you use my family as fodder for the gutter press and when the dust died down, you and I would take the money and run?'

'Not run. Settle. Here. Build a life together.'

'If that's what you want, you wouldn't be doing this.' And then it hit her. 'But that isn't what you want, is it? You've done all this because deep down you knew it would be the end of us.' Laurie shoved her chair back, anger and disappointment raging inside her as fierce as a winter storm. 'You're not used to being happy, are you, Jake?'

'What the hell are you talking about?' He gestured between them. 'What do you think this is?'

'It's nothing. Not any more, though it could've been something wonderful.' She snatched her handbag from the table and started for the door. 'If I were you, I'd stick to watching other people from now on. It's all you're really good at.'

His next words were hard as stone. 'If I don't tell this story, someone else will. Speak to Nick. Persuade him it's in his best interests to talk to me.'

A final, terrible realisation struck. She froze; turned back to face him. 'What if Nick had been involved in something illegal? What would you have done, then?' She already knew the answer.

Jake stared at her, that awful unreadable expression on his face. 'People have a right to the truth.'

The laugh that ripped from her throat had nothing to do with humour. 'Don't set yourself up as some kind of moral arbiter, Jake. I've heard your truth, and I don't want to have anything to do with it.'

The mask cracked, revealing a mirror to the desperate pain lancing through her. 'Laurie, *please*.' He held out his hand as though begging her to stay.

For an agonising moment she stood suspended between the two halves of her life. The family she owed everything to, and the man she'd begun to hope would stay for more than just one summer. But he didn't fit here; he never would, and it was time to stop pretending otherwise. He didn't understand what it took to be part of a community, part of a family.

'Publish and be damned, Jake. Isn't that what they say?' All but choking on the sob forming in her throat. Laurie wheeled from the room and slammed the door behind her.

25

Jake didn't know how long he stared at the door in the vain hope Laurie would come back. Even if it was only to yell at him a bit more, it would be better than the vast pit of nothingness yawning before him. He'd thought himself immune to criticism, but even a master manipulator like his father hadn't been able to hurt him the way she had just now.

Maybe because she was right.

Jake slumped forward, clutching his head in his hands as the weight of his own stupidity crashed into his brain. He'd based his entire approach to the evening on Laurie not being able to forgive him for lying to her about who he was. He'd been so sure it would be the end of his time here at the Point, he'd done everything in his power to make it a self-fulfilling prophesy. Her initial reaction hadn't been anything like he'd suspected, she'd even laughed at the absurdity of him chasing around after the mermaid. If it had stopped there, they might have been able to talk it out, find a way past things.

He tugged at his hair. Why the hell hadn't he minded his

own business and walked away this morning? Was she right? Had an unconscious part of him wanted this all along and used Nick as a pawn to ensure it happened? Even after he'd dug around and put the pieces of the story together there'd been a point where he could've stopped, could've turned the whole thing on its head and made it an exciting secret for him and Laurie to share while they waited to see what happened next.

There might even have been a way to still write the story and get a positive outcome. If he'd talked it through with her, maybe between them they'd have worked out a solution that gave him the scoop – and the money it would bring – while protecting Laurie and her family from any blowback. Instead, he'd chosen the path of most destruction, and for reasons, now he sat and thought about it, he simply couldn't understand. Or didn't want to.

Other than that couple of years with Jules at university, he'd never had anything resembling a relationship. He'd dated loads; met plenty of nice women and been very happy to enjoy their company while he was with them, but rarely followed up after one or two nights. Something had always come up at work, a new investigation to get his teeth stuck into, the unsociable hours making it easy to find excuses to cancel plans. Maybe he'd engineered it that way.

Even with Jules it had been clear their paths lay in different directions. The careers they'd both chosen to pursue once university ended had provided the perfect excuse to break up. Was that why it had been easy to be with her, knowing things would run their course eventually, that there was a ready-made escape cord to pull?

Jake pressed his thumbs against the unbearable pressure forming in the corners of his eyes. Growing up the way he did had taught him not to cry, what was the point when there was no one to care if he was upset. What else had it broken inside him? Shit. What had he done?

He ran to the door, wrenched it open and ran out into the yard. If he was quick, he might be able to catch up with Laurie, beg her to listen, beg her to let him explain and give him a chance to prove he could do better. Would *be* better. Somehow. But what if he couldn't? What if this was the best he was capable of being?

I've heard your truth, and I don't want to have anything to do with it.

His frantic footsteps ground to a halt not even halfway down the path to the village. If he couldn't be better than this, then he couldn't be with anyone else. Especially not someone as sweet as his Laurie, who deserved only love and kindness, and the kind of honesty he wasn't sure he had in him. He sank down beside the path, eyes fixed on the empty expanse of ocean before him.

He had no idea how much time passed with him sitting on the dampening grass until he was ready to face facts. If he loved Laurie, in whatever imitation of that emotion his stunted heart was capable of, he had to let her go. For now at least, maybe forever. He had no idea how he was going to make things right, but he knew where he needed to start – back at the very beginning. It'd been ten years since he'd shut the door to his parents' house, swearing never to return. But no matter how hard he tried, he hadn't been able to shut the door on *them*. Pride had kept him away, but what was his pride worth if it was going to cost him everything? He might not get any answers, but if he wanted to move forward with any hope of a decent future, he had to find a way to deal with his past.

He lingered a few moments longer until the last of the twilight sank below the horizon. Night's curtain of stars drew closed over the sky – and over his time in Mermaids Point. He hoped he'd be back again someday, because nowhere else had ever felt like the place he wanted to call his home. Eyes dry and burning, Jake stood and began to trudge back to his cottage.

* * *

The kitchen door stood ajar and from beyond it came the tinkling default ring of his mobile. A surge of hope sent him flying through the door to snatch up the handset, but it was only his editor. Slumping into the seat in front of his laptop, he answered the call. 'Hey, Mac.'

'Where the hell have you been? I've been ringing on and off for the past hour.'

'Sorry, I had stuff to think—'

'Never mind. We haven't got time to waste on that, this is one hell of a story you've got on your hands, kid.'

The familiar click of a disposable lighter followed by the sound of Mac sucking deep on a cigarette broke something inside him. His boss had given up smoking not long after Jake had started working at the *Comet*, but now and then he indulged himself – usually when he thought they were onto something big. Jake could picture him, perched on the back steps of the fire escape, shirt creased from a long day in the office, tie hanging limp beneath the collar he invariably unbuttoned within the first ten minutes of walking through the office door. His salt and pepper hair would be rumpled from the many frustrated shoves of his hand, his fingers stained with ink from the cheap, leaky biros he preferred when scribbling notes on the enormous jotter pad that covered most of the surface of his desk.

A sob burst from Jake's throat, cutting Mac off midstream. 'Jake? Jesus Christ, Jake, are you crying?'

'No.' The strangled croak said otherwise.

A long silence filled the air between them, interspersed with the exhalations of Mac blowing out smoke from his cigarette and the awful choking gurgles that once started, Jake seemed unable to stop.

'Tell me what's wrong, son,' Mac said, at last, which only made Jake cry harder.

How pitiful was his life that only his boss had ever been willing to claim him as such? The memory of a big, beefy hand clapping him on the shoulder filled his mind's eye, together with Andrew Morgan's booming laugh. Laurie's dad had called him that, too. Had been willing to make room in that big-hearted chest of his for the man his daughter had brought to their dinner table. It wasn't just Laurie he was losing – though that in itself was enough – it was the promise of being part of family for the first time in forever. 'I've fucked it, Mac,' he managed to gasp out between sobs. 'I've fucked everything up.'

* * *

It was a much-chastened version of Jake that made its way along the winding path to the beach the next morning. He and Mac had talked long into the night, the whole sorry story of his time in Mermaids Point coming out in fits and starts. It hadn't taken Mac long to agree to quash the story, even if he grumbled a time or two about the loss of revenue.

Knowing he was asking so much of a man who'd only

ever been good to him hadn't made Jake feel any better; local papers like theirs ran on a shoestring even in the hands of someone as proactive as Mac. He'd been the one to spot and catch the first wave of digital media, investing capital they didn't really have on building a first-class website to support their traditional print run. A story about someone as famous as Aurora Storm would drive a huge number of clicks to the *Comet*, bringing a ton of extra advertising revenue along with it.

When they'd finally run out of words, Jake had staggered to bed and fallen fast asleep, too exhausted to even bother taking off his clothes. It was only when he'd surfaced a couple of hours ago that he'd noticed the floral backpack sitting in the corner of the bedroom where Laurie must've dropped it. He'd sat on the end of the bed for a while, staring at it as regret washed through him. He was calmer now, his mind clearer.

Now he'd persuaded Mac to pull the article, there might be a way to resolve things with Laurie. *Not yet.* He needed to take some time, to sort himself out rather than expecting her to heal all the broken bits inside him. Until then, he would return her backpack and offer her nothing more than the apology she deserved.

He passed the window of the amusement arcade, the lights already flashing to tempt those with more money than sense. He paused for a moment, remembering Laurie's tale about trying to win the silly pink bear. Cupping his hand to his eyes, Jake peered through the glass, a smile forming as it spotted the ugly little thing still squatting in the corner of the claw grab machine. Deciding he needed all the help he could get, Jake entered the arcade and approached the cashier's booth at the back.

'Want some change, love?' The woman behind the window asked.

He nodded, drawing out his wallet from his back pocket. 'How much is the claw grab a go?'

'A pound.'

Jake winced as he pulled out a twenty. 'Better hope luck is on my side.'

Luck was not on his side. When he trudged back to the window for the third time, his new pal, Janice – she'd told him her name on his second visit to her window – eyed the motley collection of two rabbits, a duck, and a one-eyed green monster he dropped onto the counter as he reached once more for his wallet. 'How many prizes do you need?' she asked, shaking her head as she pulled another bag of one-pound coins from the till.

'Just the one. I'm trying to win the pink bear.' Embarrassed and not sure how to explain, he scrubbed the back of his neck. 'It's an apology thing.'

Janice threw back her head and laughed. 'Well, why didn't you just say so?' Unhooking a set of keys from a nail on the back wall, she let herself out of the booth and headed for the claw grabber. 'Which one do you want?' she asked, using a large round key to unlock the back of the machine.

'That one.' Jake tapped the glass in front of the tatty looking bear he'd grabbed and dropped a few inches from the winning slot.

'You sure?' She retrieved the pink toy and studied it, her expression sceptical. 'I can't see this making any apology better, myself.'

'That's the one,' Jake said, ignoring her remark. 'How much do I owe you?'

She shoved the bear into his hands. 'Get on with yourself, love. You've paid more than the thing is worth ten times over.'

'It'll be worth every penny.' Jake crossed his fingers behind his back, hoping he was right, then tucked the bear inside the backpack.

'Don't forget the rest of your prizes,' Janice called as he started for the door.

'Stick them back in the machine, I've got what I need, thanks.'

As he approached the café, some of the spring in his step his exchange with Janice had put there faded as he noticed the blinds were still drawn. Ignoring the CLOSED sign, he knocked on the glass. When there was no answer, he peered through the little gap between the edge of the blind and the doorframe. The room beyond was dark, no sign of life at all.

Guilt tore at his gut. Had he upset Laurie so much last night he was costing her a day's worth of trade? He strode next door, pulling up short when he realised her parents' shop was shut up tight as well. What the hell was going on?

Unsure of his next move, Jake walked back towards the café and watched as a guy gave the handle an unsuccessful rattle. 'Any idea why they're closed?' he called out to Jake, before using the newspaper he'd had tucked under his arm as a shield as he tried to peer through the window. He could only see the top half of the banner headline and half of a familiar face, but it was enough to make Jake's stomach churn.

'Mind if I have a look at that?' Jake raised a shaking hand towards the newspaper.

'Help yourself, mate.' The man thrust it towards him, more concerned with trying the door to the café once more.

Unfolding the tabloid, Jake stared in disbelief at the front page. 'BACK WITH A SPLASH!' the headline declared.

'Aurora Storm, haven't heard much of her lately,' the man said, peering over Jake's shoulder.

'No, we haven't,' Jake muttered, the response automatic as he started moving in a daze. After everything they'd talked about, he couldn't believe Mac had gone behind his back like this.

'Here, mate, where're you going with my paper?' The man yelled, grabbing his arm.

'Sorry, sorry.' Shoving it into the man's hands, Jake turned on his heel and started running. He had to find Laurie!

His chest was burning by the time Jake reached the Morgans' house at the top of the hill. He thumped the metal knocker hard, before bending at the waist to gasp breath into his aching lungs. Laurie's backpack fell from his shoulder to land at his feet as the door swung open to reveal a pair of dark work boots, too large and masculine to be hers.

'You've got a bloody nerve,' Nick hissed, drawing the door closed behind him. 'I should knock your teeth down your throat for what you've done.'

'It wasn't me.' Breathing under control a bit, Jake straightened. One look at the fury on Nick's face sent him back a couple of steps. 'I swear, mate,' he said, holding up his hands.

'Don't you mate me, you sneaky bastard. My sister's in there breaking her heart, right now.' Nick gestured angrily behind him.

Jake knew how she felt. Rubbing a weary hand over his chest, he shook his head. 'I'm so sorry, but this isn't what you think. Well, it is, but it isn't.' Jake couldn't think straight, couldn't think beyond the roaring need to get to Laurie and try to explain. 'Please, just let me speak to her.'

'No chance,' Nick snarled, reaching for him.

Jake dodged the other man's swipe just as the door behind them opened. His heart leapt for a split second before the forbidding frame of Andrew Morgan filled the door. 'Enough, Nick,' he said in a tone that brooked no argument. 'Inside with you.'

Nick glared at Jake for a long moment before shaking his head and ducking past his father back into the house.

When he met Andrew's eyes, Jake saw none of the fury of his son in them. Only sadness, and disappointment. It was almost more than he could bear. 'I'm sorry.'

Andrew shook his head. 'I think you'd better go.' When Jake took a step forward, the big man crossed his arms over his chest. 'Now, Jake.'

Defeated, Jake had no option other than to retreat to the pavement. 'Laurie left some things at my place.' He pointed at the backpack. 'Will you see that she gets them?'

Andrew stared at the bag for a long moment before stooping to retrieve it. 'I'll give it to her.'

It was the best Jake could hope for right now. She'd get the bear, at least. A paltry thing to assuage the harm he'd done, but he would text her when he got back to the cottage. But first he needed to speak to Mac and find out what the hell was going on.

His phone was barely in his hand before it started flashing Mac's name with the familiar green and red accept/reject call buttons. Why the hell wasn't it ringing? As he pressed the accept button he tilted the handset to one side and muttered a curse. He must've caught the silent mode switch at some point.

'Mac?'

'Finally! I've been trying to reach you all bloody morning.' Mac sounded flustered.

'To apologise, I assume?'

'What? Oh, you've seen the papers, then? No idea where that came from, but that's not important now.'

Not important? 'Well, it didn't come from me,' Jake yelled as he rounded the corner at the bottom of Laurie's street and reached the road running along the seafront. A couple of people turned at hearing his raised voice, but he was too angry to be bothered about drawing attention to himself. 'And you're the only other person I told...' Apart from Laurie, he realised, coming to a stop at the iron railing lining the edge of the road. But why would she leak it? It didn't make any sense.

'Shut up, Jake.' Mac's sharp tone cut into his thoughts, followed by a gusty sigh. 'Christ, son,' he said, voice softer. 'Just listen a minute. Forget about that rubbish in the papers. We had a call on the out of hours line. Mary on reception picked it up this morning. It was from some woman claiming to be your mum.'

The click of Mac's lighter filled Jake with as much dread as mention of his mum. Mac never smoked this early in the day. 'I hate to break it to you like this, but if she is who she claims to be, then your dad died last night. I'm so sorry.'

'Thanks.' Jake stared unseeing across the crowded beach. 'I'd better go.'

'Okay. Call me later, though. And you know whatever I can do to help, you only have to say the word.'

'Bye, Mac.' Jake shoved his phone back in his pocket, knowing he wouldn't call him back because there was nothing he could do. Nothing anyone could do, because it was too late. Had it already been too late last night when Jake had finally resolved to go home and look for answers? He shook his head, bitter irony making him laugh as he tucked his hands in his pockets and set his feet on the path towards the cottage. If his dad could be alive to see it, Jake had no doubt the old bastard would be thrilled to bits to thwart him to the very end.

26

It was lunchtime when Laurie emerged from her room, groggy from an enforced nap. She couldn't remember the last time her mother had sent her to bed, but after a night spent mostly crying and the shock of realising Jake had actually gone through with it when the morning paper thumped on the mat, her mum had taken one look at Laurie's face and sent her back upstairs. She'd woken a few minutes earlier needing the bathroom and realised she was starving. The pizza she'd bought had gone uneaten in Jake's fridge, and she'd been in such a state when she'd got home she hadn't thought about eating. She also needed to stop hiding out and leaving the rest of the family to handle the potential fallout.

Brushing her teeth made her feel a bit more human, though there was nothing to be done about her swollen eyes and raw nose. Tugging a sweatshirt over the vest and light cotton trousers she'd slept in, Laurie made her way down-stairs. When she entered the kitchen, it was empty except for her dad who was sitting at the table with a full set of the morning papers strewn in front of him. His hands were wrapped around a mug she'd bought him years ago that declared him to be the 'World's Best Dad'.

'Hello, my poppet, feeling any better?' When she shook her head, he stood and held out an arm to her. Cosying in to one of her very favourite places in the world, she wondered if she'd ever grow old enough to not need a hug from him, and silently hoped not.

'How bad is it?' Staying in the shelter of his arm, Laurie turned her head to gaze at the stack of papers.

'Not as bad as we expected. There's no mention of Nick by name, just a line about her being helped out by some trusted locals.' Her dad gave her a squeeze then dropped his arm. 'Fancy a cuppa?'

'Oh, yes please, Dad. And can you stick a couple of slices in the toaster for me?'

'Peanut butter or Nutella?' When she raised her eyebrows at him, her dad shook his head. 'Heathen child.'

While he pottered around, humming along to something on the radio, Laurie stole his vacant seat and started flipping through the various articles. As well as the headline article, the first tabloid she opened had pages of follow-up pieces dredging up every story they'd ever written about Aurora Storm, including speculation over her prior disappearance. She flipped back to the front page again with a frown. The byline credit was their in-house Showbiz reporter with no mention of Jake's name anywhere.

She rifled quickly through the stack and it was the same case with each paper. The front-page stories linking Aurora to the mermaid sightings were interchangeable, with key sections reproduced almost word for word. It was clear they'd come from the same source, so why no credit?

'Here you go, love.' Her dad placed a steaming mug of tea

on a coaster then handed her plate piled with quarter-squares of toast slathered in peanut butter *and* Nutella.

'Thanks, Dad, you're the best.'

'And I've got the mug to prove it,' he said, with a grin, raising a fresh brew of his own in her direction. His smile drooped as he stared down at the paper open in front of her. 'What a bloody stupid fuss over nothing.'

'Did you notice Jake's name isn't on any of the articles?' She asked around the first square of toast. The salty-sweet combination of the toppings hit her tongue and she sighed in appreciation at the old childhood treat. 'They haven't used any of the photos he showed me last night either.'

'Have they not?' Frowning, her dad sat down and flicked through one of the other papers.

She shook her head. 'They're all either old stock photos or stills taken from the viral videos.'

'Maybe Jake decided to keep them back, to at least try and keep Nick's name out of it.'

'Maybe.' Laurie sipped her tea, feeling a bit less wobbly now she had something in her stomach. 'Where's Mum?'

'She went to open the shop for a few hours. Once we were sure Nick's involvement wasn't mentioned we decided it was safe enough. She'll get the gossip, see what the general mood is.'

Laurie nodded, still not quite able to believe Nick's involvement even though he'd confirmed it the moment she'd rushed in the door and spilled out everything that had happened between her and Jake. The row Jake had witnessed had been over Aurora and her team filming at the caves beneath the Point after Nick had refused to take her there himself because of the danger. 'What about Nick?'

Her dad shrugged. 'After Jake came by earlier, he got a call from someone and stormed off. Haven't seen or heard from him since.'

Laurie dropped her half-eaten piece of toast and stared at her father. 'Jake was here? When?'

'Ten-ish, I suppose. You were asleep, and I didn't want him upsetting you again.' A fierce frown marred his usual open expression. 'He left a bag for you.'

Following his glance through the door to the hall, Laurie spotted the rucksack she'd left in Jake's bedroom the previous night. Hot tears pricked the back of her eyes and she grabbed her tea, pretending to drink while she choked them back. 'I'll take it up with me,' she said when she could speak without her voice wobbling. 'I'm going to have a shower and get dressed.'

When she started to clear her plate and mug, her dad waved her off. 'Leave them, I'll do it in a minute when I've finished my tea. You go up and sort yourself out.'

'Thanks, Dad.' She bent down to hug him around the neck. 'You really are the best.'

He tapped the side of his mug, making her laugh even though she felt like weeping all over again. It shouldn't be possible, she'd cried at least a year's worth of tears last night, but she could feel the sadness welling up inside. Capturing her hand, her dad held her in place. 'It'll be all right, my poppet.'

She nodded, unable to speak.

He eyed her for a long moment before releasing her hand with a sigh. He looked older than she'd ever seen him. Lack of sleep and worry over her had etched deep lines between his brows and cast purple shadows beneath his eyes. 'I'll be okay,' she whispered, the lie of it bitter on the back of her tongue.

'Of course, you will. You're a Morgan, and like the rocks upon the shore we endure – whatever life throws at us. We might get swamped at times, worn by some experiences and shaped anew by others, but we never break.'

Spine straightening a fraction, Laurie nodded. She would get through this. She wasn't alone. Right now things felt pretty unbearable, but that was okay because she had people around her who would carry the parts she couldn't manage until such time as she could stand on her own two feet once more. 'I love you, Daddy.'

'Love you too, my darling. Go have your shower and maybe a bit more sleep if you can manage it?' He smiled, the familiar broad grin that never failed to warm her heart and lift her spirits. 'Shepherd's pie for tea, tonight, what do you reckon?'

Warmth spread through her belly, as though filling already with comforting food, made in this kitchen where she'd only ever known safety, by the man who was the beating heart of their family. 'I reckon that sounds about perfect.'

* * *

Steam billowed in a cloud behind her as Laurie exited the bathroom in her dressing gown, a towel wrapped around her wet hair. Just like the tea and toast, the heat from the shower had added another layer of sticking plaster over the raw wound of her heart. It wasn't healed, but it was holding together and that was good enough.

Padding into the bedroom she sat on the stool in front of her dressing table and began towel-drying her hair. Blasting herself with the hairdryer would be quicker but felt like too much effort. Lethargy weighed heavy on her. The warmth from the shower combined with the aftershock of so much emotional upheaval stole through her bones until she wanted nothing more than to crawl underneath her quilt and escape from reality again. With effort, she raised her arms to twist her hair into a plait, which would tame the worst effects of going to bed with it still wet.

She'd at least had the foresight to place a clean set of pyjamas on the bed before taking her shower and she tugged them on, leaving her dressing gown in a heap on the carpet. Her foot nudged something and she looked down to see the backpack she'd tossed there. *Leave it.* The clothes she'd packed would be impossibly creased already, a few more hours wouldn't make any difference. Still, something made her sit on the edge of the bed and lift it into her lap. Unzipping the top, she could only stare at the tatty, cross-eyed little face peeking up at her.

'Oh, Jake.' When had he done this? Why had he done this, after all the terrible accusations she'd flung at him last night? Some of them he'd richly deserved, but the rest... the stuff about his family? Laurie shuddered, not liking the part of her that had been capable of such cruelty. Pulling the shocking pink teddy out of the bag she crawled up the bed to slide under the quilt, the bear tucked tight against her body.

She should probably check on Jake, find out why he'd come to the house earlier, find out why his name wasn't on any of the articles, but her limbs felt too heavy. Her eyelids drooped once, twice, and she drifted off to sleep, telling herself there was plenty of time to speak to him later.

It felt like she'd barely closed her eyes before they were startled open by her door banging followed by a heavy weight thumping against her legs. Struggling to a sitting position, Laurie cast a baleful glance at her brother, who'd plonked himself down on the end of the bed. She was about to tell him to go away, or words to that effect but then she saw the terrible, wild look in his eyes. Please, God, she didn't think she could cope with any more bad news. Settling back on her pillows, she folded her arms. 'It better be something important, or I'm going to flush all your action men down the toilet.'

Nick laughed, a little bark of surprise at the unexpected memory she'd conjured. 'God, Dad was so mad about that.' She'd got one of the figures wedged halfway around the U-bend and he'd had to drain the system and take apart the pipes to get it out. 'And worst of all, he yelled at me about it!'

'That's because you deserved it,' Laurie said, giving him the smug smile of a little sister who'd scored an unexpected victory over her big brother. 'For breaking my Barbie castle.'

'I was staging a rescue mission, not my fault it was cheap plastic and couldn't withstand the assault.' Laurie laughed with him this time. It was a pointless conversation, a diversionary tactic she'd deployed on instinct the moment she'd seen the look on Nick's face, but it had bought them a little time, relaxed him a fraction.

They fell silent, and Laurie watched Nick as he fiddled with the ribbon and lace decoration at the bottom of her quilt. Another diversionary tactic. His shoulders heaved up and down in a sigh so big it crumpled his frame a little. 'He didn't do it.'

She knew instantly what he was talking about. Jake's name not appearing anywhere had been a big red flag, but her brain had been too frazzled to slot the puzzle together. 'You're sure?'

Nick nodded, eyes still fixed on where his fingers plucked at a piece of ribbon. 'She did it herself.'

Wide awake now, Laurie bolted upright. 'Aurora leaked the story? But why?'

Leaving the ruffled decoration alone, Nick hooked his hands around his bent knee, his expression a picture of abject misery. 'To control the situation. She had a press release prepped and ready to go. Jake finding out just meant she pulled the trigger on things a bit earlier than she'd intended to. It's a big publicity stunt to promote her return to the music industry. First the viral videos, then a leak to the press to ensure maximum exposure when her new song drops in a couple of days. That's why we were out on my boat yesterday, she wanted to film a final appearance of the mermaid that was supposed to be released next week.' He dropped his eyes from hers. 'She's on her way back to London as we speak.'

Oh. 'You liked her?'

Nick was silent for a long moment, before giving a shrug that aimed for nonchalance and missed by a country mile. 'It was just a bit of fun.' He rose, shoved his hands in his pockets and wandered towards the door. 'Something to tell the grand-kids one day.' He paused on the threshold. 'What will you do about Jake?'

Retrieving the pink bear from beneath the covers, Laurie set it in her lap and stared at it. Though he'd done the right thing, probably at great financial cost and possibly damaged his career prospects in the process, she couldn't just forgive and forget. Too much had happened for that. In one brutal hour they'd shredded the delicate fabric of their relationship – and she couldn't lay the blame for that solely at his feet. They couldn't erase the past twenty-four hours and act like nothing had happened. They might not be able to pick up the pieces at all. 'I'll talk to him.' Laurie smoothed a hand over the bear's tatty pink fur. Rushing up there now when everything was still too raw would be a mistake, even though she longed to do just that. 'In the morning.'

* * *

Still pale and tired after a night spent having imaginary conversations with Jake in her head, Laurie was up and out of bed before first light. She'd found a couple of messages from him on her phone after talking to Nick last night, sent hours earlier.

It's not my story.

Read the first, followed later by:

I'll call you.

She'd sent one back:

I like my present.

She had followed that one with a bear emoji. The blue ticks had appeared to show he'd seen it, followed by the dancing ellipses to indicate he was typing a reply, but they'd stopped, and no follow-up message had appeared. Probably for the best, she'd reassured herself before finally falling asleep. What they needed to say to each other couldn't be played out on a chat app.

It was not even quarter past six when she entered the

main yard of Walkers' Farm, but several of the farmhouse windows were illuminated and the backdoor stood open. Off to the left sat Jake's little cottage, shrouded in darkness. Not surprising given the early hour, but still something seemed off about it.

'Laurie, is that you?'

Jumping at the voice from behind her, Laurie turned to see Alan Walker standing beside his Land Rover, a flask in one hand and a Tupperware box tucked under his other arm. 'Oh, morning, Alan. I'm just on my way to see Jake.' She felt like a schoolgirl who'd been caught sneaking around to meet a forbidden boyfriend and hoped it was still dark enough to hide the blush burning her cheeks.

'You've missed him, I'm afraid.' Dumping his lunch on the seat of his vehicle, Alan strolled closer. 'Got called away home yesterday, some sort of family emergency. Surprised he didn't tell you—' Alan coughed, perhaps realising the awkwardness of what he'd just said. 'I think Caro found an envelope for you when she went in to clean up. Hold on...'

Heart sinking, Laurie watched him stump back inside the farmhouse before glancing at the cottage behind her once more. The thing that hadn't looked right clicked into place. Jake's car was missing from its spot, leaving only a pale square in the dirt of the farmyard to mark its former presence.

I'll call you.

The significance of his last message struck with hideous clarity. Not the olive branch she'd assumed it to be, but a nasty little FU of a goodbye. She'd been too tired and addled to see it at the time, but why else would he choose the exact last words Matt had said to her, other than to wound? A final twist of the knife, a bit of payback for the secrets he'd shared and she'd weaponised against him during their fight. So why had he given her the bear? Nothing was making sense to her tired brain.

'Here you go, love.' Alan held out an envelope to her, bent to peer closer when she made no move to take it. 'Are you all right? Oh, you're not, are you. Hang on. Caro! Caro, come give us a hand!'

In no short order, Laurie found herself sitting at the Walkers' battered kitchen table, bundled in a blanket with a steaming mug in front of her. Carolyn had shooed her husband out and taken a seat at the other end of the table, a matching cup of tea nestled between her palms. 'Must've been a shock for him, poor lad,' she mused, taking a sip.

The words took time to penetrate the fog of pain shrouding her, but when they did, Laurie raised her head. 'Sorry? What?'

'You know, Jake, losing his dad all of a sudden. Terrible to get a call like that when you're away from home. It was the same with Alan's dad. Fit as bull, then dropped like a stone in the yard not five feet from the door. We were in Tenerife at the time. Such a rush, it was, trying to change our tickets and get home to sort it all out.'

Laurie let the woman prattle on as she tried to get her head around it all. From what Jake had told her, he hadn't seen either of his parents for ten years or more. For someone like her, who'd hardly gone a day without seeing hers, it had seemed impossible. What must he be thinking? Relief? Anger? Grief? All that and more. She stared at the unopened letter beside her mug. In the mess of everything else, would

Jake really have been in enough of his right mind to go out of his way to hurt her in the way she'd assumed? There was only one way to find out. 'Will you give me a minute, Carolyn?'

'Of course, dear.' Carolyn's understanding smile said she'd been filling the silence in order to give Laurie space to think. 'I've got a stack of washing to sort through. Leave your mug in the sink when you're done.'

Laurie stared at the envelope for a few more minutes, half-scared, half-hopeful of what it might contain. 'Just read it,' she muttered to herself. Snatching it up, she ripped it open before she could change her mind. There was a single page of cramped scrawl.

> *My darling Laurie,*
>
> *There's so much I need to say to you, but I'll start with the most important one – this isn't goodbye.*
>
> *I'm sorry for everything. I'll try and do some digging in the next couple of days, find out who broke the story, but I swear to you it wasn't me.*
>
> *Mum called my work and left a message to say my dad had died.*

Laurie paused to consider that. He hadn't been in touch with his parents enough for them to even have a current phone number for him. How awful to hear something like that second-hand.

> *I have to go home. There's nothing else for it, though it's the last thing I want to do. She won't cope on her own, never could. I thought about calling you, but I didn't want to dump my problems on you. I know you, Laurie Morgan,*

know that big heart of yours would want to take on all this,
but that's not fair to you.

This is where I'll be, and you've got my number.

A full address, including postcode was written out in block capitals beneath it, as though he hadn't wanted to risk there being any mistake in her deciphering his handwriting.

I'm not him.

Jake had ripped a little hole in the paper underlining the word.

I'm not leaving you – not forever, just for a little bit until I
can get my head on straight and be the kind of man you
might one day be proud to have at your side.

At the bottom of the page he'd scrawled a letter 'J' and a single 'x'.

A tear dripped onto the paper, blurring the ink. 'Oh, Jake,' she whispered, 'You already are.'

27

'How are you getting on, Mum?' Jake called up the stairs, more in hope than expectation.

She hadn't moved from her bed in the days since he'd come home, other than to use the bathroom. He'd had to use the spare key, still hidden under the same flowerpot by the back door, to let himself in. The state of the normally spotless kitchen had proven his worst fears about his mum's state of mind. Dirty cups and plates covered every surface, cold water filled the sink, a thin layer of scum coating it. In the tiny utility room he'd found a pile of damp, smelly washing abandoned in the machine. She'd barely lifted her head from the pillow to acknowledge his arrival, as though it had taken all her energy to make that one call to his office and she had nothing left.

Silence.

With a sigh, he headed back into the kitchen to make a bowl of soup. It was about all he could get her to eat, and even then it was only a few mouthfuls before she pushed the tray aside. As he waited for the soup to heat, he picked up his notepad and ran over the list of things he needed to do. The local undertaker he'd called had been brilliant at dealing with all the practicalities, but they'd sent him a long list of questions he had no idea how to answer about the type of service they wanted. Flowers or charity donation? What readings, and who would give them? Interment or cremation? He'd been over it a dozen times and was still no closer to a decision. His mum was in no fit state to answer any of it, and though Jake would be glad to see his father sent off without any fanfare whatsoever, he knew he had to do better than that. Once the shock passed, it would devastate his mum if things weren't handled properly.

He couldn't count the number of times he'd reached for his phone to call Laurie, to ask her advice, just to hear her voice and know he wasn't alone in all of this. Had she got his letter? He shouldn't have left it on the table, but he'd been too focused on the long drive ahead, the pull of responsibility to make sure his mum was okay, even as he'd wondered why he was bothering. Maybe he could call her this evening, after he knew she'd be finished in the café, and see if she had any suggestions on what he should do about the service.

A knock came at the door, followed by the two-toned ring of the bell. Another bloody neighbour, no doubt, he thought, turning off the gas beneath the pan. There'd been a steady trail of them calling to offer their sympathies, to drop off a pie or a casserole and no doubt get a good eyeful of the prodigal son now returned.

Forcing a polite smile he didn't feel to his lips, Jake yanked open the door.

'All right there, son?' Andrew Morgan filled the doorway, a kind smile on his open face. 'Ah, you're not, are you?' He shook his head. 'Get on in, now, the girls are just grabbing some stuff from the car.'

In the face of the big man moving towards him, there was nothing Jake could do other than backpedal into the hallway.

He'd taken only a couple of steps before Andrew enveloped him in a huge bear hug. 'It's all right, son. You don't have to do this on your own, not any more.' Hot tears scalding his cheeks, Jake gripped the back of Andrew's t-shirt and clung on for grim death while the older man patted his back. 'Take a deep breath, now.'

Doing just that, Jake let him go in time to scrub a hand across his wet face before first Laurie, then her mum entered the hallway laden down with bags and boxes. Laurie stopped a foot from him. 'Hello.'

'Hello.' It was all he could manage, but it was enough for now. She was here. She'd come, even though he'd told her not to. Stubborn, beautiful woman.

'I've told Nick to leave the suitcases in the car, as I wasn't sure there'd be enough room for all of us. He's going to Google search for a B & B,' Sylvia said, brushing past them on her way to the kitchen. She returned a moment later, burden free, to brush a kiss on Jake's cheek. 'How are you, love? Bloody awful business. How's your mum?'

Jake shook his head. 'Not great. She's upstairs in bed.'

'Like that, is it?' Sylvia raised an eyebrow. 'Right then. What's her name?'

'Linda. I was just making her some soup…'

'Leave that to us.' She patted his shoulder, before turning to her husband. 'Andrew?'

'On it, love.' Andrew Morgan headed for the kitchen while his wife marched to the bottom of the stairs, a petite general in white linen trousers and a floaty pink blouse. Jake could only stare as she began to climb the stairs, in awe of the way she'd taken complete charge of things within thirty seconds of entering the house.

'Should I be doing something?' He turned to Laurie in bemusement, still not quite able to believe she was there.

Laurie looped her arms around his waist. 'Mum's in her element, don't worry. If she needs you to do something, she'll tell you. Come on.'

With the sound of Sylvia cajoling his mother echoing down the stairs, Jake let Laurie lead him into the kitchen and push him gently into a chair. Andrew was over by the cooker, a tea towel draped over one shoulder as he poured soup into a bowl. He'd already found a tray and added a couple of slices of bread and butter to it, and the kettle was coming to a boil on the worktop, a handful of mugs stacked before it.

'I've found somewhere,' Nick said, entering the kitchen. 'Rotten news, mate.' He patted Jake on the shoulder then went to join his dad. 'What's to do?'

'Take this tray up to your mother. Leave it in the hall, mind, don't go barging in on Linda.'

Linda. He said it so casually, like he was referring to an old friend and not some stranger he'd never met. Jake glanced at Laurie, who'd taken the seat beside him and was busy tidying up his notes and the leaflets the doctor and the undertaker had dropped off during their visits. 'We'll get this sorted, don't worry,' she said, setting the stack aside.

'I'm not worried.' For the first time in a week, he felt calm. Right. Centred. Nothing had been resolved, his head was still a horrible mess, but that was okay. He'd thought he had to go it alone, but the woman sitting beside him wasn't going to let that happen.

When he opened his arms, she slid onto his lap and

settled against him with a sigh. 'They're a bit full-on, my family, I'm sorry, but there was no way they were going to let me leave them behind,' she said, shaking her head as her dad unhooked the tea towel and flicked it playfully at Nick, the pair of them laughing. 'I hope you're ready for this, because as far as they're concerned, you're part of this family now, too.'

He wasn't sure he was completely ready. Not yet. But the promise of it was enough to steal his breath. 'They're wonderful.' He captured her chin, tilted her face up to meet his. 'You're wonderful.' He kissed her, then. Soft and sweet with a promise of more. 'I can't believe you came.'

'I'll always come when you need me.' She stroked his cheek then leaned in to make sure her next words were for him alone. 'I love you.'

'I love you, too.' He whispered the words against her temple, closing his eyes as he breathed in the scent of her favourite shampoo. That was one thing he knew about her, and there were many others. Not enough to set a firm foundation beneath their relationship, but it was a start. The rest... the rest would come in time if they worked at it.

And Jake had all the time in the world for Laurie Morgan and her loud, bossy, brilliant family.

Their family.

ACKNOWLEDGMENTS

Here we are again. I'll be honest that there were times when I wasn't sure I would get to the point of writing acknowledgements for another book which is why there has been a bit of a break between this one and the last. With plenty of rest and lots of great support I am delighted that my writing mojo had just wandered off for a bit rather than leaving me forever!

I'm so excited to be starting this new series with a fabulous new publisher. Huge thanks to everyone at Boldwood Books for helping me to bring what I think will be a really fun new series to my readers. I loved bringing Mermaids Point to life and I am sure we're going to have a wonderful time getting to know the Morgans and their extended group of friends and family over the next couple of years.

Extra special thanks to my editor extraordinaire, Sarah Ritherdon. From the moment we first spoke on the phone I knew we would work well together. Thank you so much for, well, EVERYTHING! X.

Thanks to Cecily Blench (Copy Editor) and Camilla Lloyd

(Proof Reader) for adding the all-important polish and shine xx.

To Amanda, Nia, Ellie and the rest of the Boldwood team who worked so hard to put this book into your hands (or on your e-reader, or into your ears via your favourite audio app!) – thank you x.

#TeamBoldwood, who are just about the nicest bunch of fellow authors I could hope for. Thank you for all the support, shares, chats and cheerleading. Here's to a bumper year of success for all of us.

My Party People – Jules Wake, Bella Osborne, Rachel Griffiths, Phillipa Ashley. You mean the absolute world to me. I love you all and cannot wait to be able to party in the same room as you xxx.

To Rachel Burton, who gets me and is always there xxx.

To everyone who has messaged me to say they've enjoyed one of my books or taken the time to leave a review – it really makes a difference and I appreciate it x.

To the Book Bloggers who help not just me, but so many other authors to get the word out about our books. You are brilliant and I am enormously grateful for the time and care you take xx.

And my biggest and most heartfelt thanks are reserved for you, dear reader, because without you buying this book I couldn't keep doing the job I love most in the world xxx.

MORE FROM SARAH BENNETT

We hope you enjoyed reading *Summer Kisses at Mermaids Point*. If you did, please leave a review.

If you'd like to gift a copy, this book is also available as an ebook, digital audio download and audiobook CD.

Sign up to Sarah Bennett's mailing list for news, competitions and updates on future books.

https://bit.ly/SarahBennettNewsletter

ABOUT THE AUTHOR

Sarah Bennett is the bestselling author of several romantic fiction trilogies including those set in *Butterfly Cove* and *Lavender Bay*. Born and raised in a military family she is happily married to her own Officer and when not reading or writing enjoys sailing the high seas.

Visit Sarah's Website:
https://sarahbennettauthor. wordpress.com/

Follow Sarah on social media:

- facebook.com/SarahBennettAuthor
- twitter.com/Sarahlou_writes
- bookbub.com/authors/sarah-bennett-b4a48ebb-a5c3-4c39-b59a-09aa9Idc7cfa
- instagram.com/sarahlbennettauthor

ABOUT BOLDWOOD BOOKS

Boldwood Books is a fiction publishing company seeking out the best stories from around the world.

Find out more at www.boldwoodbooks.com

Sign up to the Book and Tonic newsletter for news, offers and competitions from Boldwood Books!

http://www.bit.ly/bookandtonic

We'd love to hear from you, follow us on social media:

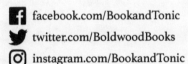

facebook.com/BookandTonic

twitter.com/BoldwoodBooks

instagram.com/BookandTonic

COMING SOON ...

Autumn Dreams at Mermaids Point

Sarah Bennett

PROLOGUE

'Ah, Gareth, you should see the way he makes her smile. It's like a light comes on inside her.' Nerissa closed her eyes for a moment, picturing her niece, Laurie, as she'd seen her in the pub the previous evening, head tilted as she listened to whatever Jake was whispering in her ear. It had been a rare night out for the whole family, a chance to welcome Jake's mother to Mermaids Point and introduce her around. Nerissa still wasn't sure what to make of Linda – wasn't at all convinced it was good thing for Jake to have her back in his life especially when his relationship with Laurie was still finding its feet, but she'd held her peace until now.

Shifting to ease the ache in her hip from sitting cross-legged on the ground too long, Nerissa confessed her doubts to the one person she was always able to speak her heart to. 'Honestly, Gar, she's such a mousy thing it's a struggle to make even the most basic conversation. I don't think the woman's had an opinion of her own all her life.' She sighed, knowing she was being unfair given the little her sister-in-law, Sylvia, had told her about what both Jake and his mother had been through over the years. 'At least she's free of that awful man now. Given time she might come out of her shell a bit more. If anyone can help her, it'll be Sylvia.'

Nerissa loved her sister-in-law with all her heart, but she knew from personal experience what Sylvia was like once she found a pet project. Glancing down at the bunch of sunny yellow daffodils in her hand, Nerissa gave a small laugh. 'With any luck she'll be so busy with Linda she won't have time to try and fix me up with anyone for a bit. I don't know why she's still bothering after all these years.' She rearranged the bouquet to release one of the golden trumpet flowers that had twisted at an odd angle. Other women might prefer roses or extravagant lilies, but daffodils had been Nerissa's favourite since the first time Gareth had turned up on her doorstep. Tanned and fit after weeks of basic training, he'd presented her with a bunch of daffodils, a nervous smile tugging at his gorgeous full lips. He'd kissed her for the first time that day, down by the caves on the beach where he'd taken her for a walk. He'd told her he loved her that day, too, that he was tired of waiting for her to notice him, that she was his girl now. Forever.

She raised her free hand and pressed it to the echo of the warm glow that had heated her cheeks when he'd said those words. She'd been noticing her brother's best friend from the moment he'd picked her up and brushed gravel off her knees when she'd tripped over by the swings in the park. He'd been eleven to her seven, had interrupted a noisy kick-about with her brother and the rest of their pals to set her back on her feet and wipe away her tears with the sleeve of his sweatshirt. Her heart had been his from that moment on, though of course she'd been too young to understand or articulate anything beyond the feelings of security and happiness she felt whenever he was near.

Those fledging feelings had developed into a full-blown crush once her hormones caught up with her heart. Her early teens had been an excruciating torture of unspoken adoration and blushes whenever he popped around to the Morgan family home – which had been practically every day, especially during the holidays. When he'd announced at twenty-one that a life on the fishing boats wasn't for him and that he was off to join the army, the scandal of it had rushed around the village like wildfire. Nerissa had lain on her bed and wept silent tears into her pillow thinking him lost to her forever. And then he'd come home on leave to reveal those messy, wonderful things she'd been feeling for him weren't unrequited after all.

Swallowing around the tight ball in her throat, Nerissa laid the daffodils on the square of neatly clipped grass in front of the plain white headstone. 'I love you, Gareth,' she whispered, touching her fingers to her lips before pressing them to the engraved letters of his name. 'Happy birthday, sweetheart.' Rising to her feet, Nerissa turned away before the first tear dripped down her cheek. Gareth had always hated to see her cry, and though it'd been nearly twenty years since he'd last been able to brush them from her cheeks, she still didn't like to do it here in the little graveyard behind the parish church where he'd been laid to rest after a road accident during a peacekeeping mission in the Balkans. Such a waste of a life, of the promise of their life, their future together. She clutched the diamond and sapphire ring dangling from a chain around her neck, squeezing it until the imprint of the stones hurt. She'd taken it off when the band had grown too tight but hadn't been able to let it go. To let Gareth go.

With the ghosts of memories they'd never share swirling around her head, Nerissa ducked her head and hurried along the path to the lych gate guarding the entrance to the churchyard. So fixated was she on the past, she didn't notice the woman coming the other way until they were practically on top of one another.

'Nerissa.' The lack of inflection in the word sent a chill rippling down Nerissa's spine.

'Hello, Margot. How are you?' She winced the moment the stupid, automatic words left her lips. The death of the man they'd both loved above all others could've brought them together in solace and mutual grief, if only Gareth's mother had been willing.

She'd never forgiven Nerissa for him joining the army, even though it'd been a decision he'd made on his own. Gareth had told his mum of his plans for a future with Nerissa before he'd said so much as word to her, therefore, it was her fault he'd quit the boats and left the village in hopes of giving them both a better, brighter future. Two decades had hardened that initial irrational, if understandable, need to blame someone for the loss of Margot's son into a lasting bitterness.

Desperate for a way to cut through the frigidity spreading between them, Nerissa nodded to the enormous bouquet of white lilies and roses Margot carried. 'Those are nice.'

'They're the ones I always get. The same as for his funeral.' Margot didn't meet her eyes, every stiff inch of her posture radiating a fervent desire for Nerissa to go away. Not that she'd ever say as much because Margot's disdain was as polite as it was cold. Nerissa wished just once she'd let it all out, scream and rail and call curses down upon her head. Perhaps if Margot could give voice to all that bitterness, she could finally let it go, instead of letting it consume her from the inside out.

Holding back a sigh, Nerissa took a step back and to the side, clearing a path for the other woman to pass through the lych gate. 'I'll leave you in peace, Margot. You know where I am if you ever need anything.'

The only response was the sharp click of Margot's heels on the path as she strode away. Shaking her head, Nerissa passed beneath the roof of the gate, trying not to think about that awful rainy day when the pall bearers had paused beneath it with Gareth's coffin on their shoulders as they marked the symbolic passage of his life from this to the next. Margot was never going to change, and it was way past time for Nerissa to stop trying. As she paused at the curb to check for passing cars, she knew it was a fruitless thought. It wasn't in her nature to let someone hurt if she could help it.

With that in mind, she changed direction and headed away from the path leading to her niece's pretty seafront café, which had been her intended destination. Both Laurie and Sylvia were waiting for her there with hugs that would ease the ache in her heart and a slice of her favourite Victoria sponge to lift her spirits. As much as she needed that right now, there was someone who needed it more. Linda had rented one of the small holiday cottages in the centre of the village while she tried to decide if she wanted to make a more permanent move to Mermaids Point. With a little coaxing perhaps Nerissa could get her to join her for a walk on the beach and onto the café where they would both be welcome. Though her beloved Gareth had been nothing like the awful bully Linda had been tied to for years, she understood loss better than most. So, she would extend the hand of friendship and offer what comfort she could to the recently widowed woman.

And just maybe they'd both feel a little better afterwards.